ELFQUEST™

STARGAZER'S
HUNT

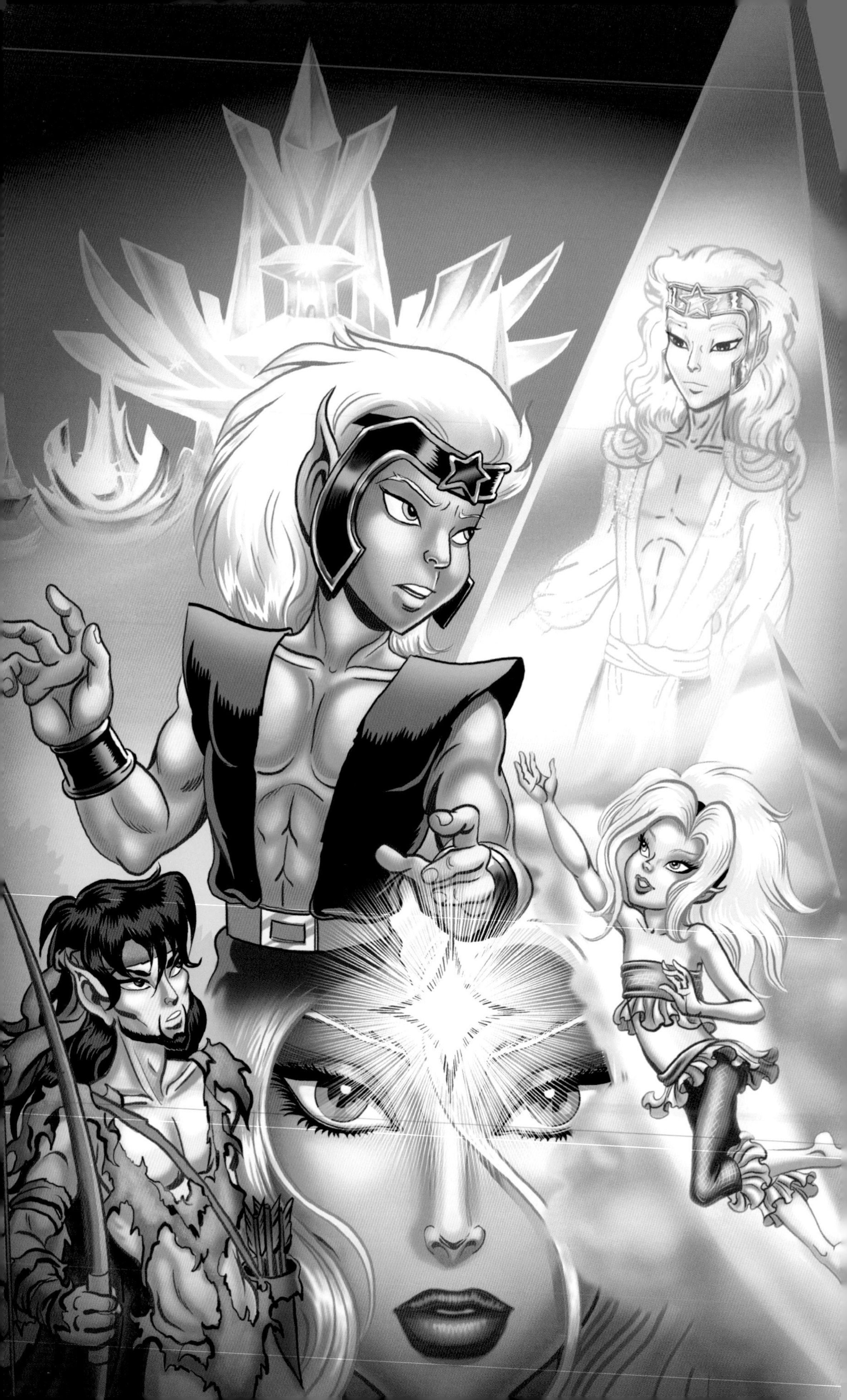

ElfQuest™
STARGAZER'S HUNT

VOLUME ONE

STORY BY
WENDY AND **RICHARD PINI**

SCRIPT AND LAYOUTS BY
WENDY PINI

ART AND COLORS BY
SONNY STRAIT

LETTERS BY
NATE PIEKOS OF **BLAMBOT®**

COVER BY
WENDY PINI

DARK HORSE BOOKS

PUBLISHER **MIKE RICHARDSON**

EDITOR **RACHEL ROBERTS**

ASSISTANT EDITOR **JENNY BLENK**

COLLECTION DESIGNER **SKYLER WEISSENFLUH**

DIGITAL ART TECHNICIAN **ALLYSON HALLER**

NEIL HANKERSON Executive Vice President • TOM WEDDLE Chief Financial Officer • RANDY STRADLEY Vice President of Publishing • NICK McWHORTER Chief Business Development Officer • DALE LaFOUNTAIN Chief Information Officer • MATT PARKINSON Vice President of Marketing • VANESSA TODD-HOLMES Vice President of Production and Scheduling • MARK BERNARDI Vice President of Book Trade and Digital Sales • KEN LIZZI General Counsel • DAVE MARSHALL Editor in Chief • DAVEY ESTRADA Editorial Director • CHRIS WARNER Senior Books Editor • CARY GRAZZINI Director of Specialty Projects • LIA RIBACCHI Art Director • MATT DRYER Director of Digital Art and Prepress MICHAEL GOMBOS Senior Director of Licensed Publications • KARI YADRO Director of Custom Programs • KARI TORSON Director of International Licensing • SEAN BRICE Director of Trade Sales

Published by Dark Horse Books
A division of Dark Horse Comics LLC
10956 SE Main Street
Milwaukie, OR 97222

DarkHorse.com
Comic Shop Locator Service: Comicshoplocator.com

First edition: March 2021
eBOOK ISBN 978-1-50671-960-3
ISBN 978-1-50671-476-9

1 3 5 7 9 10 8 6 4 2
Printed in China

ELFQUEST: STARGAZER'S HUNT VOLUME ONE

This book collects *ElfQuest: Stargazer's Hunt* #1-#4.

Library of Congress Cataloging-in-Publication Data

Names: Pini, Wendy, author, cover artist. | Pini, Richard, author. |
   Strait, Sonny, artist. | Piekos, Nate, letterer.
Title: ElfQuest : stargazer's hunt / story by Wendy and Richard Pini ; art
   by Sonny Strait ; letters by Nate Piekos ; cover by Wendy Pini.
Other titles: Stargazer's hunt
Description: First edition. | Milwaukie, OR : Dark Horse Books, 2021- |
   "This book collects ElfQuest: Stargazer's Hunt #1-#4." | Summary: "When
   ElfQuest: The Final Quest concluded, it ended the hero's journey of
   Cutter Kinseeker, chief of the Wolfriders. But that was only the start
   of a new adventure for Cutter's "brother in all but blood," Skywise. Now
   the stargazer elf, who thought he knew everything about Cutter,
   discovers how mistaken he was. In times past, whenever he has felt lost
   or empty, he has turned to the starry skies for guidance. Now is no
   exception. Once again Skywise sets his sights on the cosmic horizon for
   answers, sending him on his own epic quest from the elves' ancestral
   Star Home through uncharted space, and back to the World of Two Moons"--
   Provided by publisher.
Identifiers: LCCN 2020046084 (print) | LCCN 2020046085 (ebook) | ISBN
   9781506714769 (v. 1 ; trade paperback) | ISBN 9781506719603 (v. 1 ;
   ebook)
Subjects: LCSH: Comic books, strips, etc.
Classification: LCC PN6728 .E45 P5637 2021 (print) | LCC PN6728 .E45
   (ebook) | DDC 741.5/973--dc23
LC record available at https://lccn.loc.gov/2020046084
LC ebook record available at https://lccn.loc.gov/2020046085

LOST IN THE STARS

by Richard Pini

Someone recently asked, "So what part of 'final' did I miss when you said you were wrapping up *ElfQuest: The Final Quest*?" Granted, the speaker was being playful–I think–but all in all, it's still a valid question. We–Wendy and I as the creative backbone of a massive forty-year point-eared oeuvre, at times ably assisted by others–had spent all that time building, issue by issue, the saga of Cutter, Blood of Ten Chiefs, literally following him through his entire mortal life. *ElfQuest* was conceived from the beginning, in time-honored Joseph Campbell tradition, as Cutter's "hero's journey." We had known from the get-go how this long and winding tale must conclude, and you may find hints and clues in the words and art contained within installments of *ElfQuest* going back 20 or 30 years and more.

(Aside: Just because we knew where the story had to start and end, it doesn't mean we didn't allow ourselves the freedom to wander hither and yon now and again. Even though your road trip begins in Boston and your final destination is San Francisco, doesn't mean you can't get off the interstate and poke around the landscape. And we discovered over time that *ElfQuest*'s cast of hundreds of characters certainly had some serious roving they wanted to do.)

Thus it was on February 28, 2018, four decades to the day after the first appearance of *ElfQuest* in print, our publisher Dark Horse Comics released the final issue in the twenty-five-chapter series we called "*The Final Quest*." The title had premiered in 2013, so for nearly five years, our fans had been vocal about their feelings of apprehension. "***Final*** Quest?" they wrote in emails and posted on social media. "Does that mean *ElfQuest* itself is going to end?" And we, as we'd done from day one, teased them. We told them that *The Final Quest* was the culmination of a huge story arc we'd planned from the start, and that it would provide a satisfying (we hoped) closure to the adventures of one of the major characters. But, we hinted–again, teasingly–how could *ElfQuest* itself possibly disappear, since

we'd already created and published stories about the World of Two Moons in centuries yet to come? These were the tales of elfin shapeshifter Jink, and the rambunctious group the Rebels, collectively known as *FutureQuest*.

There was always more to tell post-*Final Quest*. There had to be, because *ElfQuest* was not and is not only a hero's journey; it has also been an ongoing love story. Not, as you might suspect, between Cutter and Leetah (although that deep connection certainly played a momentous role throughout the series). But rather, between Cutter and Skywise, the two elfin "brothers in all but blood." If Cutter has been the archetypal hero, then Skywise has been no less the classic companion-to-the-hero–Samwise Gamgee to Frodo Baggins, Doctor Watson to Sherlock Holmes. Long before the Wolfrider chief met and Recognized the Sun Village healer, Cutter and Skywise were united by the unexpected but inevitable exchange of their soul names that remains unique in all of *ElfQuest*. If the connection between Cutter and Leetah throughout the tale has been steady and calm, like the flow of a wide, deep river, then the bond between wolf-chief and stargazer is a mountain freshet, rushing headlong, with occasional still pools giving way to stretches of wild whitewater.

So while Cutter was able to accept his own passing at the conclusion of *The Final Quest* as "perfect," Skywise was left with questions and doubts, too many and too profound to allow him to go on living without his best friend and other half. Their love story is incomplete, because Skywise himself is incomplete. Even in the paradise that is the Star Home, even as part of a loving family with High One Timmain and fabulous daughter Jink, there seem to be fragments missing from his soul. He needs to be made whole, or else true peace will never be his.

That's why "The Final Quest" didn't mean no more *ElfQuest*. And that's what *Stargazer's Hunt* is all about.

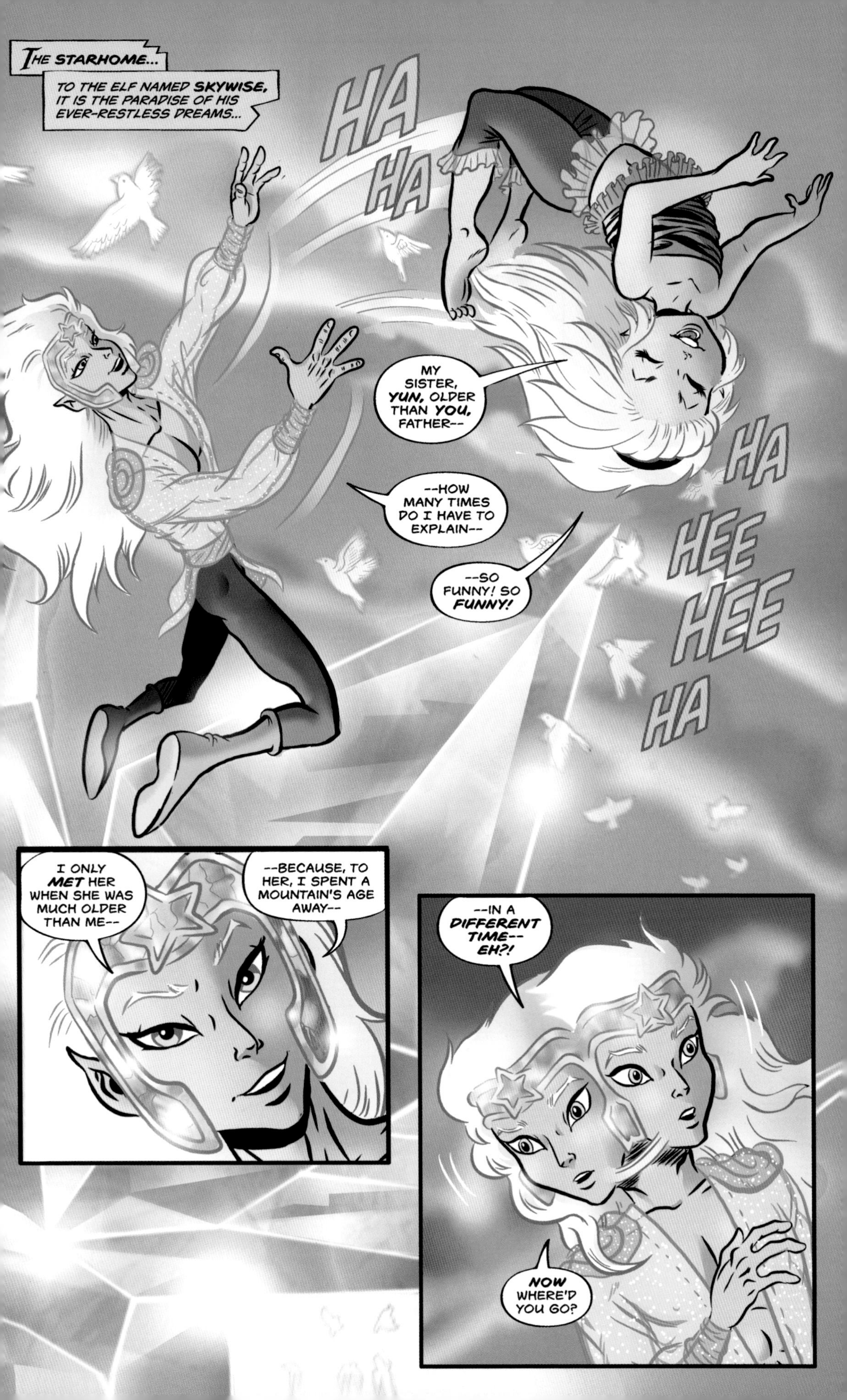
THE STARHOME...
TO THE ELF NAMED SKYWISE, IT IS THE PARADISE OF HIS EVER-RESTLESS DREAMS...
HA HA
MY SISTER, YUN, OLDER THAN YOU, FATHER--
--HOW MANY TIMES DO I HAVE TO EXPLAIN--
--SO FUNNY! SO FUNNY!
HA HEE HEE HA
I ONLY MET HER WHEN SHE WAS MUCH OLDER THAN ME--
--BECAUSE, TO HER, I SPENT A MOUNTAIN'S AGE AWAY--
--IN A DIFFERENT TIME--EH?!
NOW WHERE'D YOU GO?

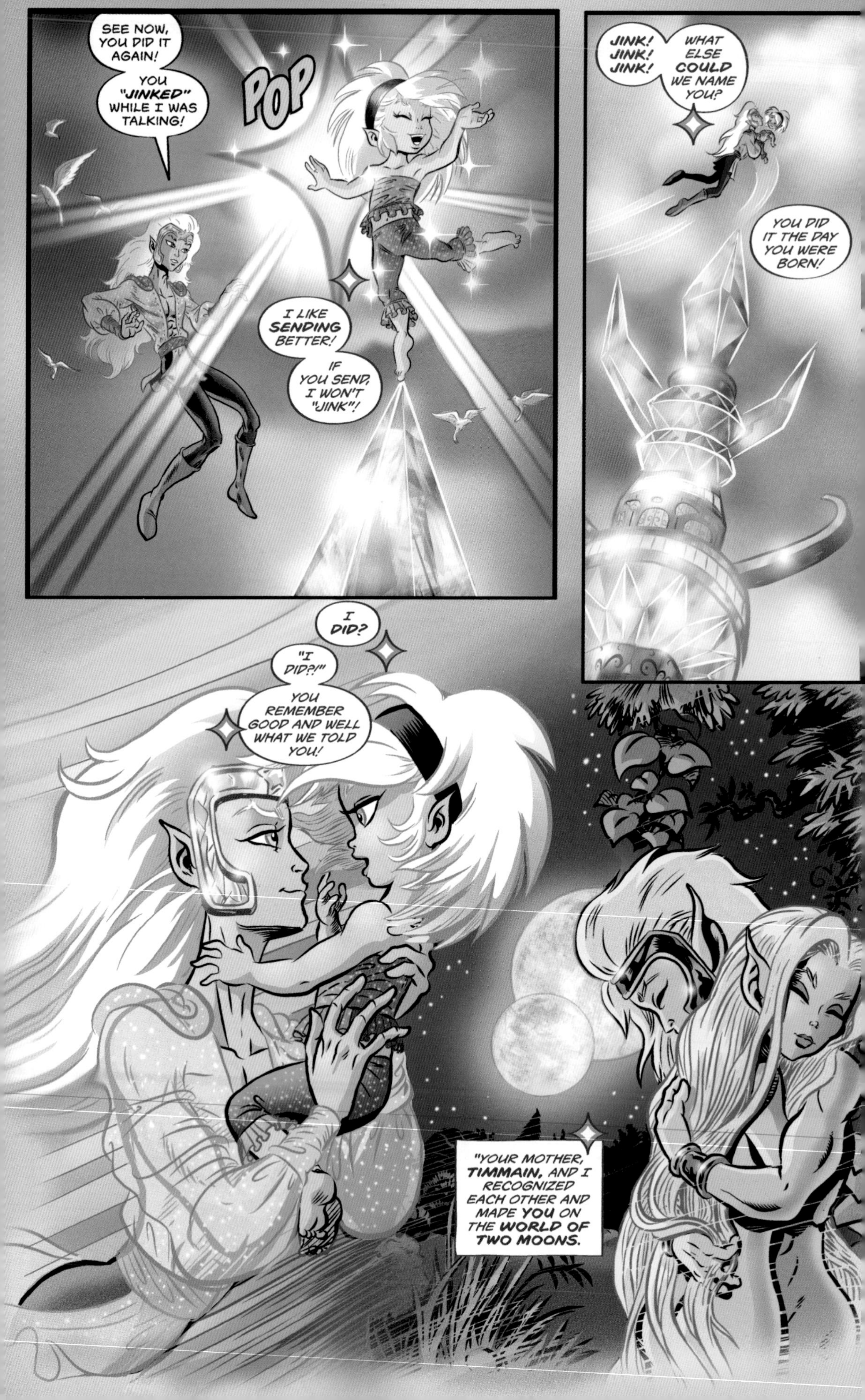
SEE NOW, YOU DID IT AGAIN!
YOU "JINKED" WHILE I WAS TALKING!
POP
I LIKE SENDING BETTER!
IF YOU SEND, I WON'T "JINK"!
JINK! JINK! JINK!
WHAT ELSE COULD WE NAME YOU?
YOU DID IT THE DAY YOU WERE BORN!
I DID?
"I DID?!"
YOU REMEMBER GOOD AND WELL WHAT WE TOLD YOU!
"YOUR MOTHER, TIMMAIN, AND I RECOGNIZED EACH OTHER AND MADE YOU ON THE WORLD OF TWO MOONS.

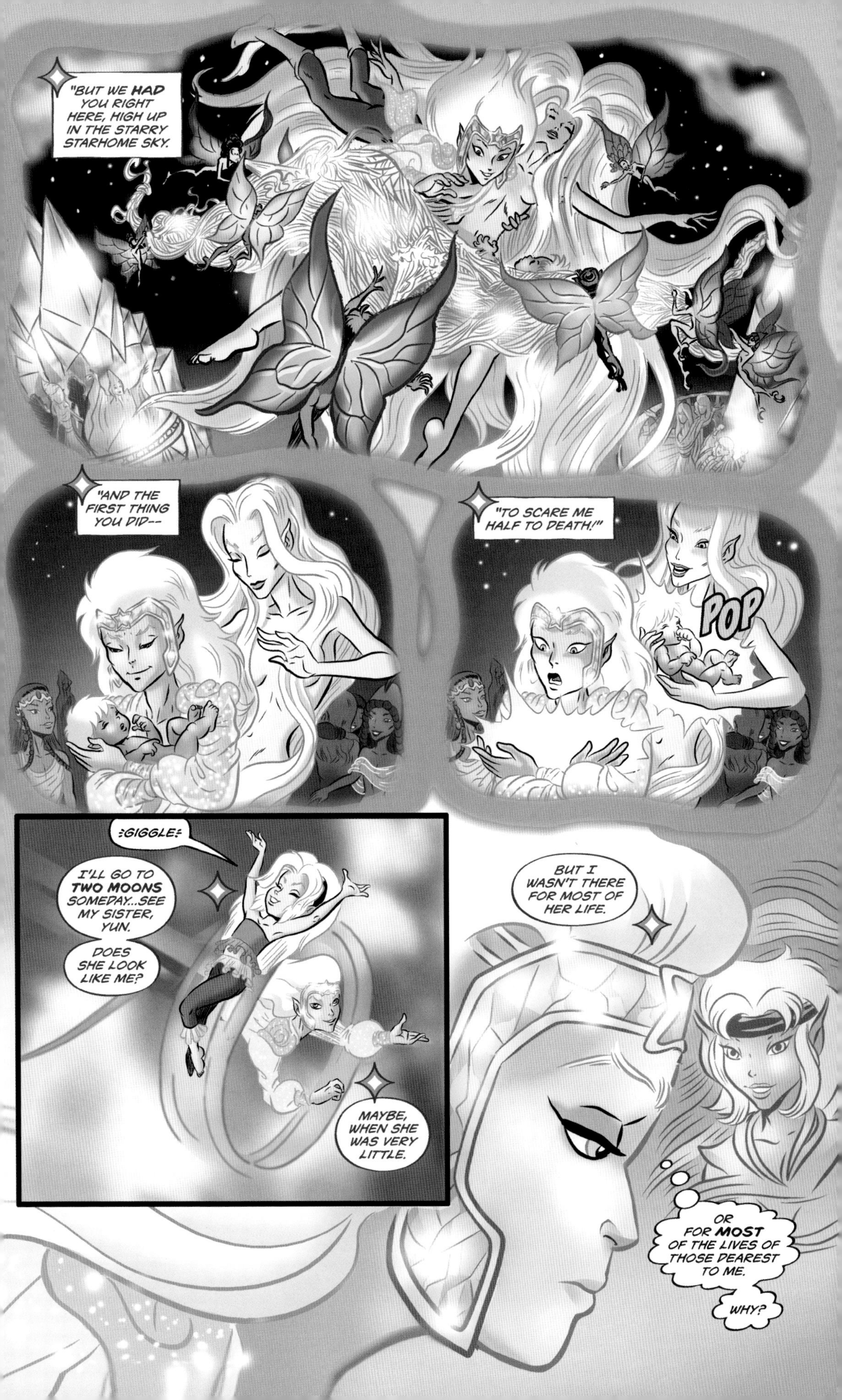
"BUT WE **HAD** YOU RIGHT HERE, HIGH UP IN THE STARRY STARHOME SKY.
"AND THE FIRST THING YOU DID--
"TO SCARE ME HALF TO DEATH!"
POP
:GIGGLE:
I'LL GO TO **TWO MOONS** SOMEDAY...SEE MY SISTER, YUN.
DOES SHE LOOK LIKE ME?
MAYBE, WHEN SHE WAS VERY LITTLE.
BUT I WASN'T THERE FOR MOST OF HER LIFE.
OR FOR **MOST** OF THE LIVES OF THOSE DEAREST TO ME.
WHY?

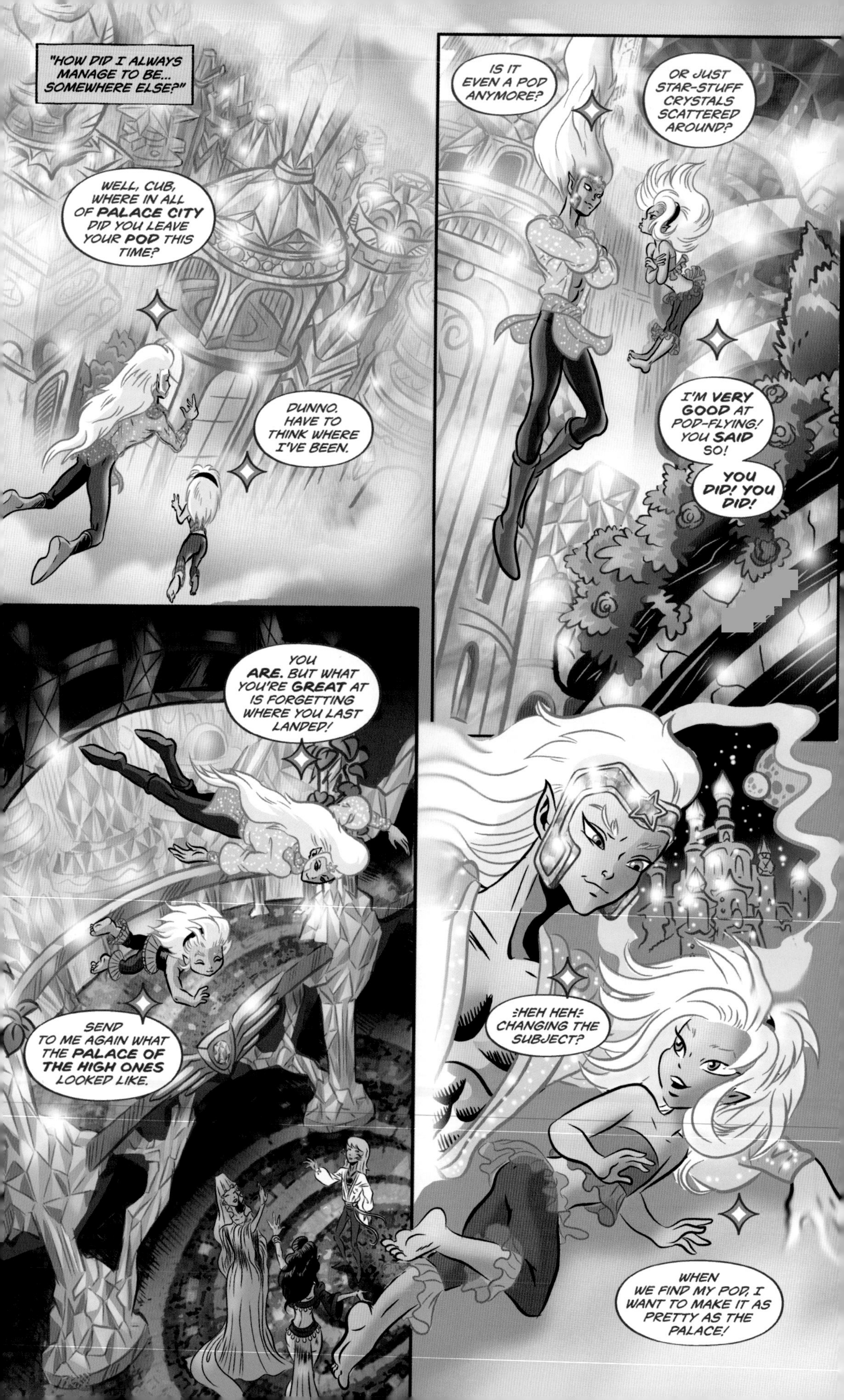
"HOW DID I ALWAYS MANAGE TO BE... SOMEWHERE ELSE?"
WELL, CUB, WHERE IN ALL OF PALACE CITY DID YOU LEAVE YOUR POD THIS TIME?
DUNNO. HAVE TO THINK WHERE I'VE BEEN.
IS IT EVEN A POD ANYMORE?
OR JUST STAR-STUFF CRYSTALS SCATTERED AROUND?
I'M VERY GOOD AT POD-FLYING! YOU SAID SO!
YOU DID! YOU DID!
YOU ARE. BUT WHAT YOU'RE GREAT AT IS FORGETTING WHERE YOU LAST LANDED!
SEND TO ME AGAIN WHAT THE PALACE OF THE HIGH ONES LOOKED LIKE.
:HEH HEH: CHANGING THE SUBJECT?
WHEN WE FIND MY POD, I WANT TO MAKE IT AS PRETTY AS THE PALACE!

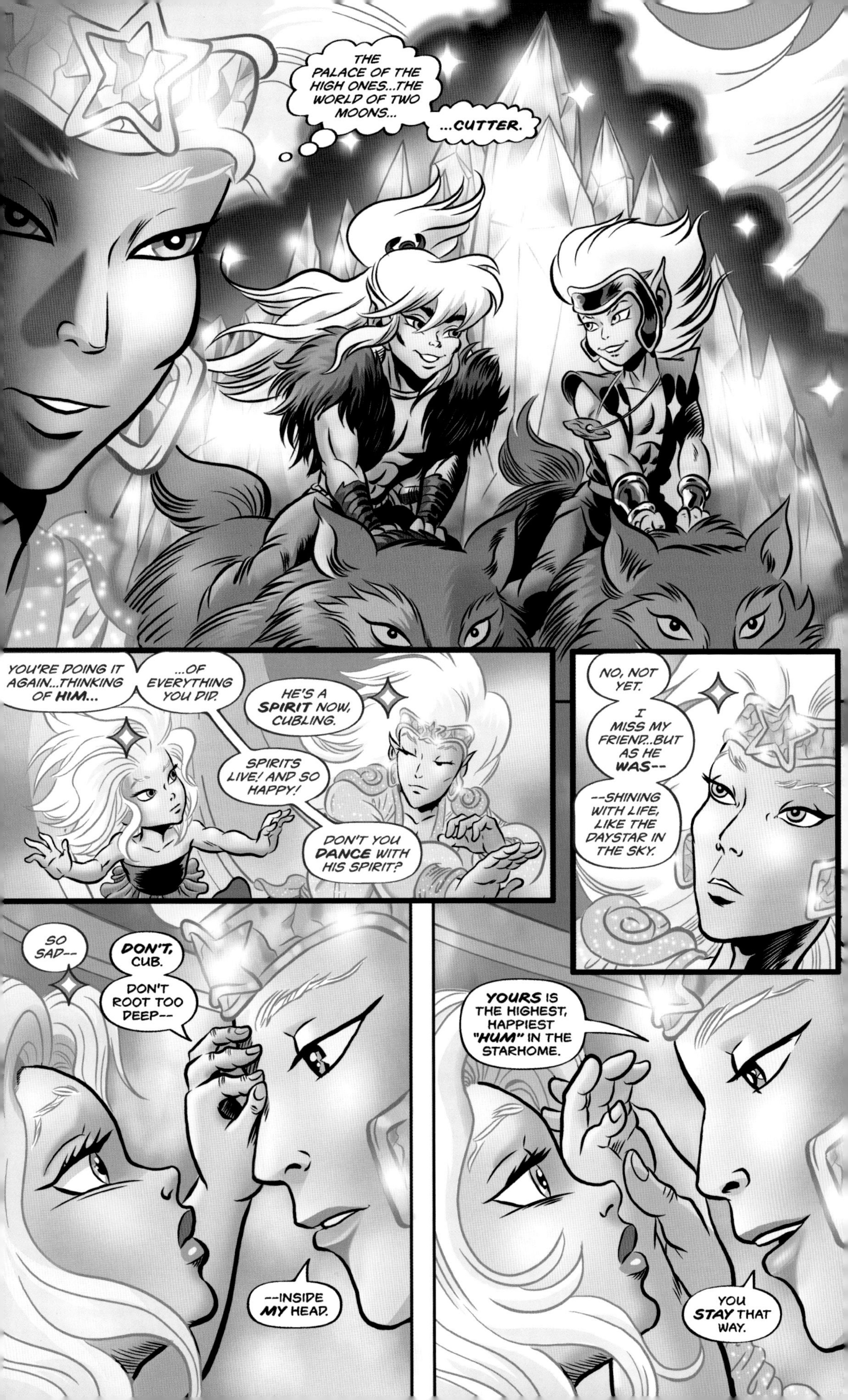
THE PALACE OF THE HIGH ONES...THE WORLD OF TWO MOONS...
...CUTTER.
YOU'RE DOING IT AGAIN...THINKING OF HIM...
...OF EVERYTHING YOU DID.
HE'S A SPIRIT NOW, CUBLING.
SPIRITS LIVE! AND SO HAPPY!
DON'T YOU DANCE WITH HIS SPIRIT?
NO, NOT YET.
I MISS MY FRIEND...BUT AS HE WAS--
--SHINING WITH LIFE, LIKE THE DAYSTAR IN THE SKY.
SO SAD--
DON'T, CUB.
DON'T ROOT TOO DEEP--
--INSIDE MY HEAD.
YOURS IS THE HIGHEST, HAPPIEST "HUM" IN THE STARHOME.
YOU STAY THAT WAY.

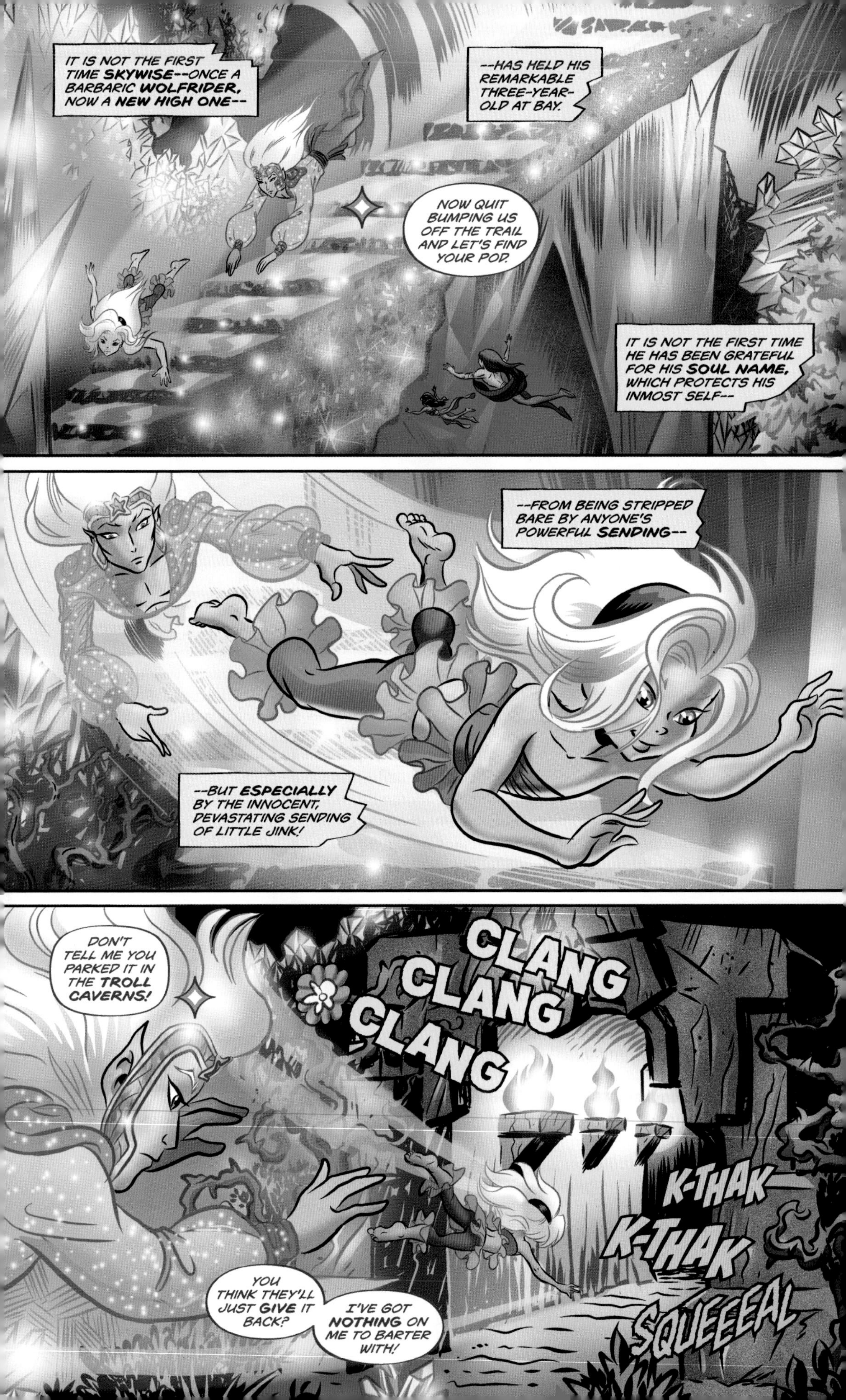
IT IS NOT THE FIRST TIME SKYWISE--ONCE A BARBARIC WOLFRIDER, NOW A NEW HIGH ONE--
--HAS HELD HIS REMARKABLE THREE-YEAR-OLD AT BAY.
NOW QUIT BUMPING US OFF THE TRAIL AND LET'S FIND YOUR POD.
IT IS NOT THE FIRST TIME HE HAS BEEN GRATEFUL FOR HIS SOUL NAME, WHICH PROTECTS HIS INMOST SELF--
--FROM BEING STRIPPED BARE BY ANYONE'S POWERFUL SENDING--
--BUT ESPECIALLY BY THE INNOCENT, DEVASTATING SENDING OF LITTLE JINK!
DON'T TELL ME YOU PARKED IT IN THE TROLL CAVERNS!
CLANG
CLANG
CLANG
K-THAK
K-THAK
SQUEEEAL
YOU THINK THEY'LL JUST GIVE IT BACK?
I'VE GOT NOTHING ON ME TO BARTER WITH!

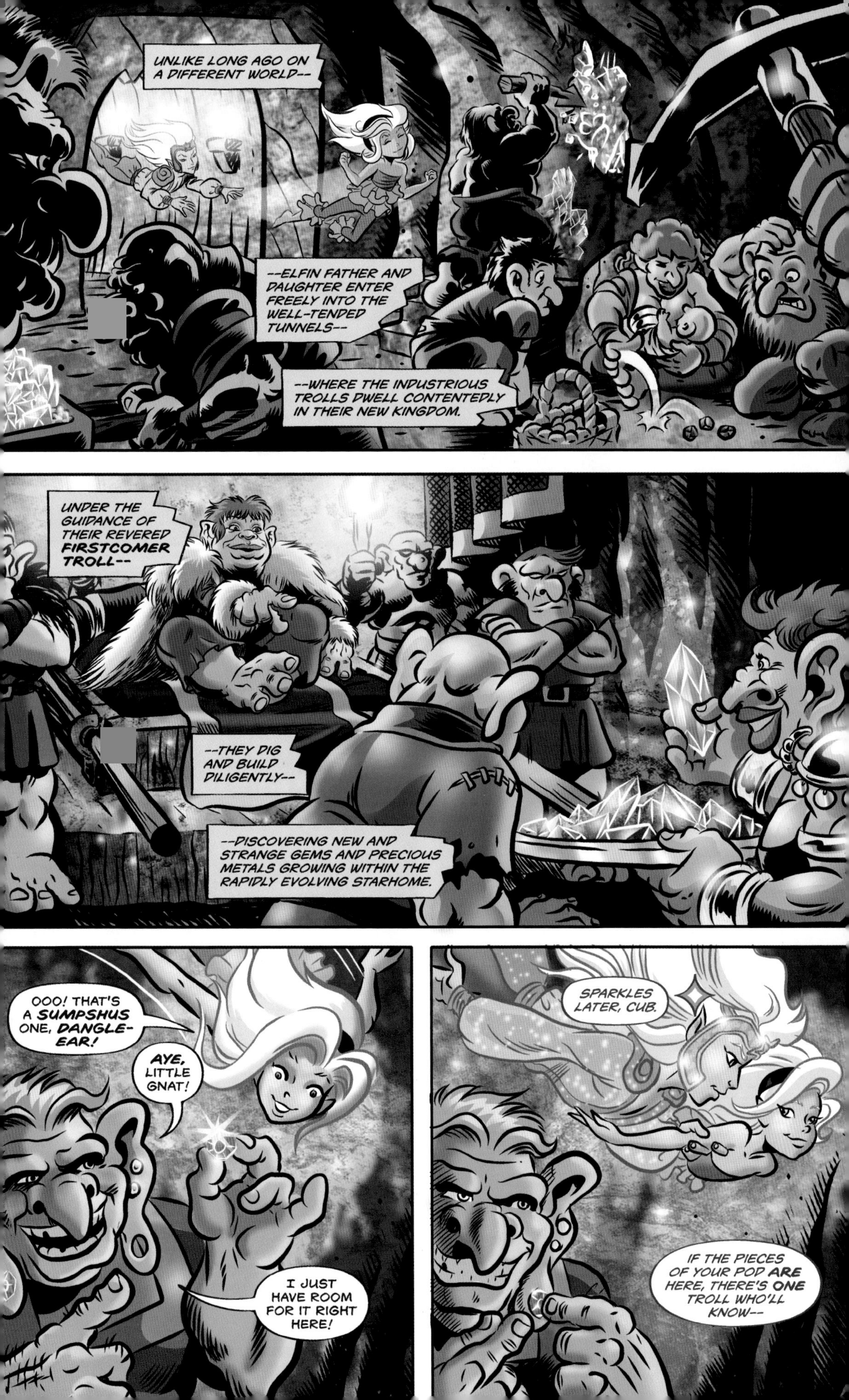
UNLIKE LONG AGO ON A DIFFERENT WORLD--
--ELFIN FATHER AND DAUGHTER ENTER FREELY INTO THE WELL-TENDED TUNNELS--
--WHERE THE INDUSTRIOUS TROLLS DWELL CONTENTEDLY IN THEIR NEW KINGDOM.
UNDER THE GUIDANCE OF THEIR REVERED FIRSTCOMER TROLL--
--THEY DIG AND BUILD DILIGENTLY--
--DISCOVERING NEW AND STRANGE GEMS AND PRECIOUS METALS GROWING WITHIN THE RAPIDLY EVOLVING STARHOME.
OOO! THAT'S A SUMPSHUS ONE, DANGLE-EAR!
AYE, LITTLE GNAT!
I JUST HAVE ROOM FOR IT RIGHT HERE!
SPARKLES LATER, CUB.
IF THE PIECES OF YOUR POD ARE HERE, THERE'S ONE TROLL WHO'LL KNOW--

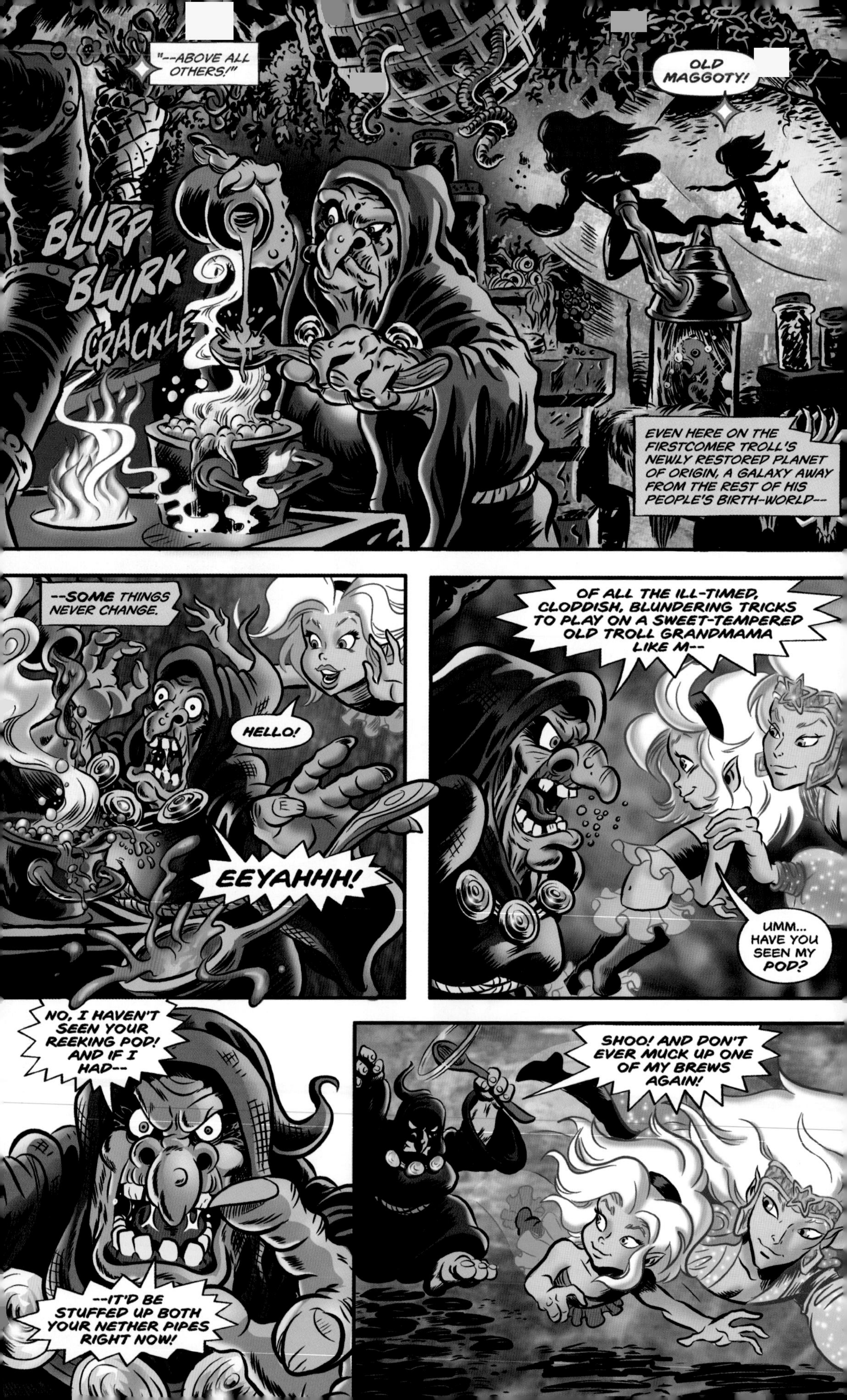
"--ABOVE ALL OTHERS!"
OLD MAGGOTY!
BLURP
BLURK
CRACKLE
EVEN HERE ON THE FIRSTCOMER TROLL'S NEWLY RESTORED PLANET OF ORIGIN, A GALAXY AWAY FROM THE REST OF HIS PEOPLE'S BIRTH-WORLD--
--SOME THINGS NEVER CHANGE.
HELLO!
EEYAHHH!
OF ALL THE ILL-TIMED, CLODDISH, BLUNDERING TRICKS TO PLAY ON A SWEET-TEMPERED OLD TROLL GRANDMAMA LIKE M--
UMM... HAVE YOU SEEN MY POD?
NO, I HAVEN'T SEEN YOUR REEKING POD! AND IF I HAD--
--IT'D BE STUFFED UP BOTH YOUR NETHER PIPES RIGHT NOW!
SHOO! AND DON'T EVER MUCK UP ONE OF MY BREWS AGAIN!

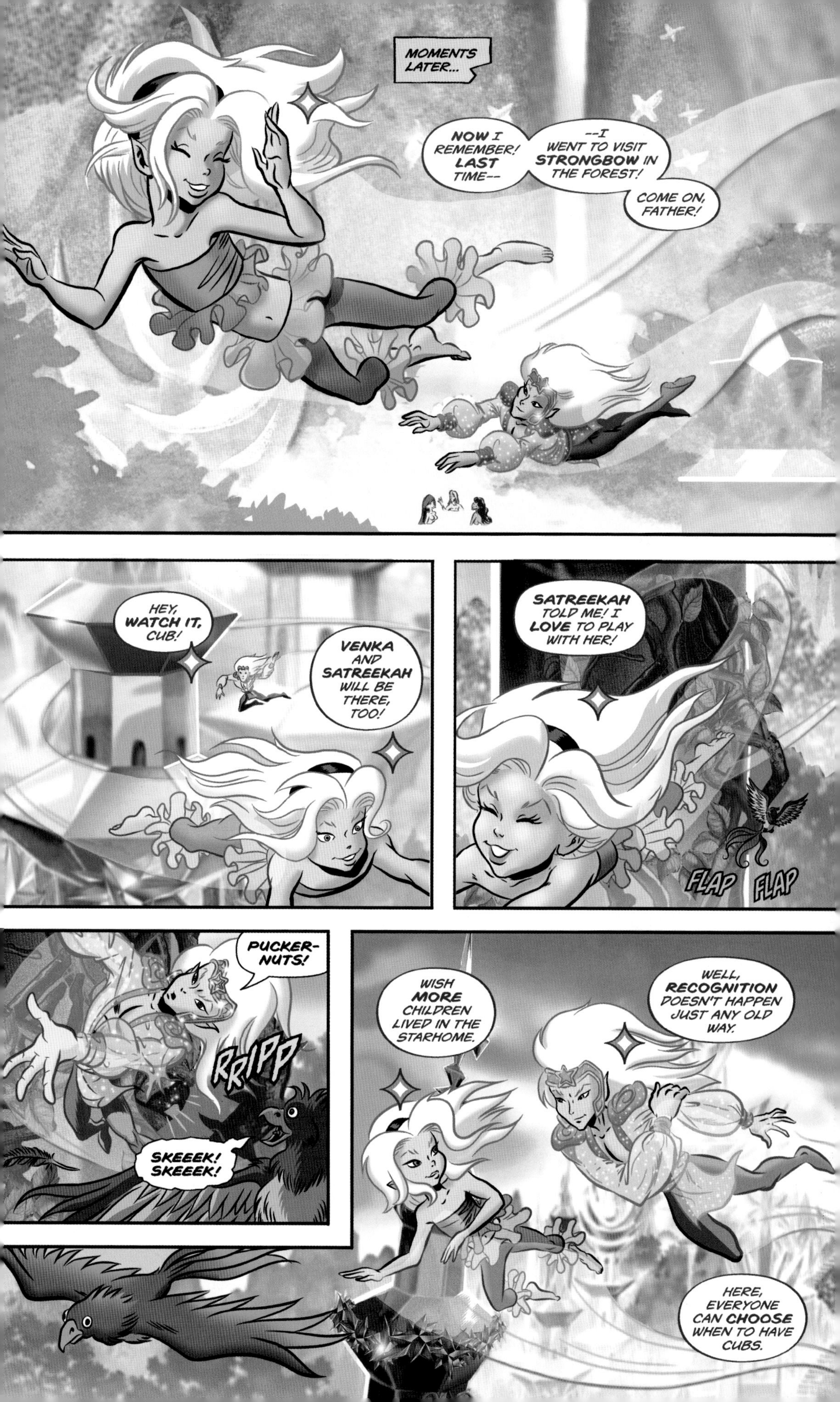
MOMENTS LATER...
NOW I REMEMBER! LAST TIME--
--I WENT TO VISIT STRONGBOW IN THE FOREST!
COME ON, FATHER!
HEY, WATCH IT, CUB!
VENKA AND SATREEKAH WILL BE THERE, TOO!
SATREEKAH TOLD ME! I LOVE TO PLAY WITH HER!
FLAP FLAP
PUCKER-NUTS!
RRIPP
SKEEEK! SKEEEK!
WISH MORE CHILDREN LIVED IN THE STARHOME.
WELL, RECOGNITION DOESN'T HAPPEN JUST ANY OLD WAY.
HERE, EVERYONE CAN CHOOSE WHEN TO HAVE CUBS.

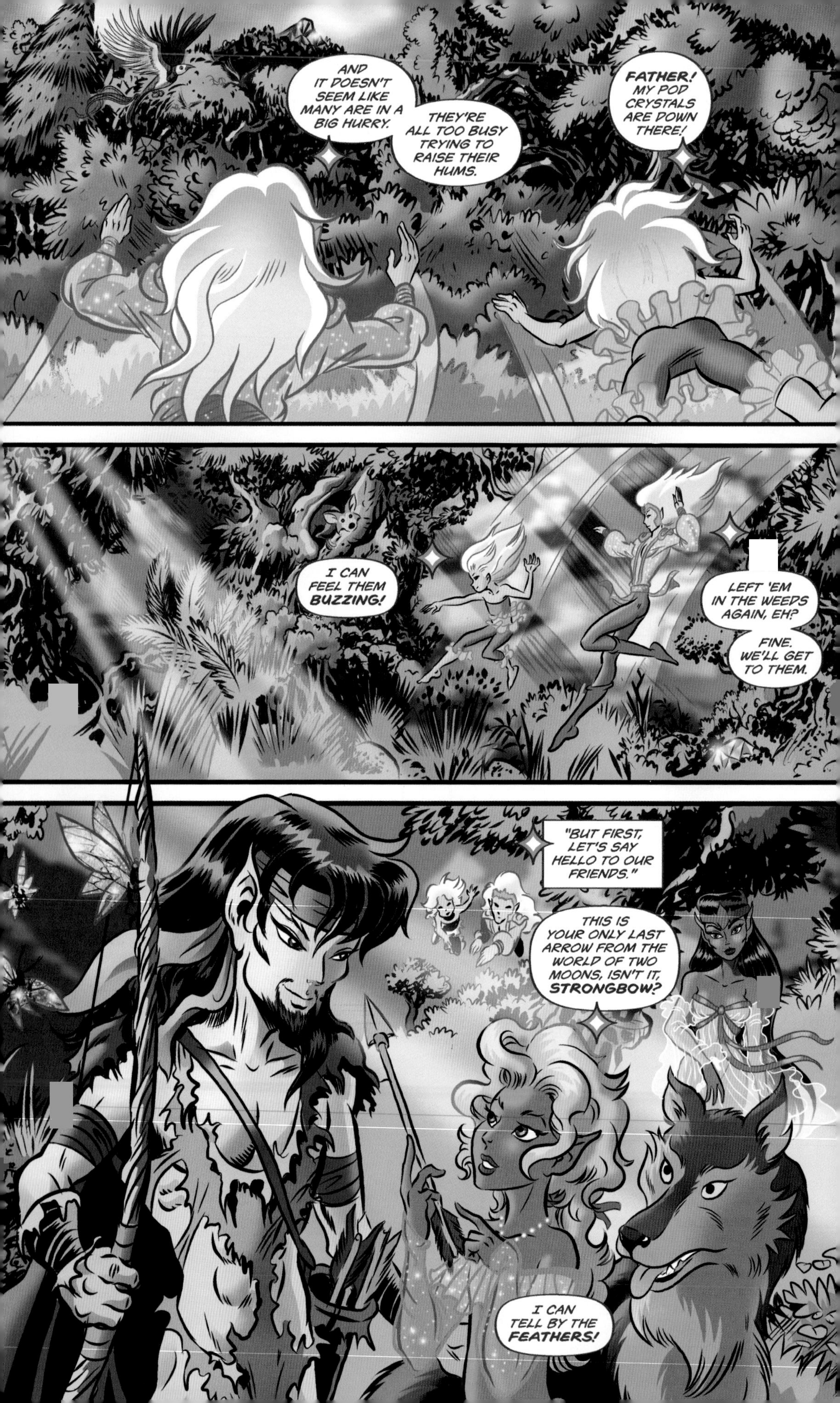
AND IT DOESN'T SEEM LIKE MANY ARE IN A BIG HURRY.
THEY'RE ALL TOO BUSY TRYING TO RAISE THEIR HUMS.
FATHER! MY POD CRYSTALS ARE DOWN THERE!
I CAN FEEL THEM BUZZING!
LEFT 'EM IN THE WEEDS AGAIN, EH?
FINE. WE'LL GET TO THEM.
"BUT FIRST, LET'S SAY HELLO TO OUR FRIENDS."
THIS IS YOUR ONLY LAST ARROW FROM THE WORLD OF TWO MOONS, ISN'T IT, STRONGBOW?
I CAN TELL BY THE FEATHERS!

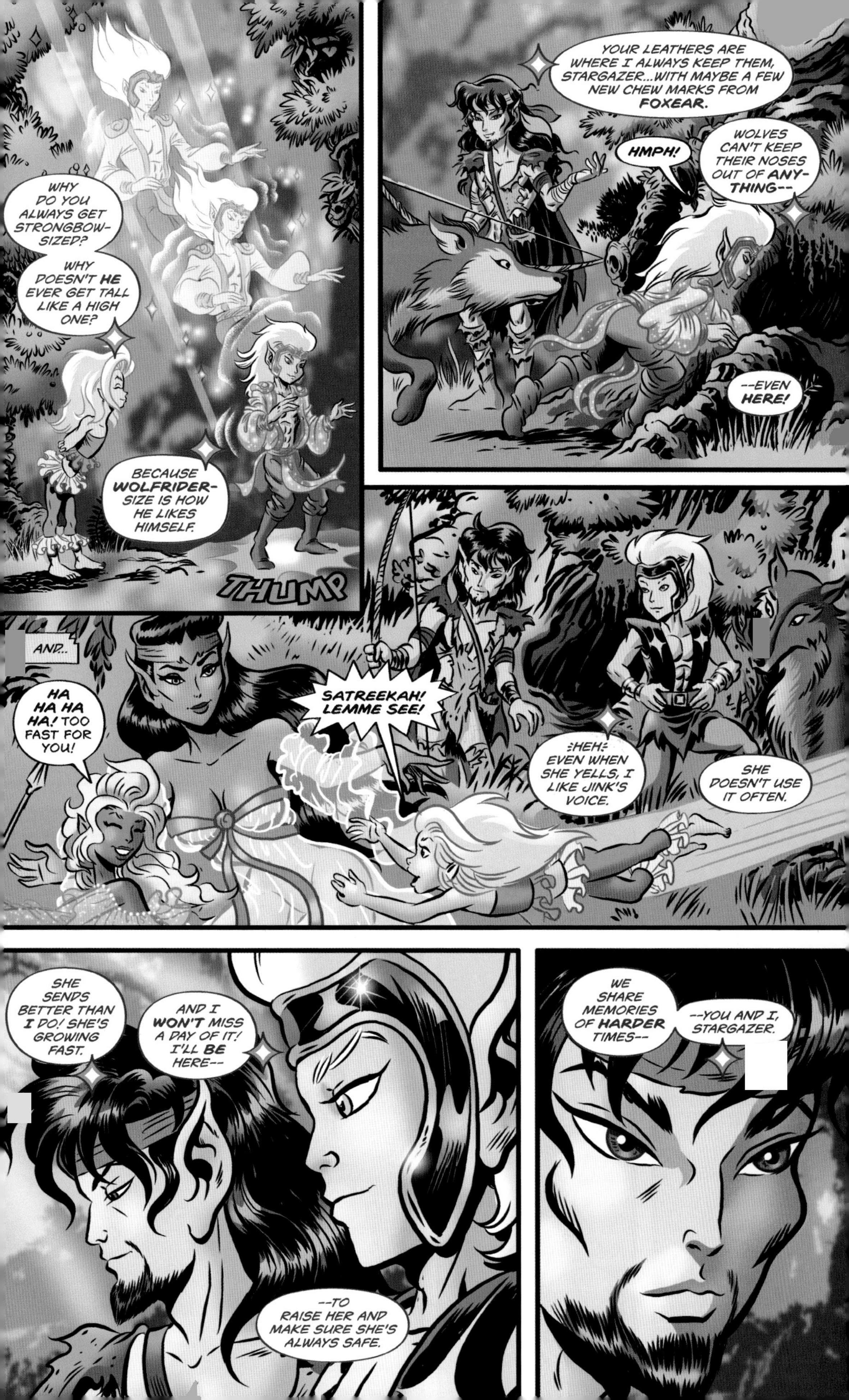
WHY DO YOU ALWAYS GET STRONGBOW-SIZED?
WHY DOESN'T HE EVER GET TALL LIKE A HIGH ONE?
BECAUSE WOLFRIDER-SIZE IS HOW HE LIKES HIMSELF.
THUMP
YOUR LEATHERS ARE WHERE I ALWAYS KEEP THEM, STARGAZER...WITH MAYBE A FEW NEW CHEW MARKS FROM FOXEAR.
HMPH!
WOLVES CAN'T KEEP THEIR NOSES OUT OF ANY-THING--
--EVEN HERE!
AND..
HA HA HA HA! TOO FAST FOR YOU!
SATREEKAH! LEMME SEE!
HEH EVEN WHEN SHE YELLS, I LIKE JINK'S VOICE.
SHE DOESN'T USE IT OFTEN.
SHE SENDS BETTER THAN I DO! SHE'S GROWING FAST.
AND I WON'T MISS A DAY OF IT! I'LL BE HERE--
--TO RAISE HER AND MAKE SURE SHE'S ALWAYS SAFE.
WE SHARE MEMORIES OF HARDER TIMES--
--YOU AND I, STARGAZER.

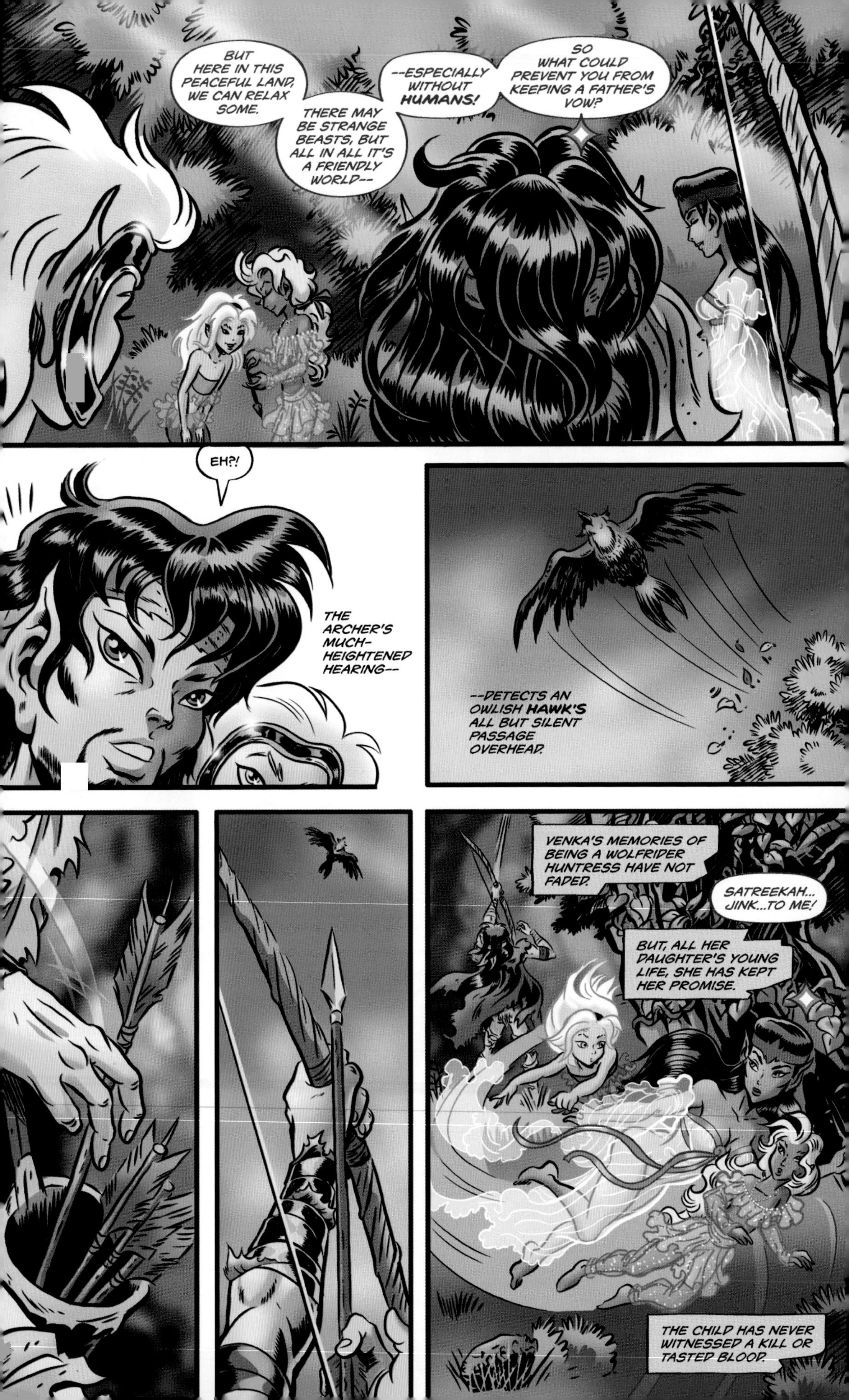
BUT HERE IN THIS PEACEFUL LAND, WE CAN RELAX SOME.
THERE MAY BE STRANGE BEASTS, BUT ALL IN ALL IT'S A FRIENDLY WORLD--
--ESPECIALLY WITHOUT HUMANS!
SO WHAT COULD PREVENT YOU FROM KEEPING A FATHER'S VOW?
EH?!
THE ARCHER'S MUCH-HEIGHTENED HEARING--
--DETECTS AN OWLISH HAWK'S ALL BUT SILENT PASSAGE OVERHEAD.
VENKA'S MEMORIES OF BEING A WOLFRIDER HUNTRESS HAVE NOT FADED.
SATREEKAH... JINK...TO ME!
BUT, ALL HER DAUGHTER'S YOUNG LIFE, SHE HAS KEPT HER PROMISE.
THE CHILD HAS NEVER WITNESSED A KILL OR TASTED BLOOD.

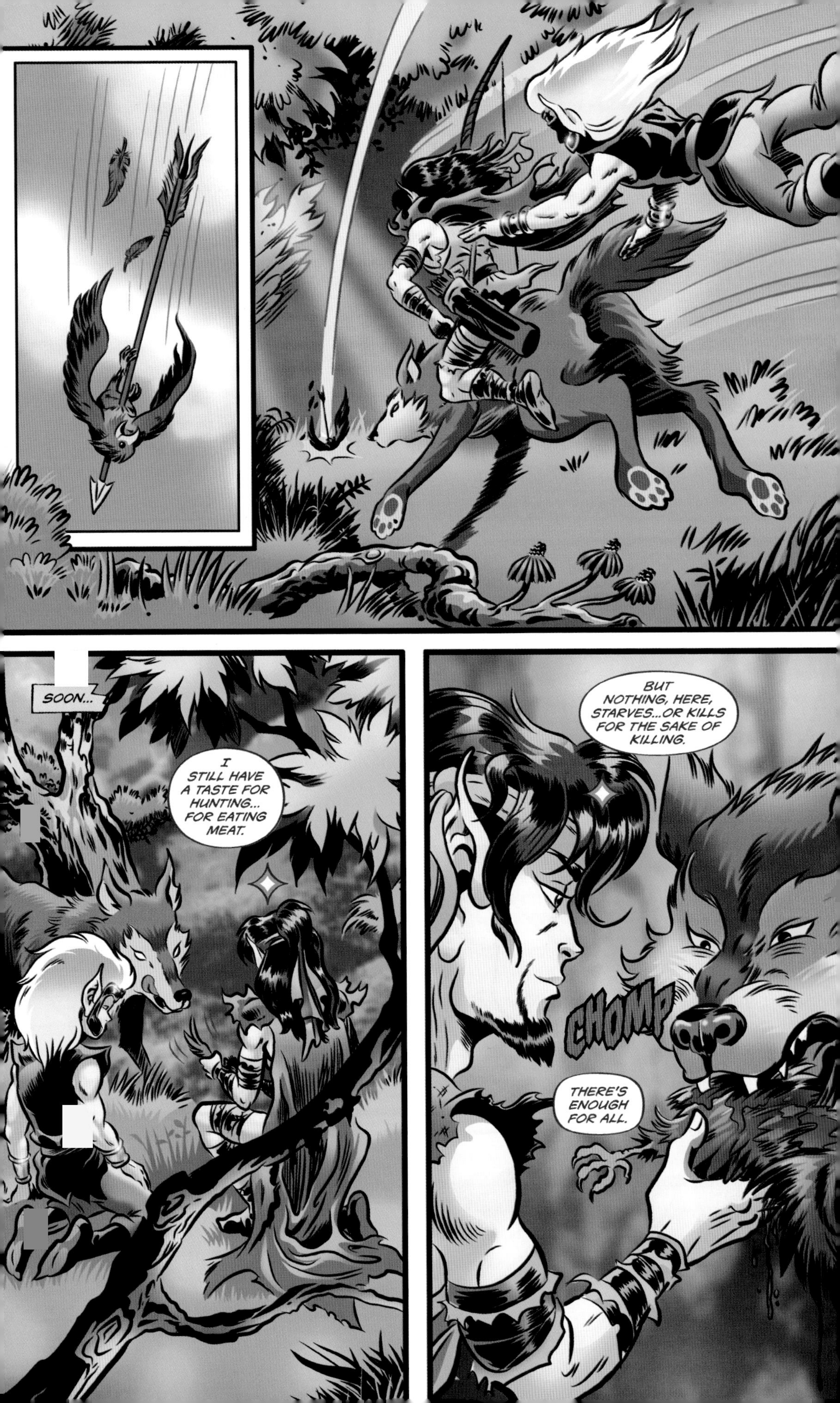
SOON...
I STILL HAVE A TASTE FOR HUNTING... FOR EATING MEAT.
BUT NOTHING, HERE, STARVES...OR KILLS FOR THE SAKE OF KILLING.
CHOMP
THERE'S ENOUGH FOR ALL.

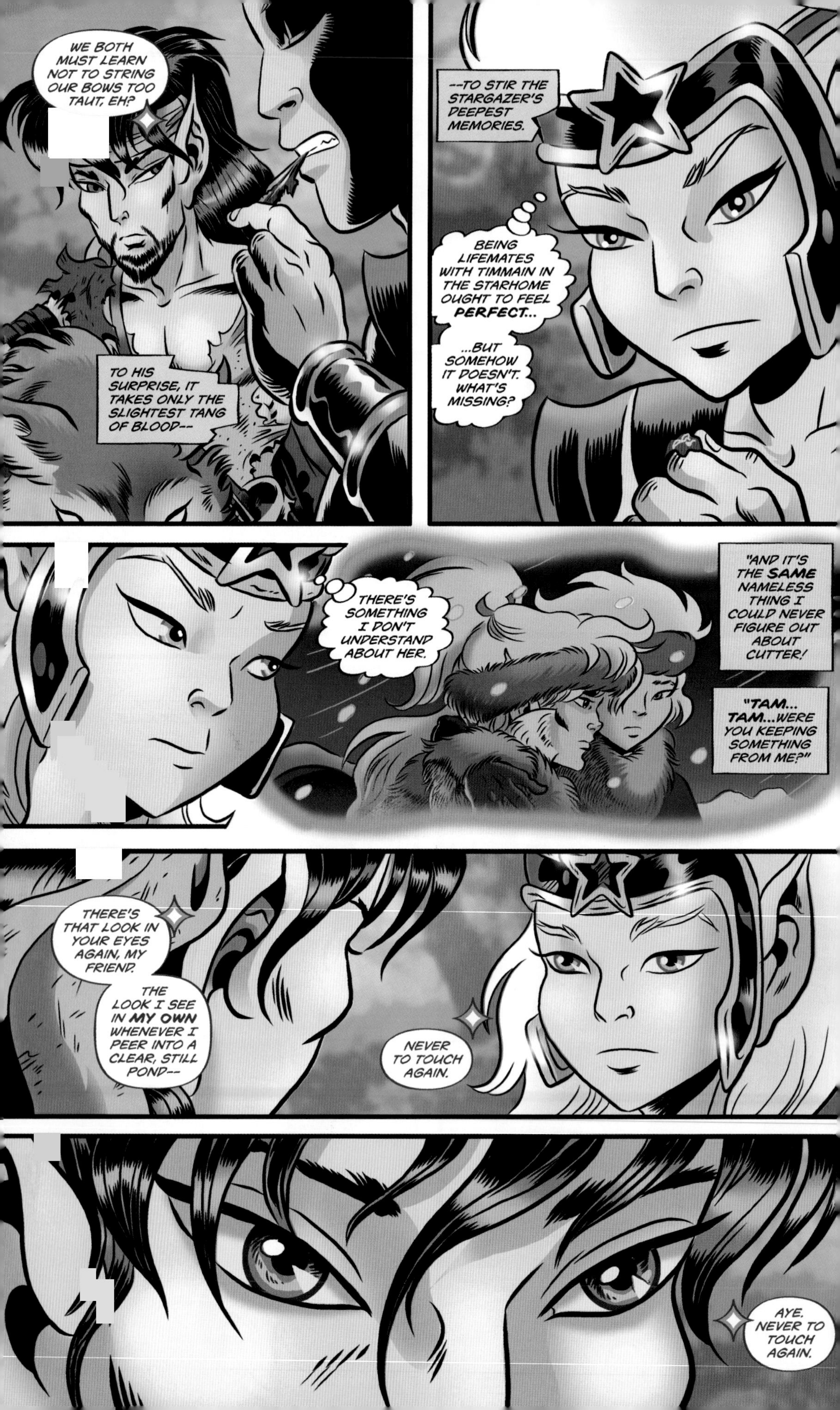
WE BOTH MUST LEARN NOT TO STRING OUR BOWS TOO TAUT, EH?
TO HIS SURPRISE, IT TAKES ONLY THE SLIGHTEST TANG OF BLOOD--
--TO STIR THE STARGAZER'S DEEPEST MEMORIES.
BEING LIFEMATES WITH TIMMAIN IN THE STARHOME OUGHT TO FEEL PERFECT...
...BUT SOMEHOW IT DOESN'T. WHAT'S MISSING?
THERE'S SOMETHING I DON'T UNDERSTAND ABOUT HER.
"AND IT'S THE SAME NAMELESS THING I COULD NEVER FIGURE OUT ABOUT CUTTER!
"TAM... TAM...WERE YOU KEEPING SOMETHING FROM ME?"
THERE'S THAT LOOK IN YOUR EYES AGAIN, MY FRIEND.
THE LOOK I SEE IN MY OWN WHENEVER I PEER INTO A CLEAR, STILL POND--
NEVER TO TOUCH AGAIN.
AYE. NEVER TO TOUCH AGAIN.

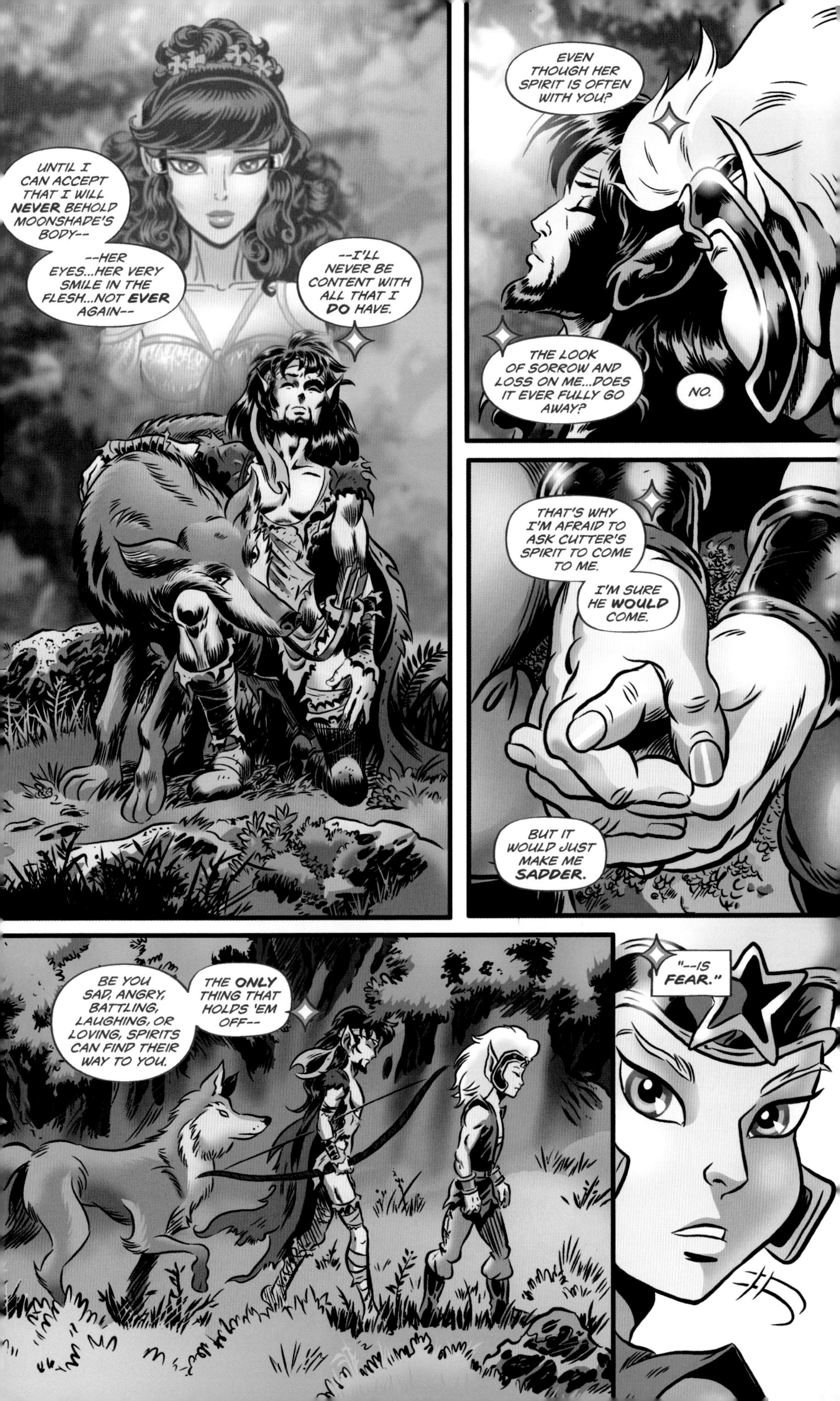

UNTIL I CAN ACCEPT THAT I WILL NEVER BEHOLD MOONSHADE'S BODY--
--HER EYES...HER VERY SMILE IN THE FLESH...NOT EVER AGAIN--
--I'LL NEVER BE CONTENT WITH ALL THAT I DO HAVE.
EVEN THOUGH HER SPIRIT IS OFTEN WITH YOU?
THE LOOK OF SORROW AND LOSS ON ME...DOES IT EVER FULLY GO AWAY?
NO.
THAT'S WHY I'M AFRAID TO ASK CUTTER'S SPIRIT TO COME TO ME.
I'M SURE HE WOULD COME.
BUT IT WOULD JUST MAKE ME SADDER.
BE YOU SAD, ANGRY, BATTLING, LAUGHING, OR LOVING, SPIRITS CAN FIND THEIR WAY TO YOU.
THE ONLY THING THAT HOLDS 'EM OFF--
"--IS FEAR."

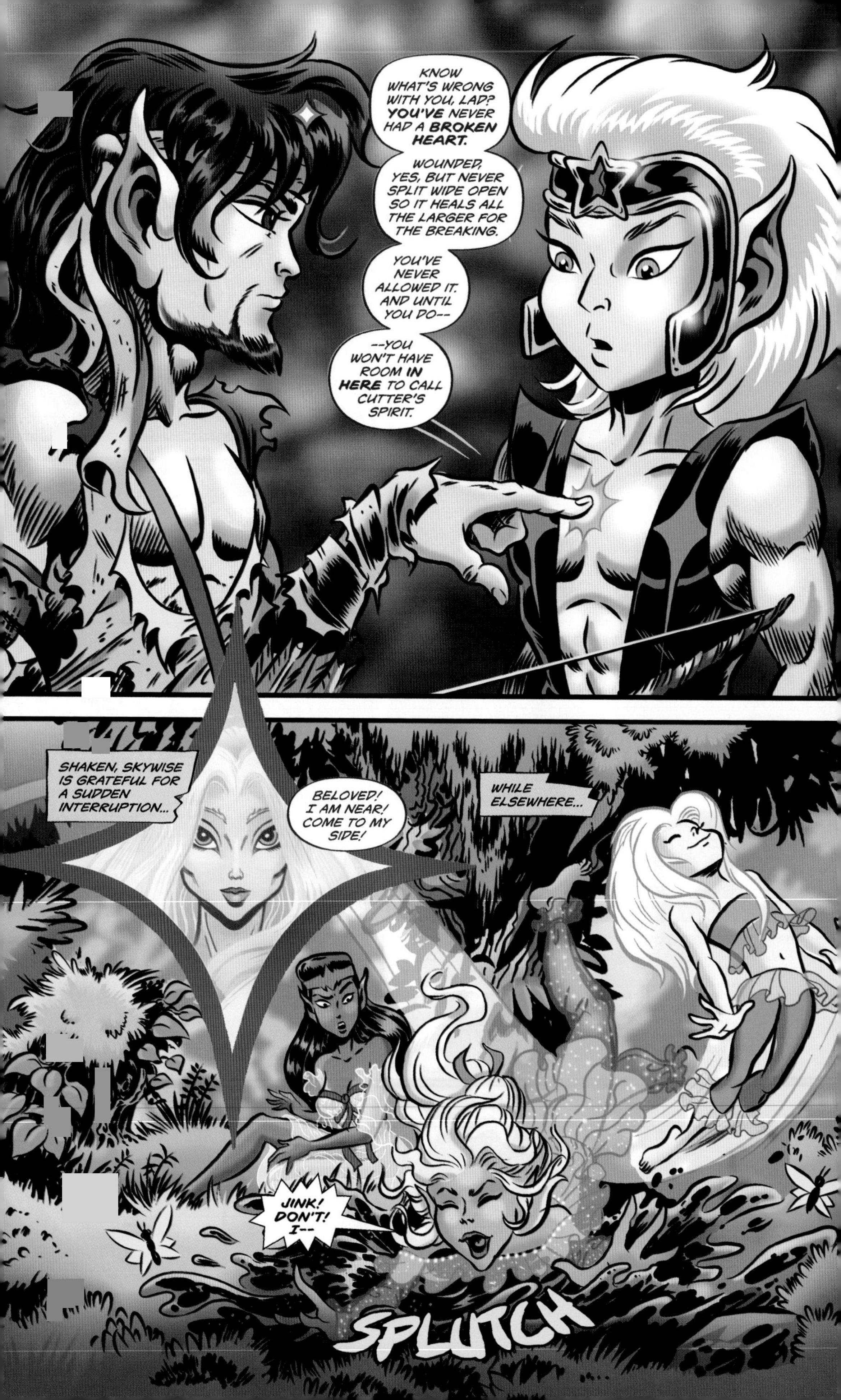
KNOW WHAT'S WRONG WITH YOU, LAD? YOU'VE NEVER HAD A BROKEN HEART.
WOUNDED, YES, BUT NEVER SPLIT WIDE OPEN SO IT HEALS ALL THE LARGER FOR THE BREAKING.
YOU'VE NEVER ALLOWED IT. AND UNTIL YOU DO--
--YOU WON'T HAVE ROOM IN HERE TO CALL CUTTER'S SPIRIT.
SHAKEN, SKYWISE IS GRATEFUL FOR A SUDDEN INTERRUPTION...
BELOVED! I AM NEAR! COME TO MY SIDE!
WHILE ELSEWHERE...
JINK! DON'T! I--
SPLUTCH

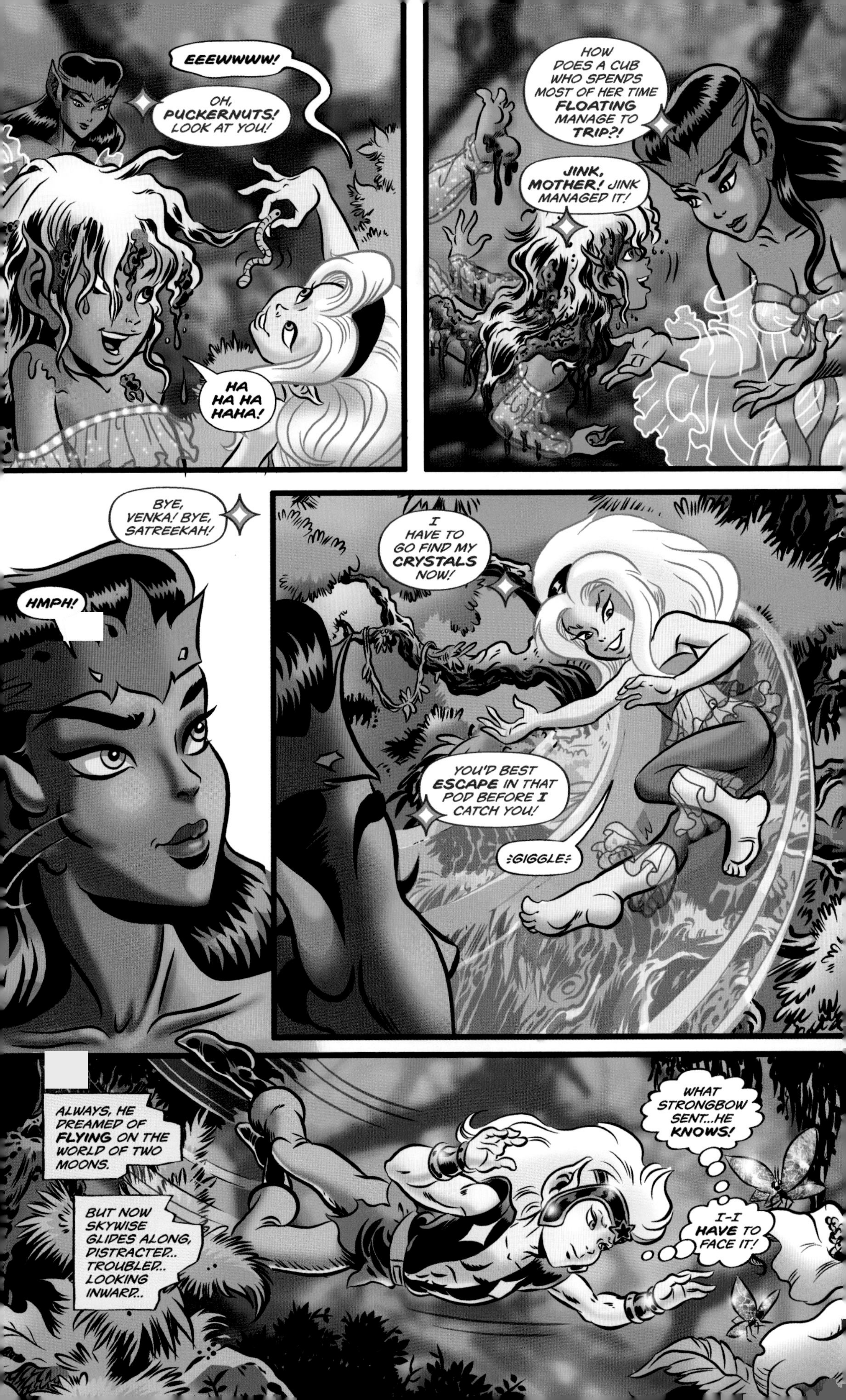
EEEWWWW!
OH, PUCKERNUTS! LOOK AT YOU!
HA HA HA HAHA!
HOW DOES A CUB WHO SPENDS MOST OF HER TIME FLOATING MANAGE TO TRIP?!
JINK, MOTHER! JINK MANAGED IT!
BYE, VENKA! BYE, SATREEKAH!
HMPH!
I HAVE TO GO FIND MY CRYSTALS NOW!
YOU'D BEST ESCAPE IN THAT POD BEFORE I CATCH YOU!
GIGGLE
ALWAYS, HE DREAMED OF FLYING ON THE WORLD OF TWO MOONS.
BUT NOW SKYWISE GLIDES ALONG, DISTRACTED.. TROUBLED.. LOOKING INWARD..
WHAT STRONGBOW SENT...HE KNOWS!
I-I HAVE TO FACE IT!

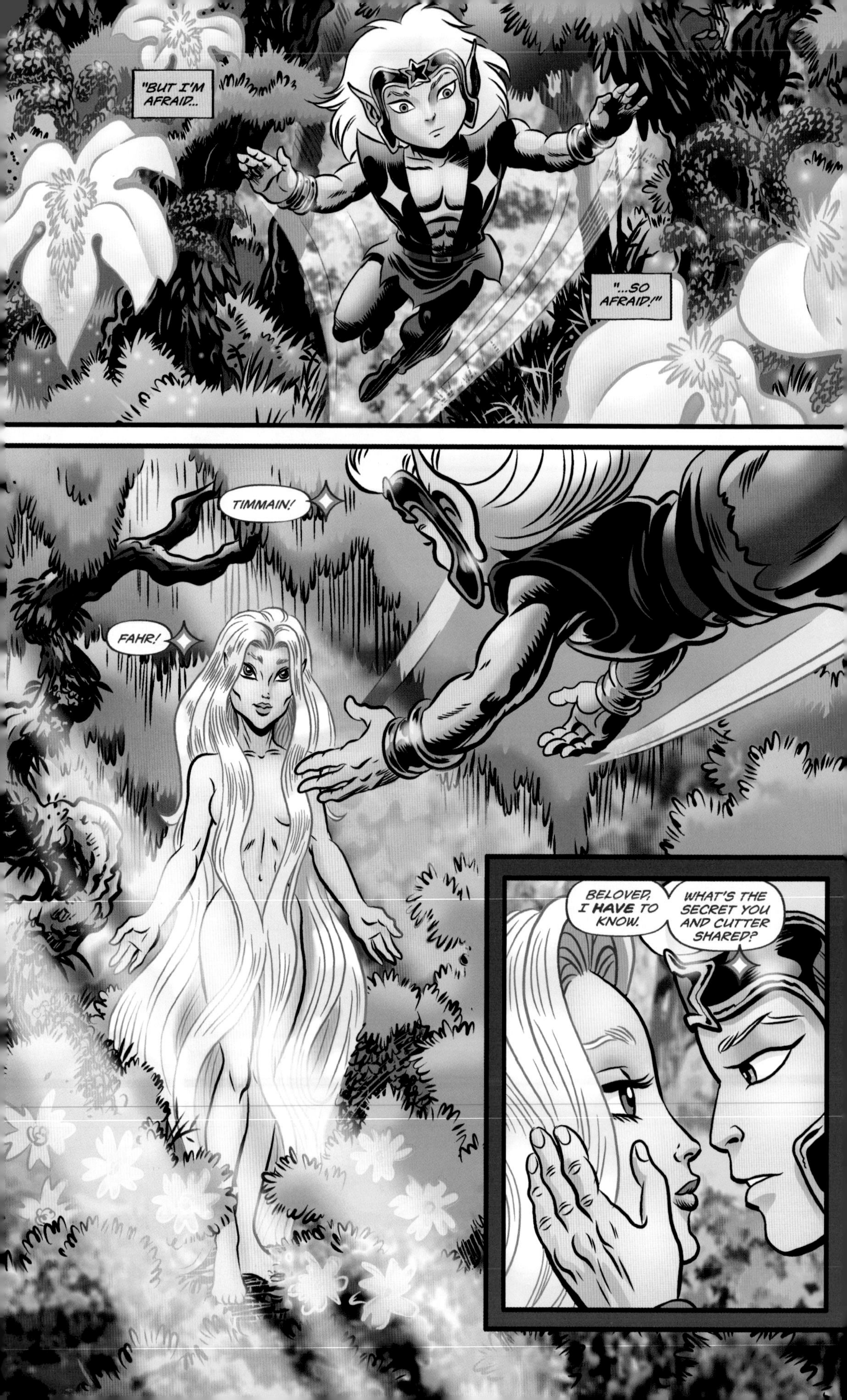
"BUT I'M AFRAID...
"...SO AFRAID!"
TIMMAIN!
FAHR!
BELOVED, I **HAVE** TO KNOW.
WHAT'S THE SECRET YOU AND CUTTER SHARED?

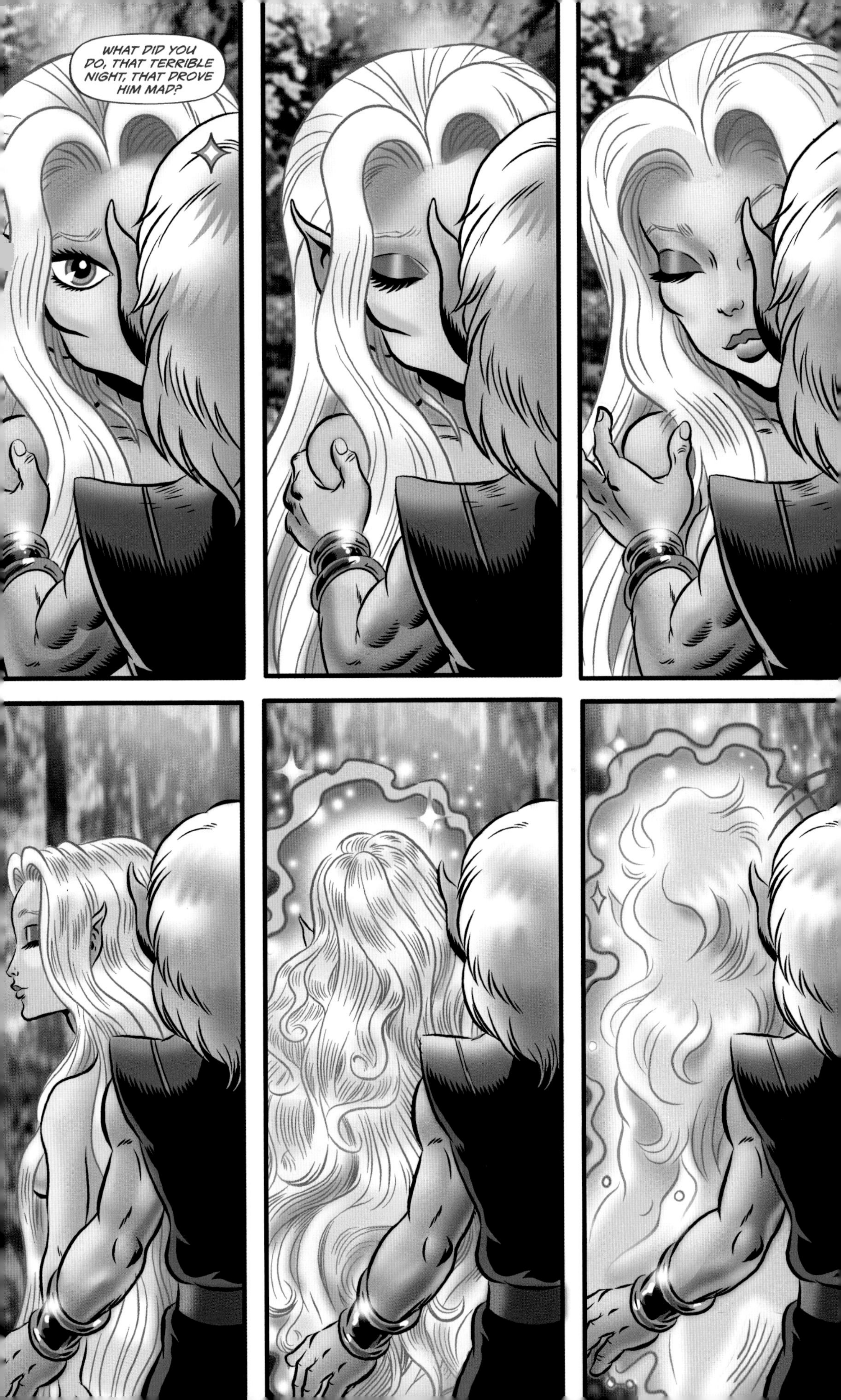
WHAT DID YOU DO, THAT TERRIBLE NIGHT, THAT DROVE HIM MAD?

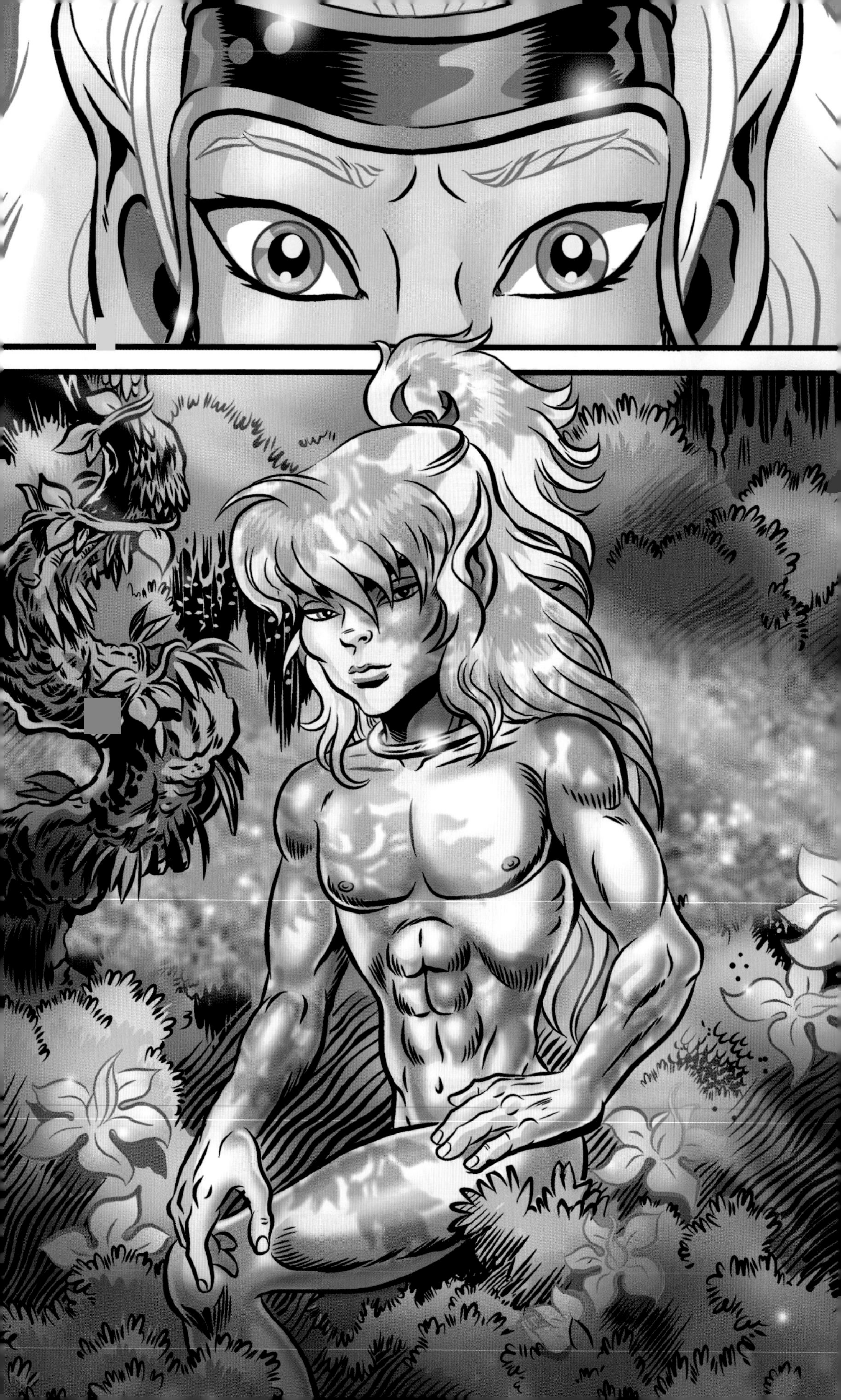

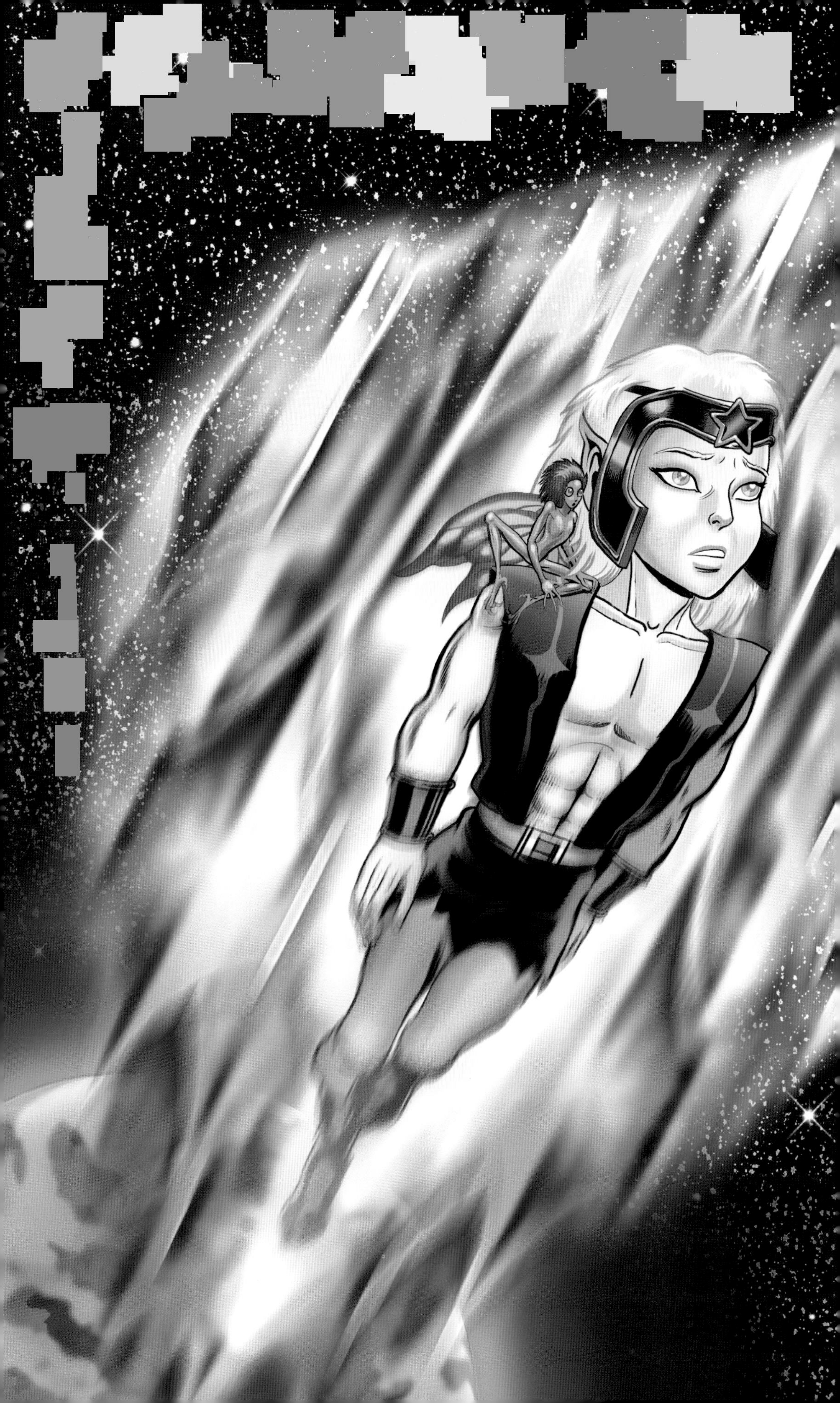

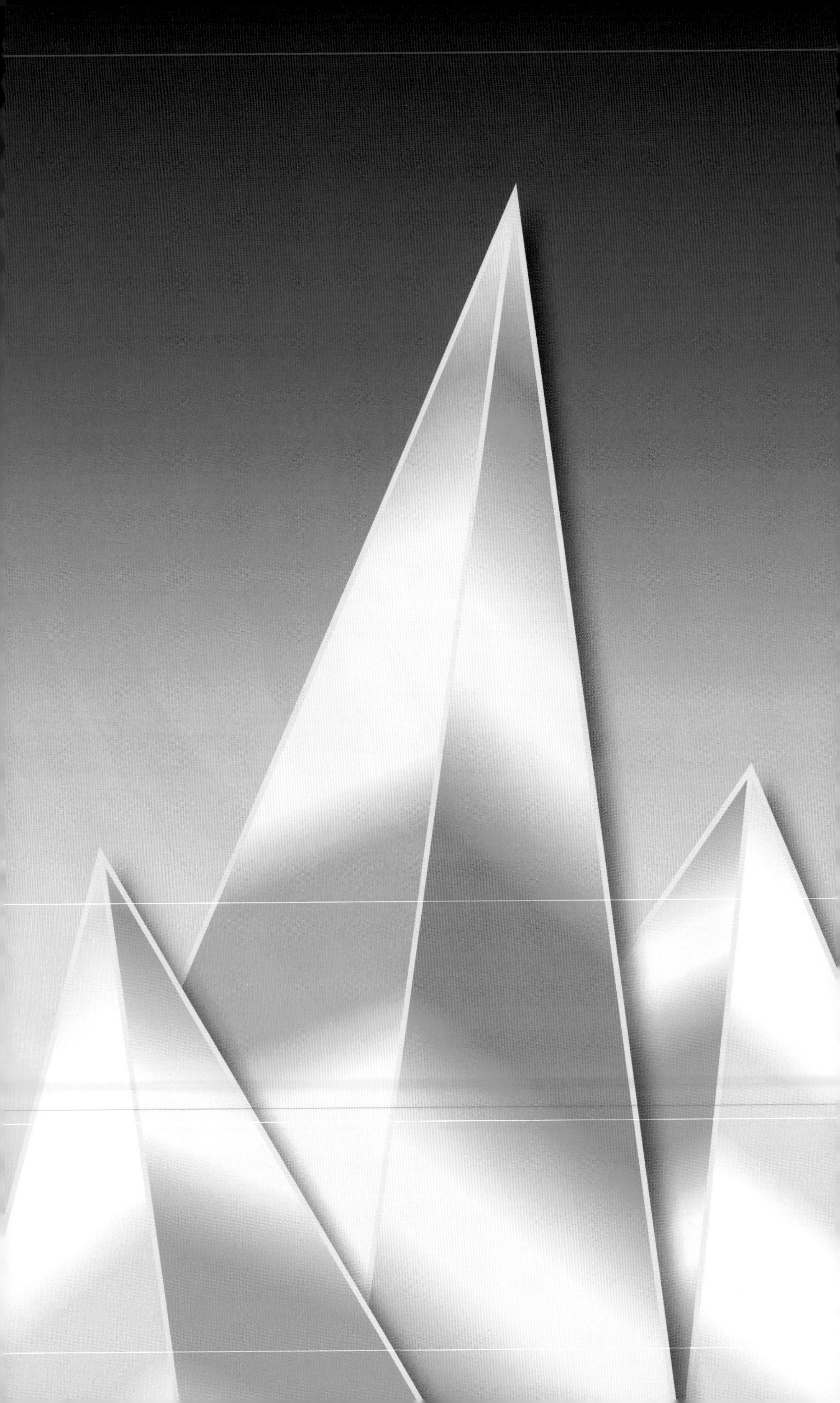

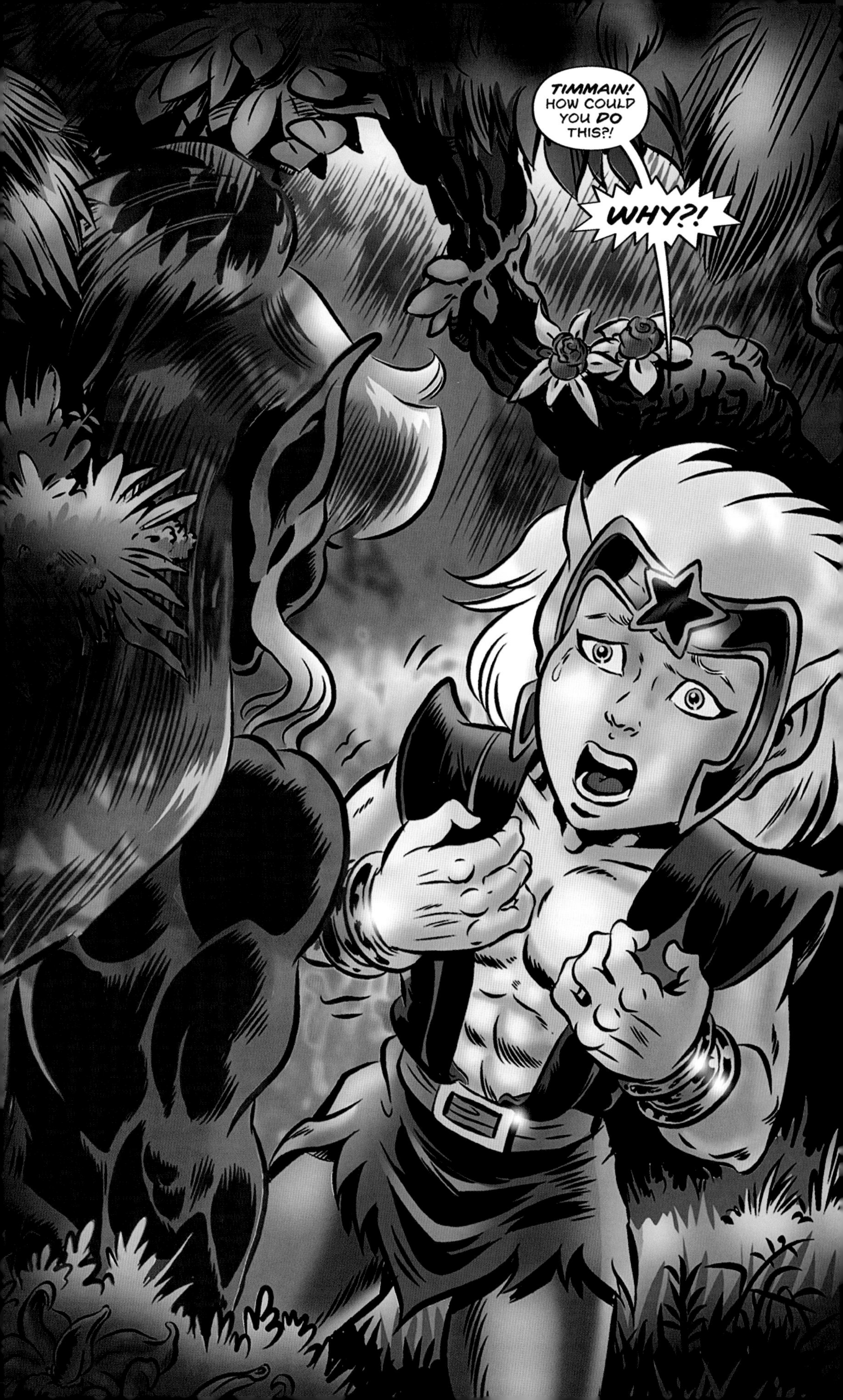
TIMMAIN! HOW COULD YOU DO THIS?!
WHY?!

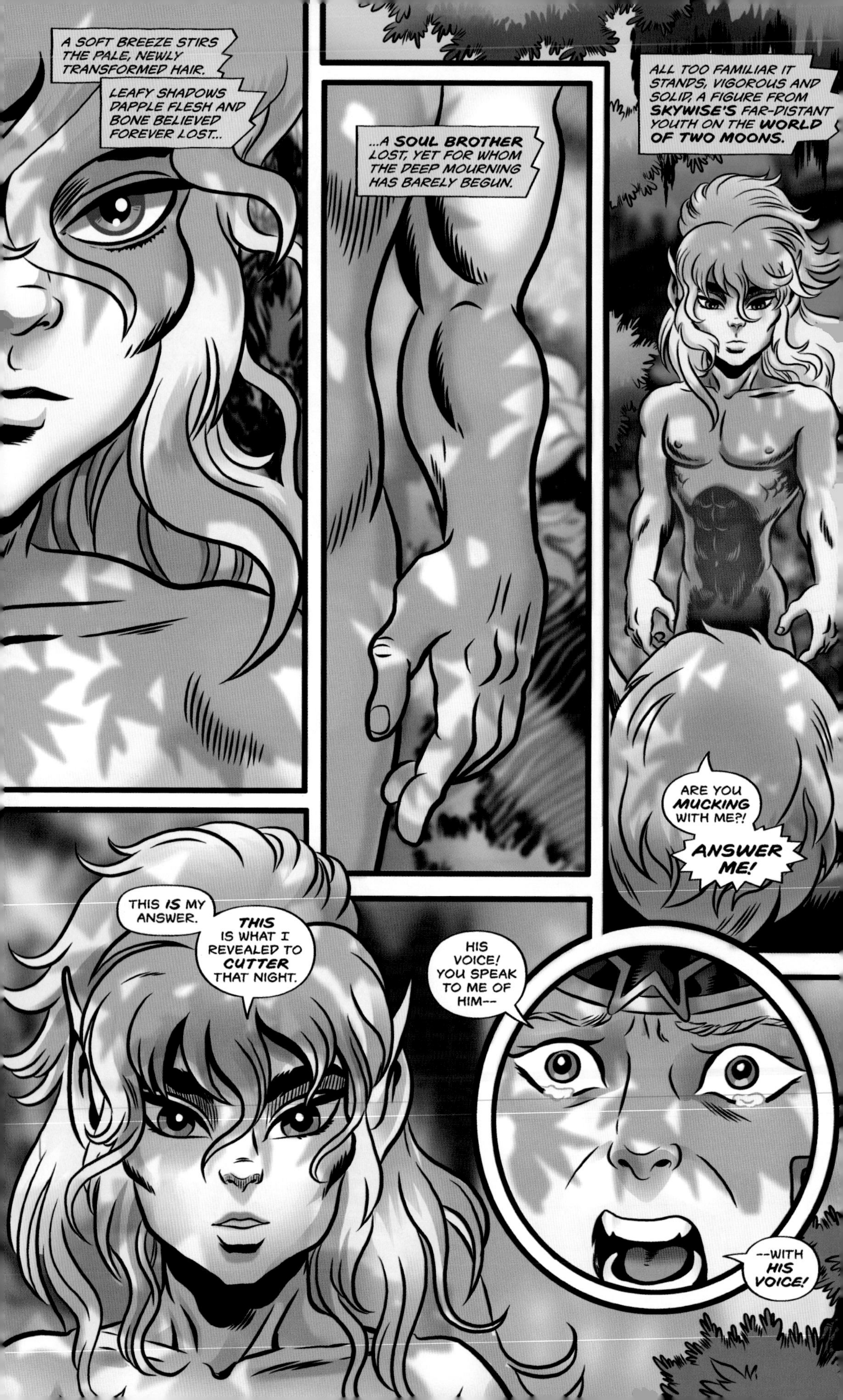
A SOFT BREEZE STIRS THE PALE, NEWLY TRANSFORMED HAIR.
LEAFY SHADOWS DAPPLE FLESH AND BONE BELIEVED FOREVER LOST...
...A SOUL BROTHER LOST, YET FOR WHOM THE DEEP MOURNING HAS BARELY BEGUN.
ALL TOO FAMILIAR IT STANDS, VIGOROUS AND SOLID, A FIGURE FROM SKYWISE'S FAR-DISTANT YOUTH ON THE WORLD OF TWO MOONS.
ARE YOU MUCKING WITH ME?!
ANSWER ME!
THIS IS MY ANSWER.
THIS IS WHAT I REVEALED TO CUTTER THAT NIGHT.
HIS VOICE! YOU SPEAK TO ME OF HIM--
--WITH HIS VOICE!

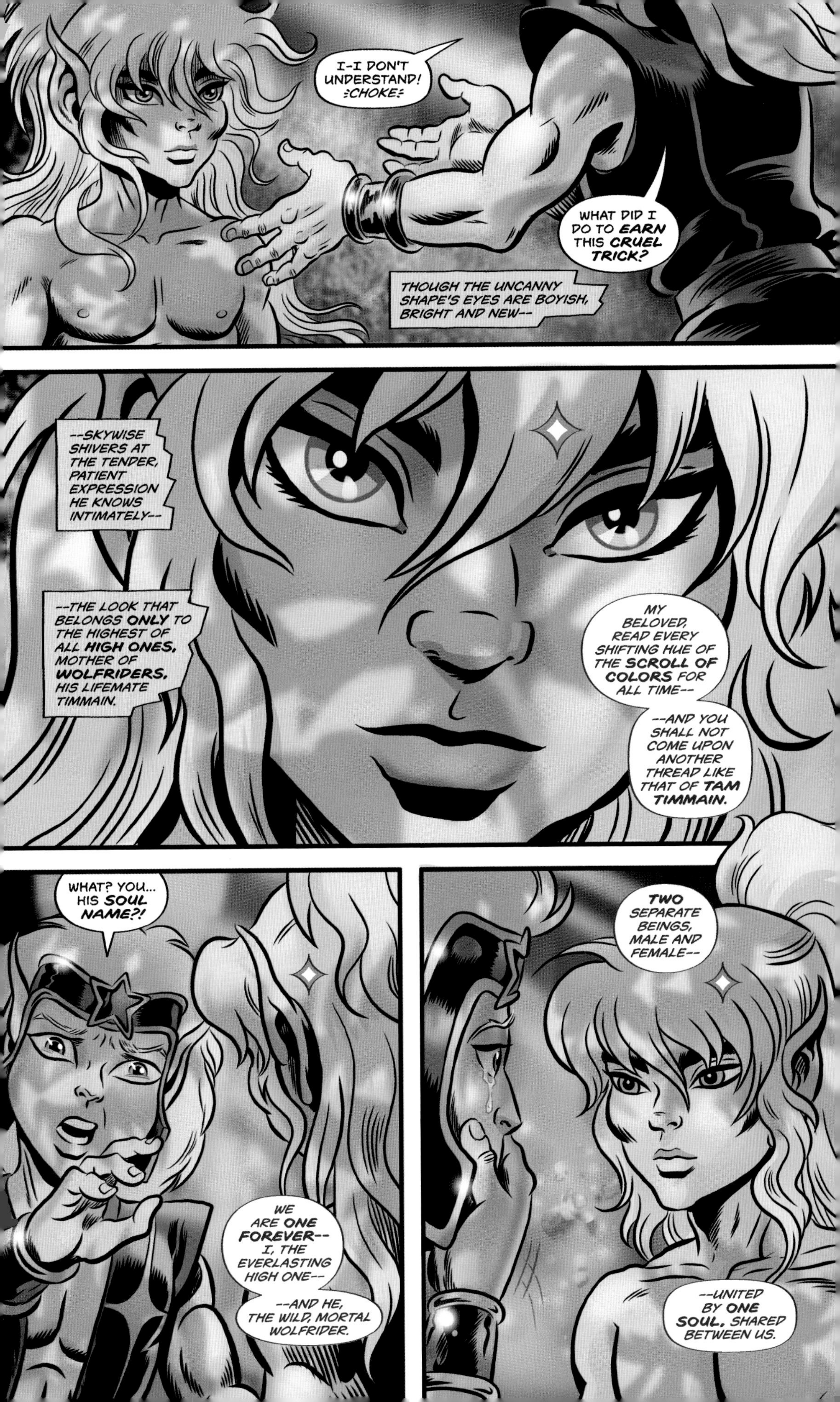
I-I DON'T UNDERSTAND! CHOKE
WHAT DID I DO TO EARN THIS CRUEL TRICK?
THOUGH THE UNCANNY SHAPE'S EYES ARE BOYISH, BRIGHT AND NEW--
--SKYWISE SHIVERS AT THE TENDER, PATIENT EXPRESSION HE KNOWS INTIMATELY--
--THE LOOK THAT BELONGS ONLY TO THE HIGHEST OF ALL HIGH ONES, MOTHER OF WOLFRIDERS, HIS LIFEMATE TIMMAIN.
MY BELOVED, READ EVERY SHIFTING HUE OF THE SCROLL OF COLORS FOR ALL TIME--
--AND YOU SHALL NOT COME UPON ANOTHER THREAD LIKE THAT OF TAM TIMMAIN.
WHAT? YOU... HIS SOUL NAME?!
WE ARE ONE FOREVER-- I, THE EVERLASTING HIGH ONE--
--AND HE, THE WILD, MORTAL WOLFRIDER.
TWO SEPARATE BEINGS, MALE AND FEMALE--
--UNITED BY ONE SOUL, SHARED BETWEEN US.

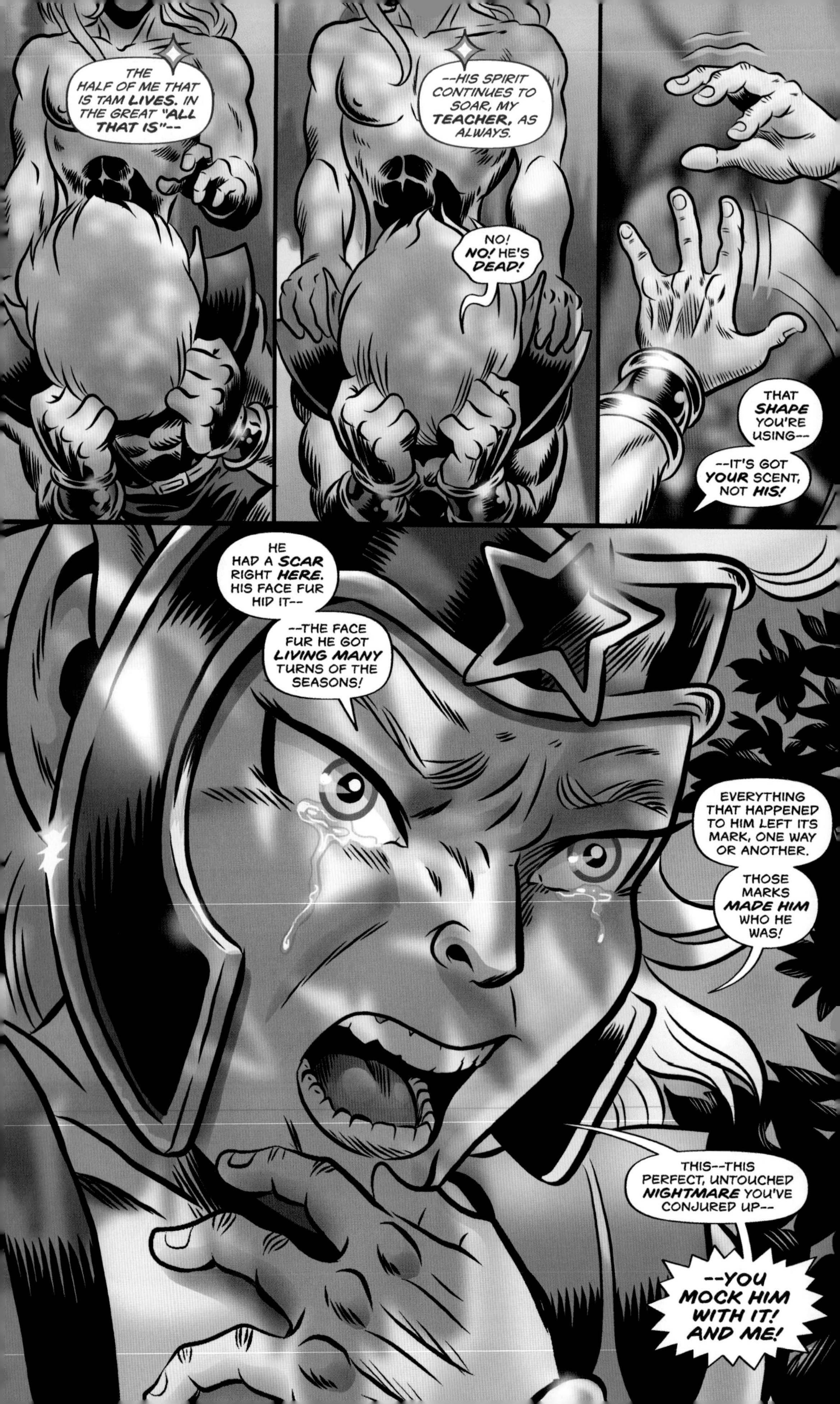
THE HALF OF ME THAT IS TAM LIVES. IN THE GREAT "ALL THAT IS"--
--HIS SPIRIT CONTINUES TO SOAR, MY TEACHER, AS ALWAYS.
NO! NO! HE'S DEAD!
THAT SHAPE YOU'RE USING--
--IT'S GOT YOUR SCENT, NOT HIS!
HE HAD A SCAR RIGHT HERE. HIS FACE FUR HID IT--
--THE FACE FUR HE GOT LIVING MANY TURNS OF THE SEASONS!
EVERYTHING THAT HAPPENED TO HIM LEFT ITS MARK, ONE WAY OR ANOTHER.
THOSE MARKS MADE HIM WHO HE WAS!
THIS--THIS PERFECT, UNTOUCHED NIGHTMARE YOU'VE CONJURED UP--
--YOU MOCK HIM WITH IT! AND ME!

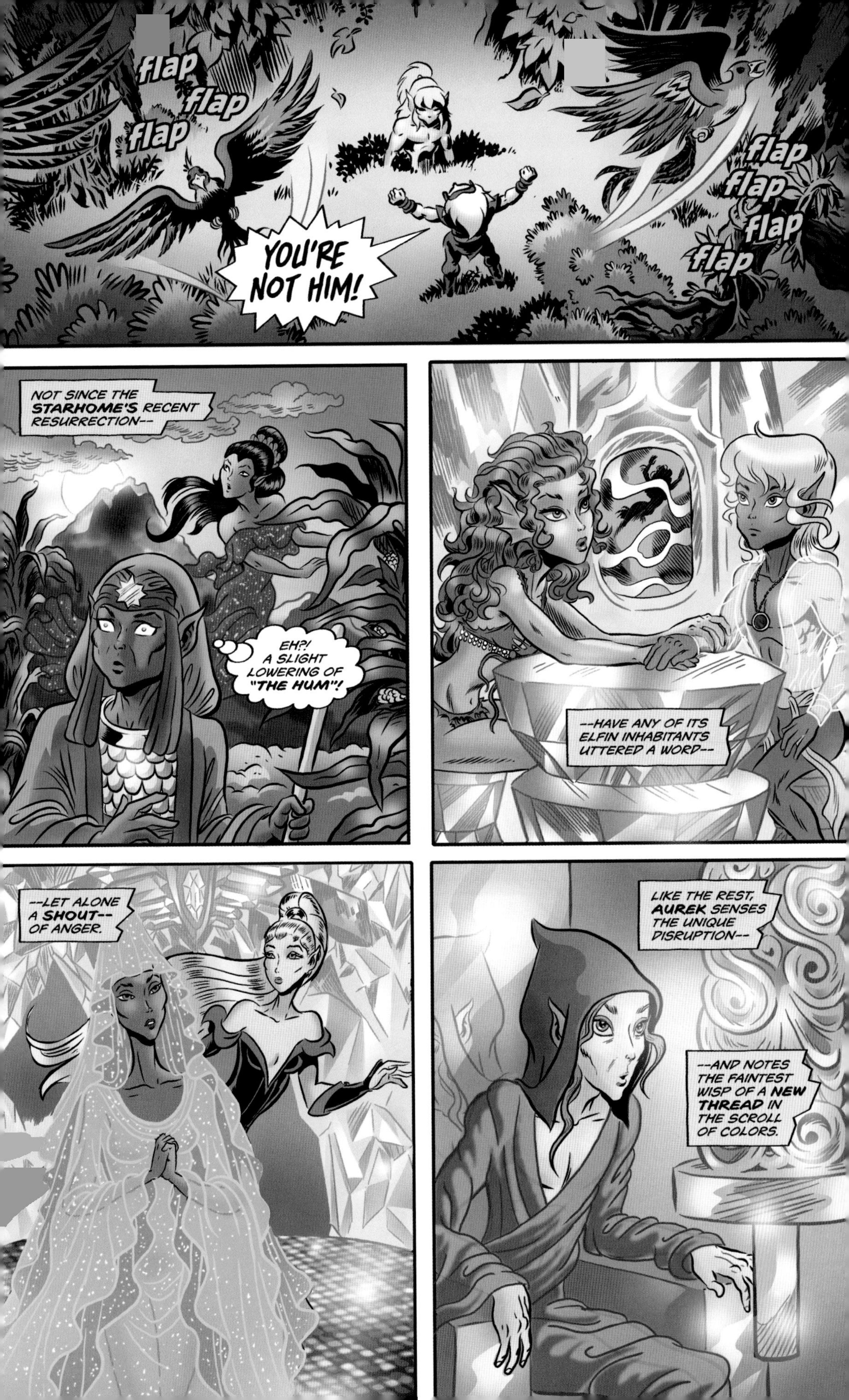

flap
flap
flap
flap
flap
flap
flap
YOU'RE NOT HIM!
NOT SINCE THE STARHOME'S RECENT RESURRECTION--
EH?! A SLIGHT LOWERING OF "THE HUM"!
--HAVE ANY OF ITS ELFIN INHABITANTS UTTERED A WORD--
--LET ALONE A SHOUT-- OF ANGER.
LIKE THE REST, AUREK SENSES THE UNIQUE DISRUPTION--
--AND NOTES THE FAINTEST WISP OF A NEW THREAD IN THE SCROLL OF COLORS.

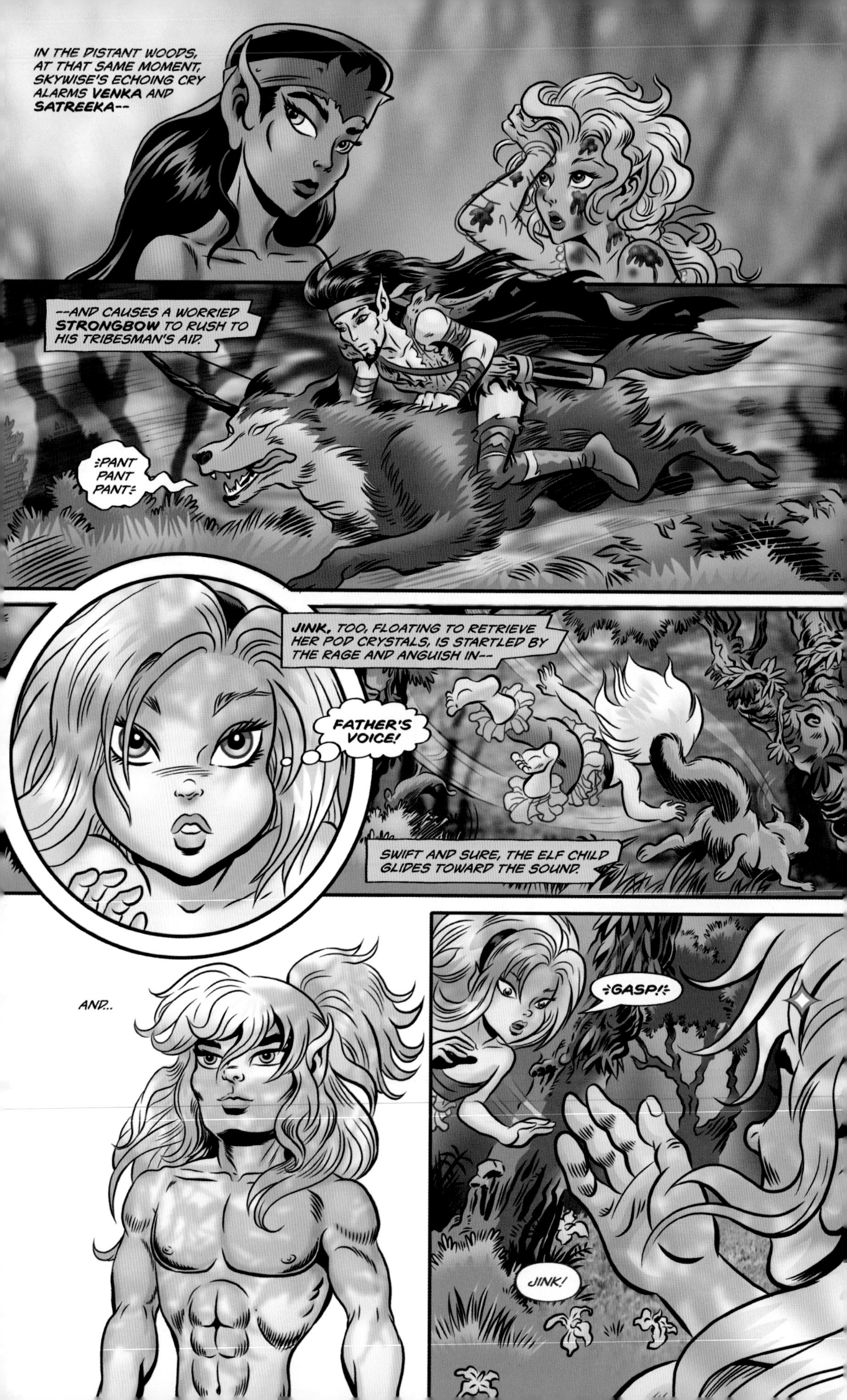
IN THE DISTANT WOODS, AT THAT SAME MOMENT, SKYWISE'S ECHOING CRY ALARMS VENKA AND SATREEKA--
--AND CAUSES A WORRIED STRONGBOW TO RUSH TO HIS TRIBESMAN'S AID.
PANT PANT PANT
JINK, TOO, FLOATING TO RETRIEVE HER POD CRYSTALS, IS STARTLED BY THE RAGE AND ANGUISH IN--
FATHER'S VOICE!
SWIFT AND SURE, THE ELF CHILD GLIDES TOWARD THE SOUND.
AND...
GASP!
JINK!

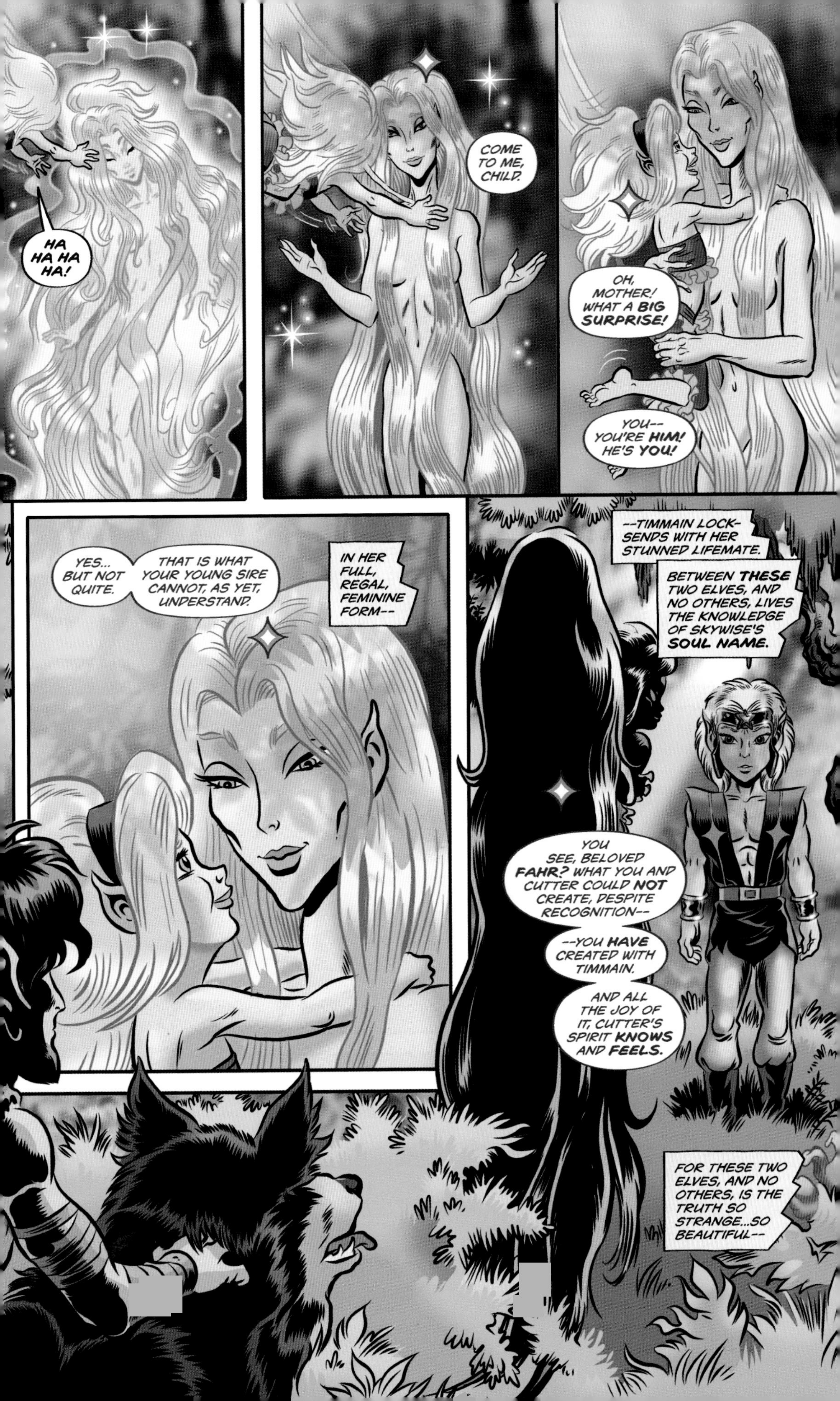
HA HA HA HA!
COME TO ME, CHILD.
OH, MOTHER! WHAT A BIG SURPRISE!
YOU-- YOU'RE HIM! HE'S YOU!
YES... BUT NOT QUITE.
THAT IS WHAT YOUR YOUNG SIRE CANNOT, AS YET, UNDERSTAND.
IN HER FULL, REGAL, FEMININE FORM--
--TIMMAIN LOCK-SENDS WITH HER STUNNED LIFEMATE.
BETWEEN THESE TWO ELVES, AND NO OTHERS, LIVES THE KNOWLEDGE OF SKYWISE'S SOUL NAME.
YOU SEE, BELOVED FAHR? WHAT YOU AND CUTTER COULD NOT CREATE, DESPITE RECOGNITION--
--YOU HAVE CREATED WITH TIMMAIN.
AND ALL THE JOY OF IT, CUTTER'S SPIRIT KNOWS AND FEELS.
FOR THESE TWO ELVES, AND NO OTHERS, IS THE TRUTH SO STRANGE...SO BEAUTIFUL--

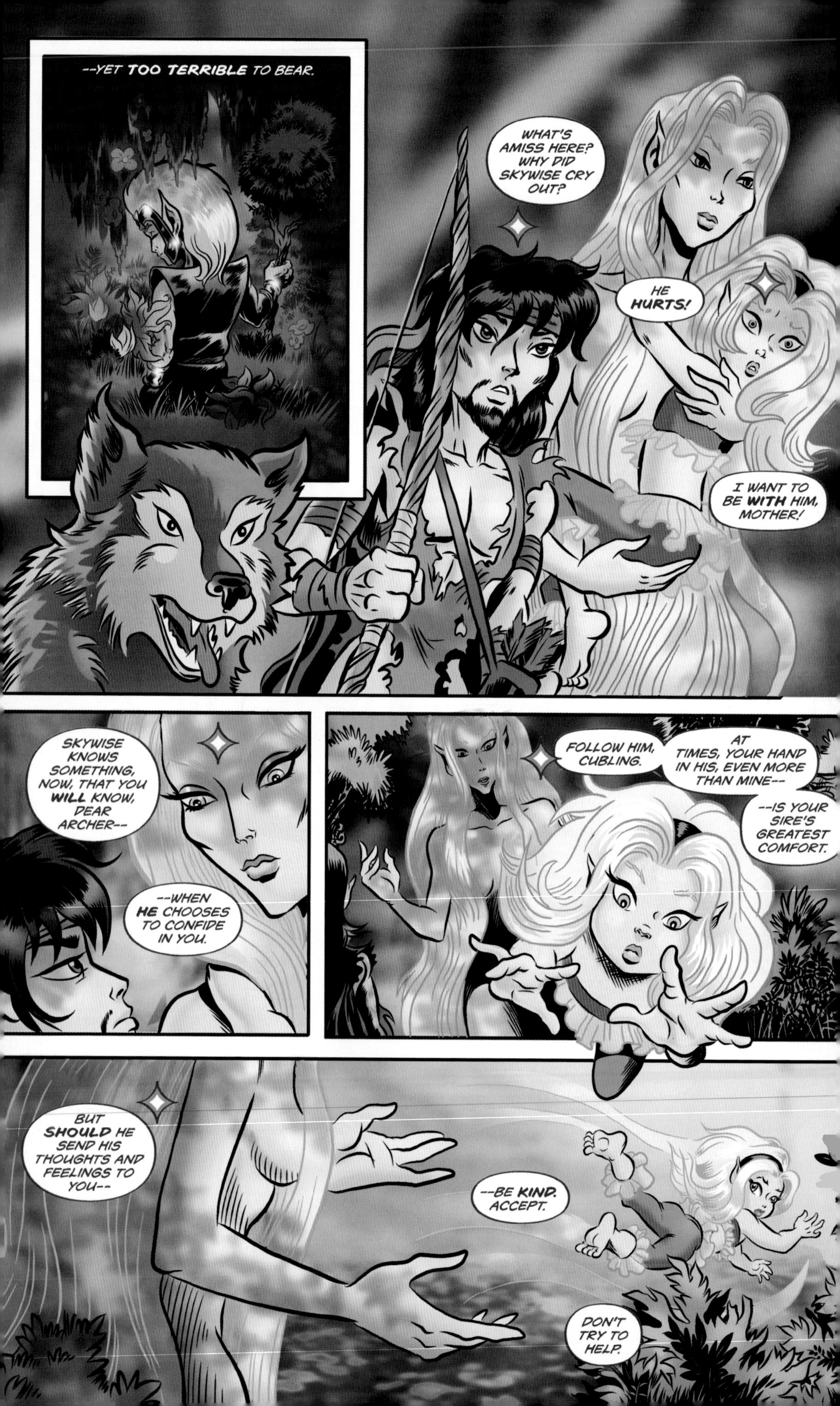
--YET **TOO TERRIBLE** TO BEAR.
WHAT'S AMISS HERE? WHY DID SKYWISE CRY OUT?
HE **HURTS!**
I WANT TO BE **WITH** HIM, MOTHER!
SKYWISE KNOWS SOMETHING, NOW, THAT YOU **WILL** KNOW, DEAR ARCHER--
--WHEN **HE** CHOOSES TO CONFIDE IN YOU.
FOLLOW HIM, CUBLING.
AT TIMES, YOUR HAND IN HIS, EVEN MORE THAN MINE--
--IS YOUR SIRE'S GREATEST COMFORT.
BUT **SHOULD** HE SEND HIS THOUGHTS AND FEELINGS TO YOU--
--BE **KIND.** ACCEPT.
DON'T TRY TO HELP.

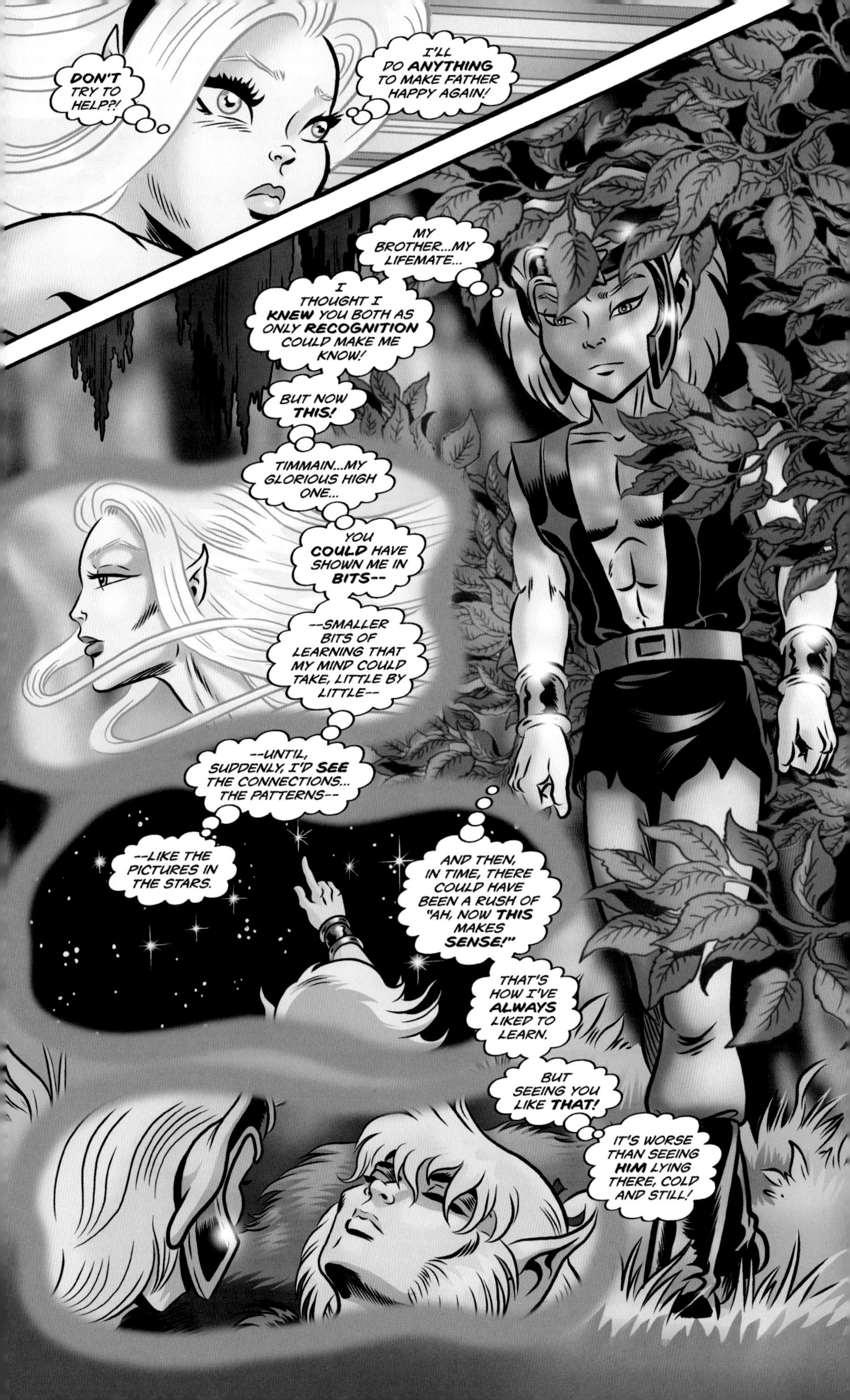
DON'T TRY TO HELP?!
I'LL DO ANYTHING TO MAKE FATHER HAPPY AGAIN!
MY BROTHER...MY LIFEMATE...
I THOUGHT I KNEW YOU BOTH AS ONLY RECOGNITION COULD MAKE ME KNOW!
BUT NOW THIS!
TIMMAIN...MY GLORIOUS HIGH ONE...
YOU COULD HAVE SHOWN ME IN BITS--
--SMALLER BITS OF LEARNING THAT MY MIND COULD TAKE, LITTLE BY LITTLE--
--UNTIL, SUDDENLY, I'D SEE THE CONNECTIONS... THE PATTERNS--
--LIKE THE PICTURES IN THE STARS.
AND THEN, IN TIME, THERE COULD HAVE BEEN A RUSH OF "AH, NOW THIS MAKES SENSE!"
THAT'S HOW I'VE ALWAYS LIKED TO LEARN.
BUT SEEING YOU LIKE THAT!
IT'S WORSE THAN SEEING HIM LYING THERE, COLD AND STILL!

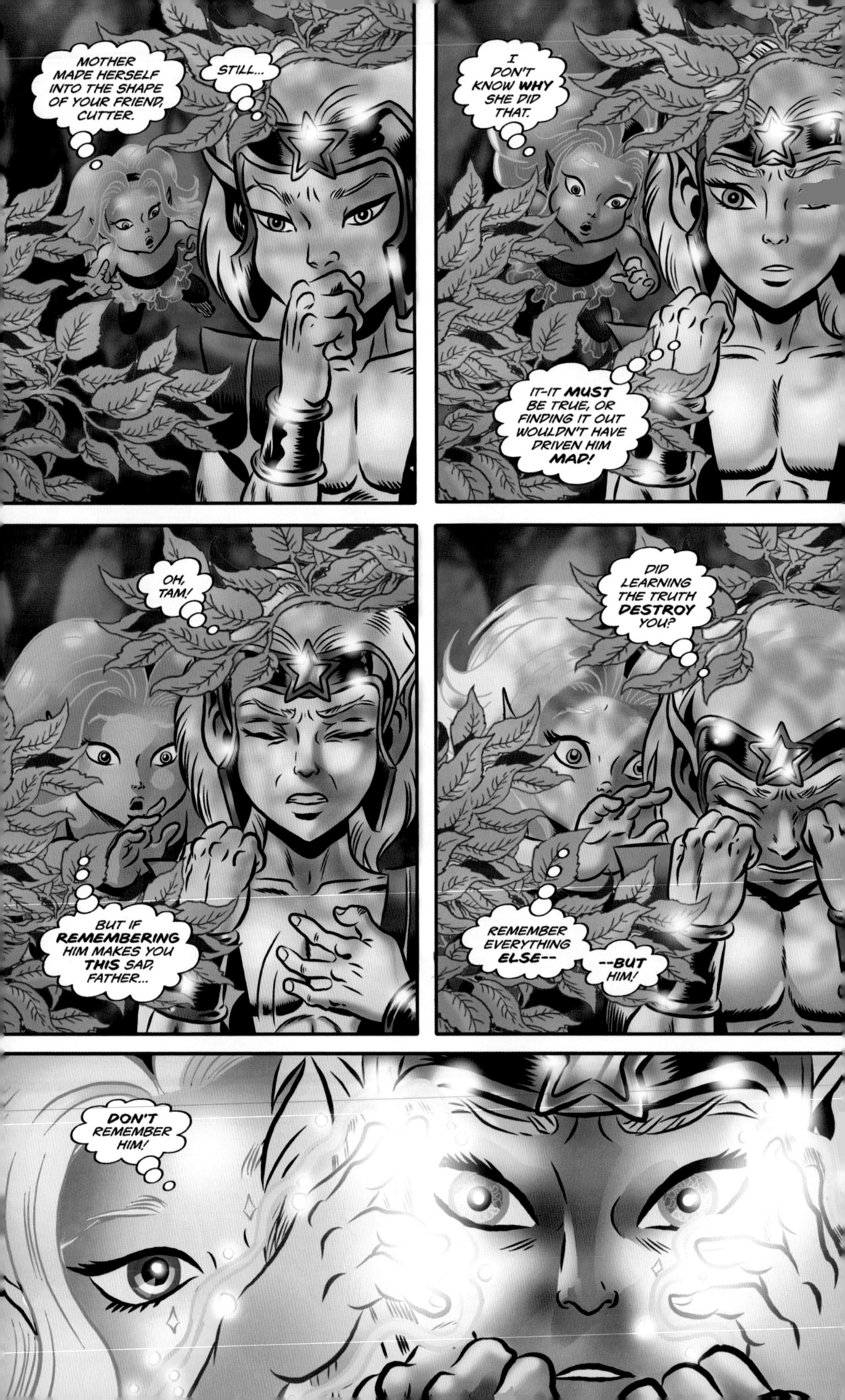
MOTHER MADE HERSELF INTO THE SHAPE OF YOUR FRIEND, CUTTER.
STILL...
I DON'T KNOW **WHY** SHE DID THAT.
IT-IT **MUST** BE TRUE, OR FINDING IT OUT WOULDN'T HAVE DRIVEN HIM **MAD!**
OH, TAM!
BUT IF **REMEMBERING** HIM MAKES YOU **THIS** SAD, FATHER...
DID LEARNING THE TRUTH **DESTROY** YOU?
REMEMBER EVERYTHING **ELSE--**
--BUT HIM!
DON'T REMEMBER HIM!

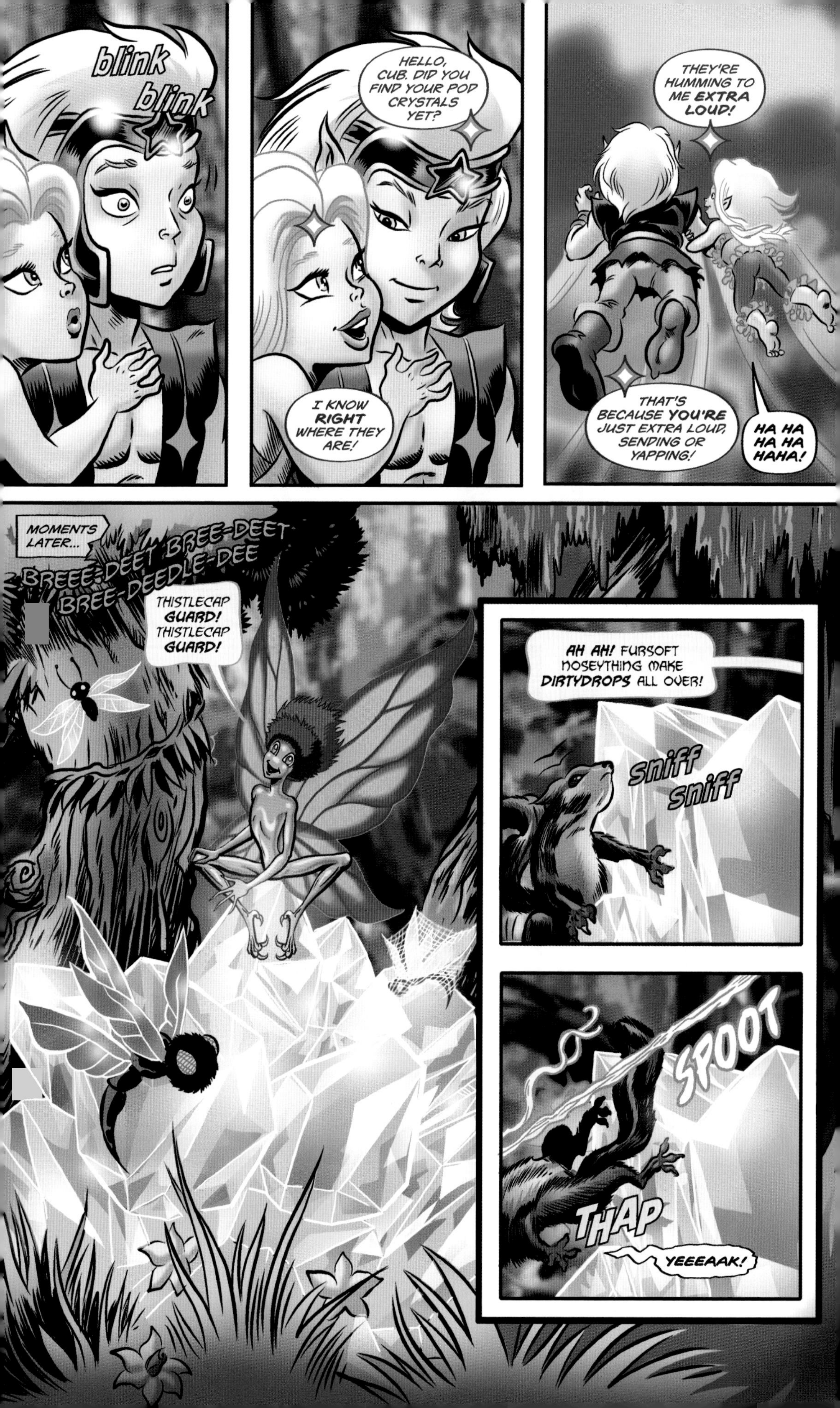

blink
blink
HELLO, CUB. DID YOU FIND YOUR POD CRYSTALS YET?
I KNOW RIGHT WHERE THEY ARE!
THEY'RE HUMMING TO ME EXTRA LOUD!
THAT'S BECAUSE YOU'RE JUST EXTRA LOUD, SENDING OR YAPPING!
HA HA HA HA HAHA!
MOMENTS LATER...
BREEE-DEET BREE-DEET
BREE-DEEDLE-DEE
THISTLECAP GUARD! THISTLECAP GUARD!
AH AH! FURSOFT NOSEYTHING MAKE DIRTYDROPS ALL OVER!
Sniff
Sniff
SPOOT
THAP
YEEEAAK!

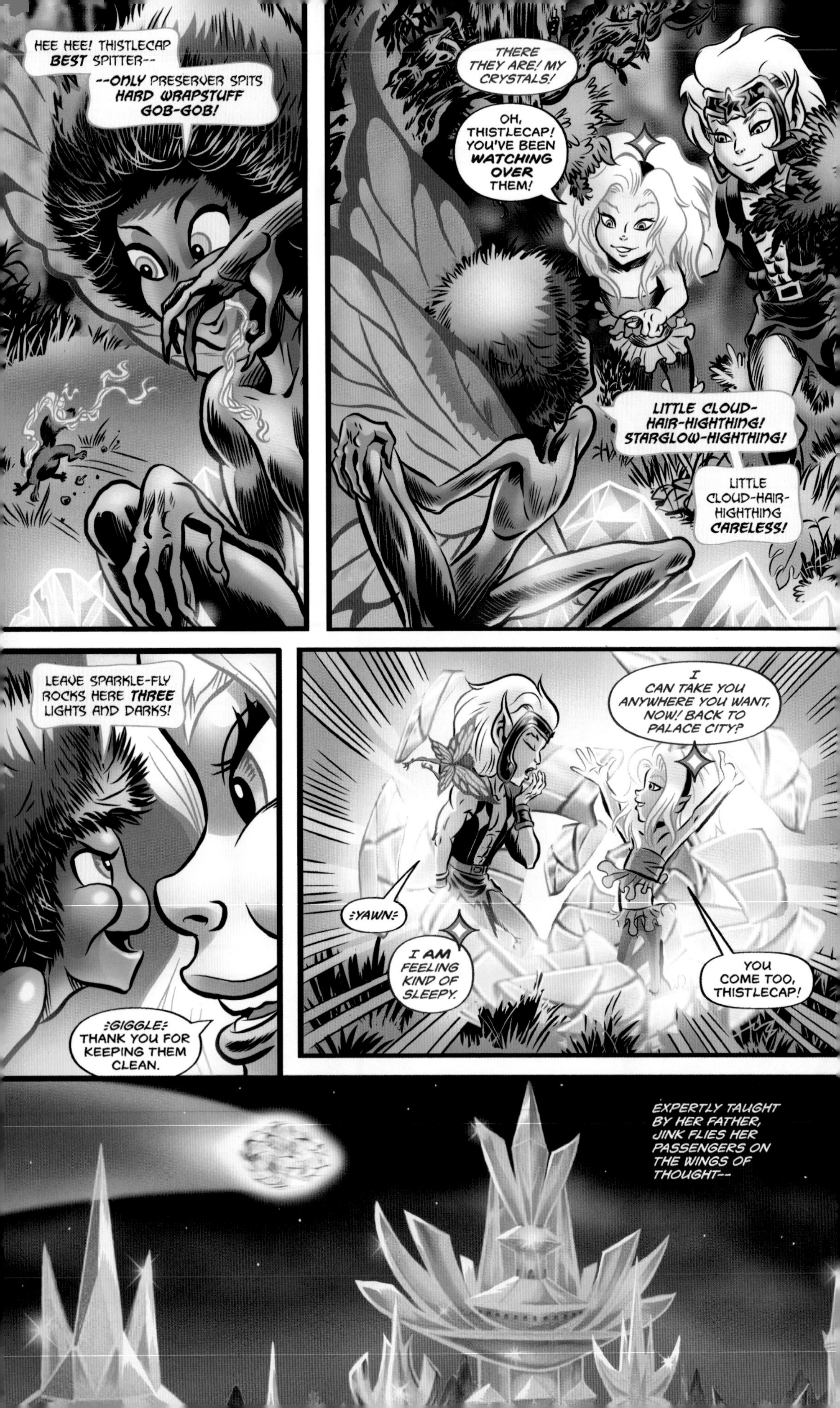
HEE HEE! THISTLECAP BEST SPITTER--
--ONLY PRESERVER SPITS HARD WRAPSTUFF GOB-GOB!
THERE THEY ARE! MY CRYSTALS!
OH, THISTLECAP! YOU'VE BEEN WATCHING OVER THEM!
LITTLE CLOUD-HAIR-HIGHTHING! STARGLOW-HIGHTHING!
LITTLE CLOUD-HAIR-HIGHTHING CARELESS!
LEAVE SPARKLE-FLY ROCKS HERE THREE LIGHTS AND DARKS!
GIGGLE THANK YOU FOR KEEPING THEM CLEAN.
I CAN TAKE YOU ANYWHERE YOU WANT, NOW! BACK TO PALACE CITY?
YAWN
I AM FEELING KIND OF SLEEPY.
YOU COME TOO, THISTLECAP!
EXPERTLY TAUGHT BY HER FATHER, JINK FLIES HER PASSENGERS ON THE WINGS OF THOUGHT--

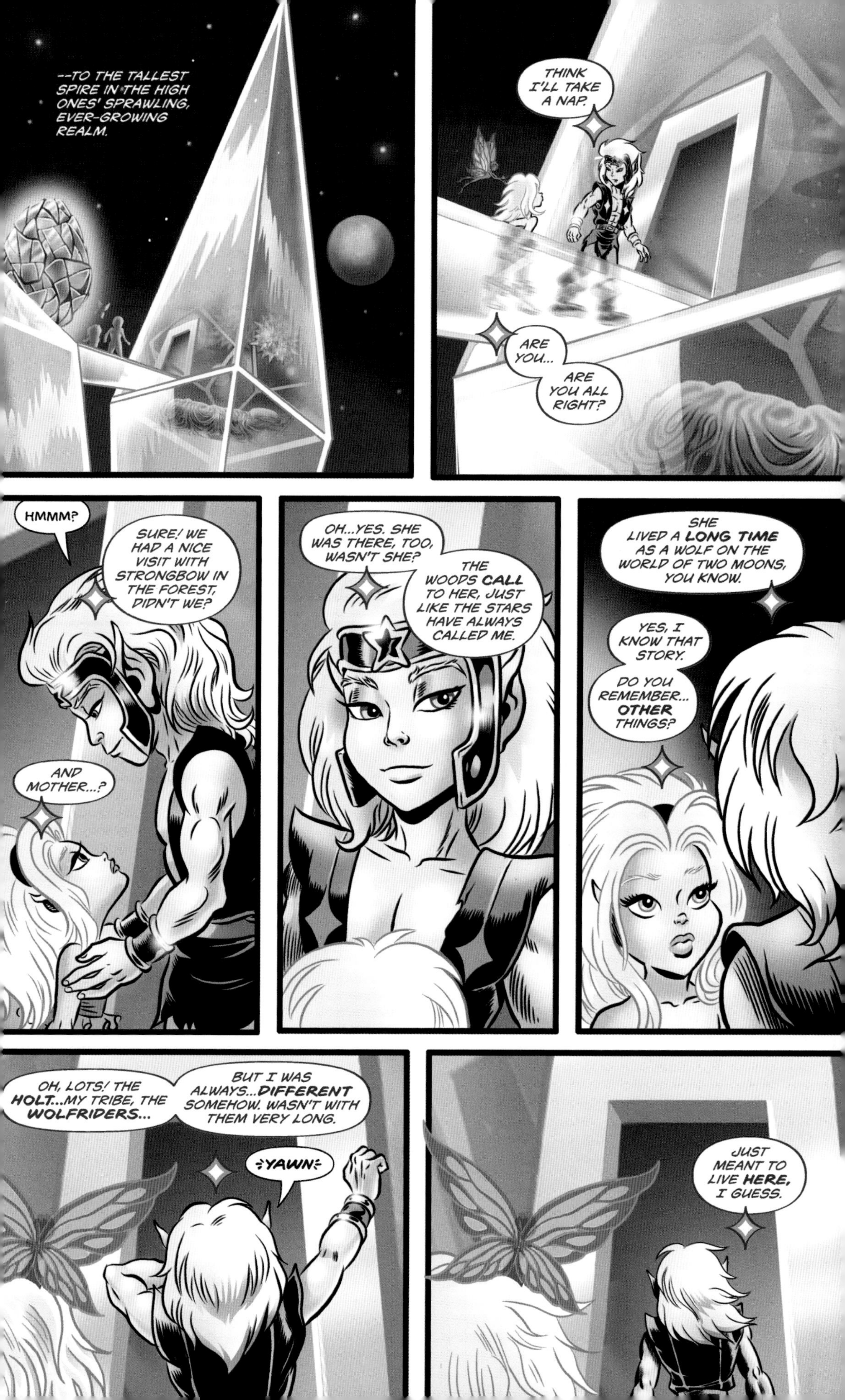
--TO THE TALLEST SPIRE IN THE HIGH ONES' SPRAWLING, EVER-GROWING REALM.
THINK I'LL TAKE A NAP.
ARE YOU...
ARE YOU ALL RIGHT?
HMMM?
SURE! WE HAD A NICE VISIT WITH STRONGBOW IN THE FOREST, DIDN'T WE?
AND MOTHER...?
OH...YES. SHE WAS THERE, TOO, WASN'T SHE?
THE WOODS CALL TO HER, JUST LIKE THE STARS HAVE ALWAYS CALLED ME.
SHE LIVED A LONG TIME AS A WOLF ON THE WORLD OF TWO MOONS, YOU KNOW.
YES, I KNOW THAT STORY.
DO YOU REMEMBER... OTHER THINGS?
OH, LOTS! THE HOLT...MY TRIBE, THE WOLFRIDERS...
BUT I WAS ALWAYS...DIFFERENT SOMEHOW. WASN'T WITH THEM VERY LONG.
YAWN
JUST MEANT TO LIVE HERE, I GUESS.

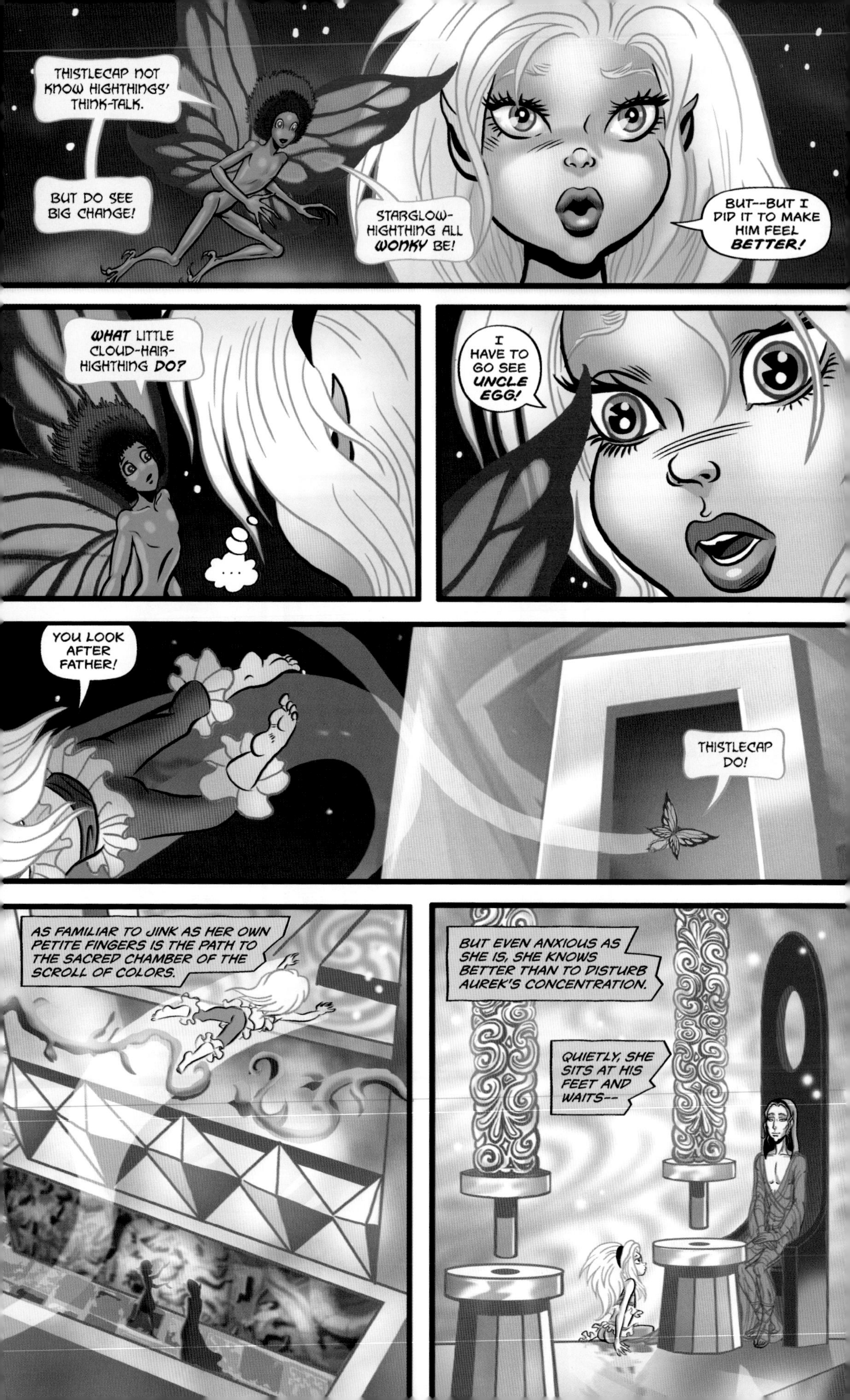
THISTLECAP NOT KNOW HIGHTHINGS' THINK-TALK.
BUT DO SEE BIG CHANGE!
STARGLOW-HIGHTHING ALL WONKY BE!
BUT--BUT I DID IT TO MAKE HIM FEEL BETTER!
WHAT LITTLE CLOUD-HAIR-HIGHTHING DO?
...
I HAVE TO GO SEE UNCLE EGG!
YOU LOOK AFTER FATHER!
THISTLECAP DO!
AS FAMILIAR TO JINK AS HER OWN PETITE FINGERS IS THE PATH TO THE SACRED CHAMBER OF THE SCROLL OF COLORS.
BUT EVEN ANXIOUS AS SHE IS, SHE KNOWS BETTER THAN TO DISTURB AUREK'S CONCENTRATION.
QUIETLY, SHE SITS AT HIS FEET AND WAITS--

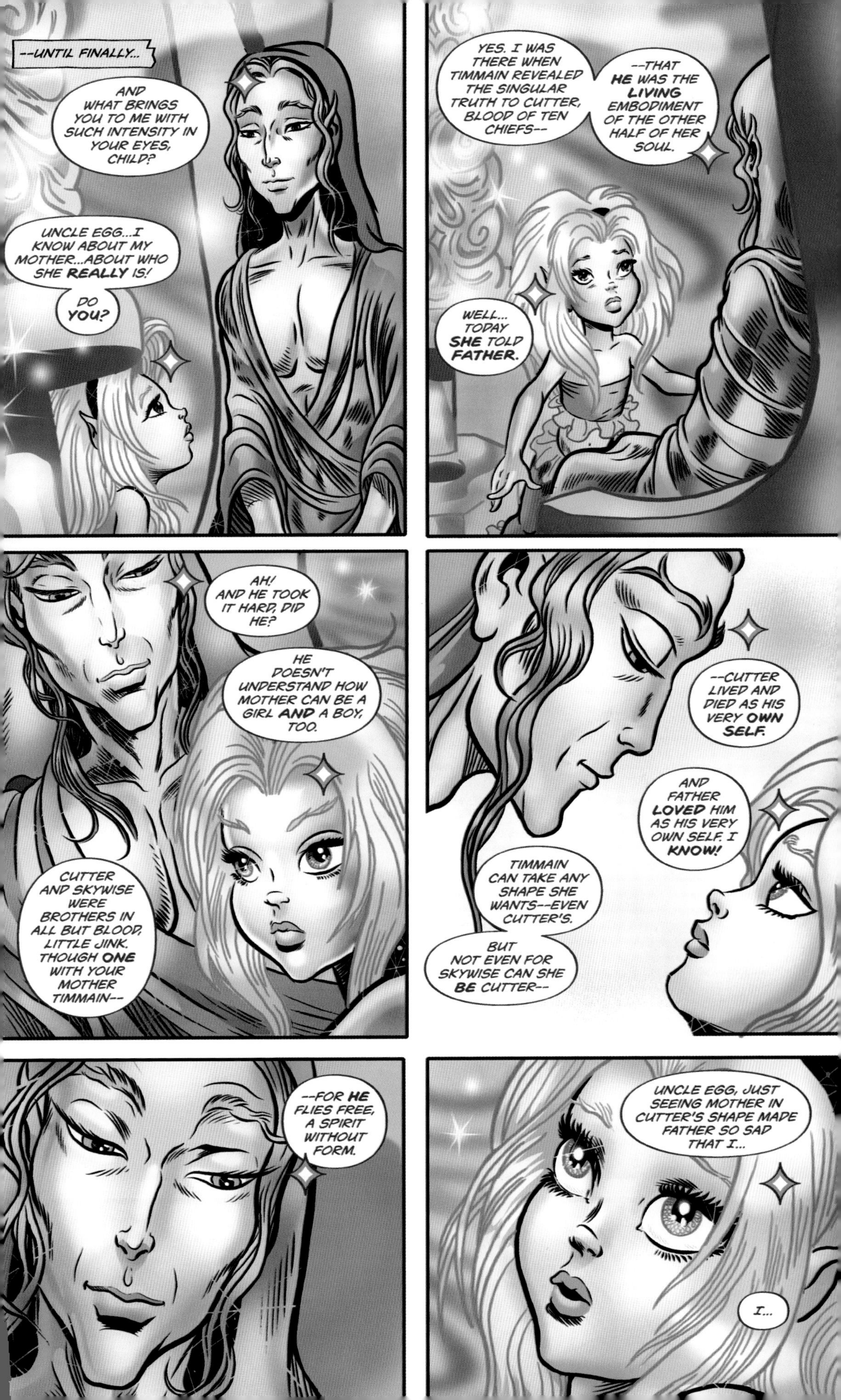

--UNTIL FINALLY...
AND WHAT BRINGS YOU TO ME WITH SUCH INTENSITY IN YOUR EYES, CHILD?
UNCLE EGG...I KNOW ABOUT MY MOTHER...ABOUT WHO SHE REALLY IS!
DO YOU?
YES. I WAS THERE WHEN TIMMAIN REVEALED THE SINGULAR TRUTH TO CUTTER, BLOOD OF TEN CHIEFS--
--THAT HE WAS THE LIVING EMBODIMENT OF THE OTHER HALF OF HER SOUL.
WELL... TODAY SHE TOLD FATHER.
AH! AND HE TOOK IT HARD, DID HE?
HE DOESN'T UNDERSTAND HOW MOTHER CAN BE A GIRL AND A BOY, TOO.
CUTTER AND SKYWISE WERE BROTHERS IN ALL BUT BLOOD, LITTLE JINK. THOUGH ONE WITH YOUR MOTHER TIMMAIN--
--CUTTER LIVED AND DIED AS HIS VERY OWN SELF.
AND FATHER LOVED HIM AS HIS VERY OWN SELF. I KNOW!
TIMMAIN CAN TAKE ANY SHAPE SHE WANTS--EVEN CUTTER'S.
BUT NOT EVEN FOR SKYWISE CAN SHE BE CUTTER--
--FOR HE FLIES FREE, A SPIRIT WITHOUT FORM.
UNCLE EGG, JUST SEEING MOTHER IN CUTTER'S SHAPE MADE FATHER SO SAD THAT I...
I...

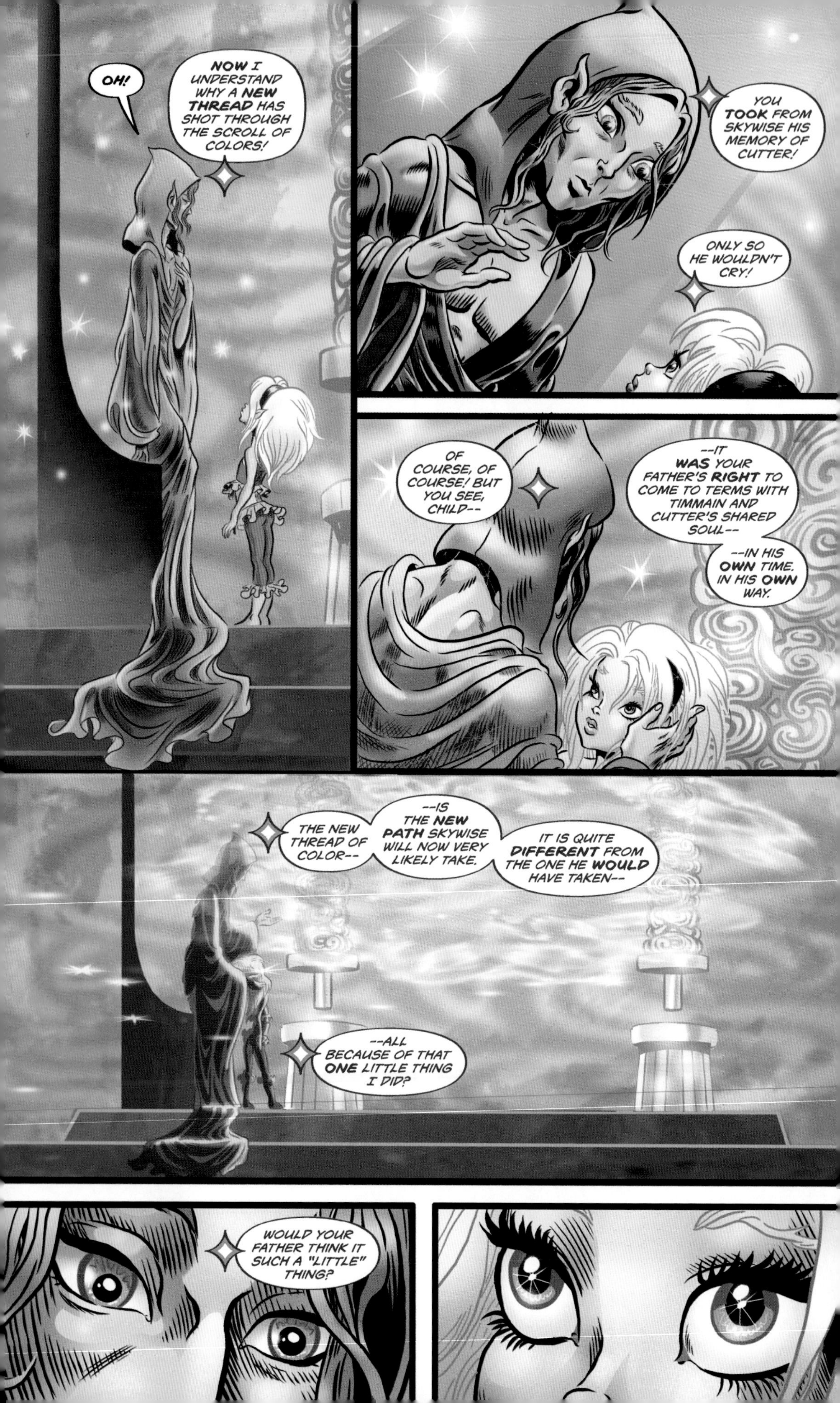

OH!
NOW I UNDERSTAND WHY A NEW THREAD HAS SHOT THROUGH THE SCROLL OF COLORS!
YOU TOOK FROM SKYWISE HIS MEMORY OF CUTTER!
ONLY SO HE WOULDN'T CRY!
OF COURSE, OF COURSE! BUT YOU SEE, CHILD--
--IT WAS YOUR FATHER'S RIGHT TO COME TO TERMS WITH TIMMAIN AND CUTTER'S SHARED SOUL--
--IN HIS OWN TIME. IN HIS OWN WAY.
THE NEW THREAD OF COLOR--
--IS THE NEW PATH SKYWISE WILL NOW VERY LIKELY TAKE.
IT IS QUITE DIFFERENT FROM THE ONE HE WOULD HAVE TAKEN--
--ALL BECAUSE OF THAT ONE LITTLE THING I DID?
WOULD YOUR FATHER THINK IT SUCH A "LITTLE" THING?

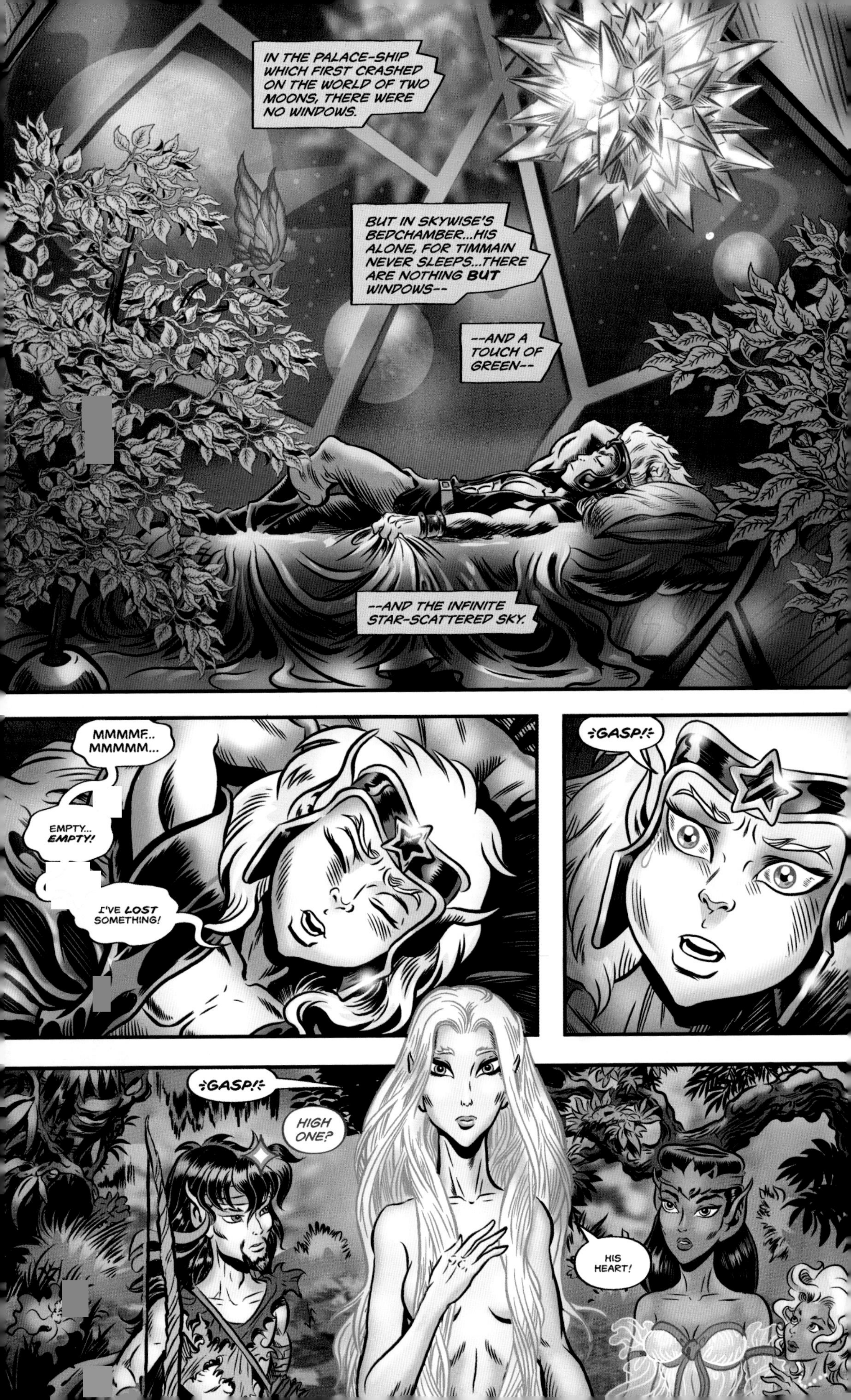
IN THE PALACE-SHIP WHICH FIRST CRASHED ON THE WORLD OF TWO MOONS, THERE WERE NO WINDOWS.
BUT IN SKYWISE'S BEDCHAMBER...HIS ALONE, FOR TIMMAIN NEVER SLEEPS...THERE ARE NOTHING BUT WINDOWS--
--AND A TOUCH OF GREEN--
--AND THE INFINITE STAR-SCATTERED SKY.
MMMMF.. MMMMM...
EMPTY... EMPTY!
I'VE LOST SOMETHING!
GASP!
GASP!
HIGH ONE?
HIS HEART!

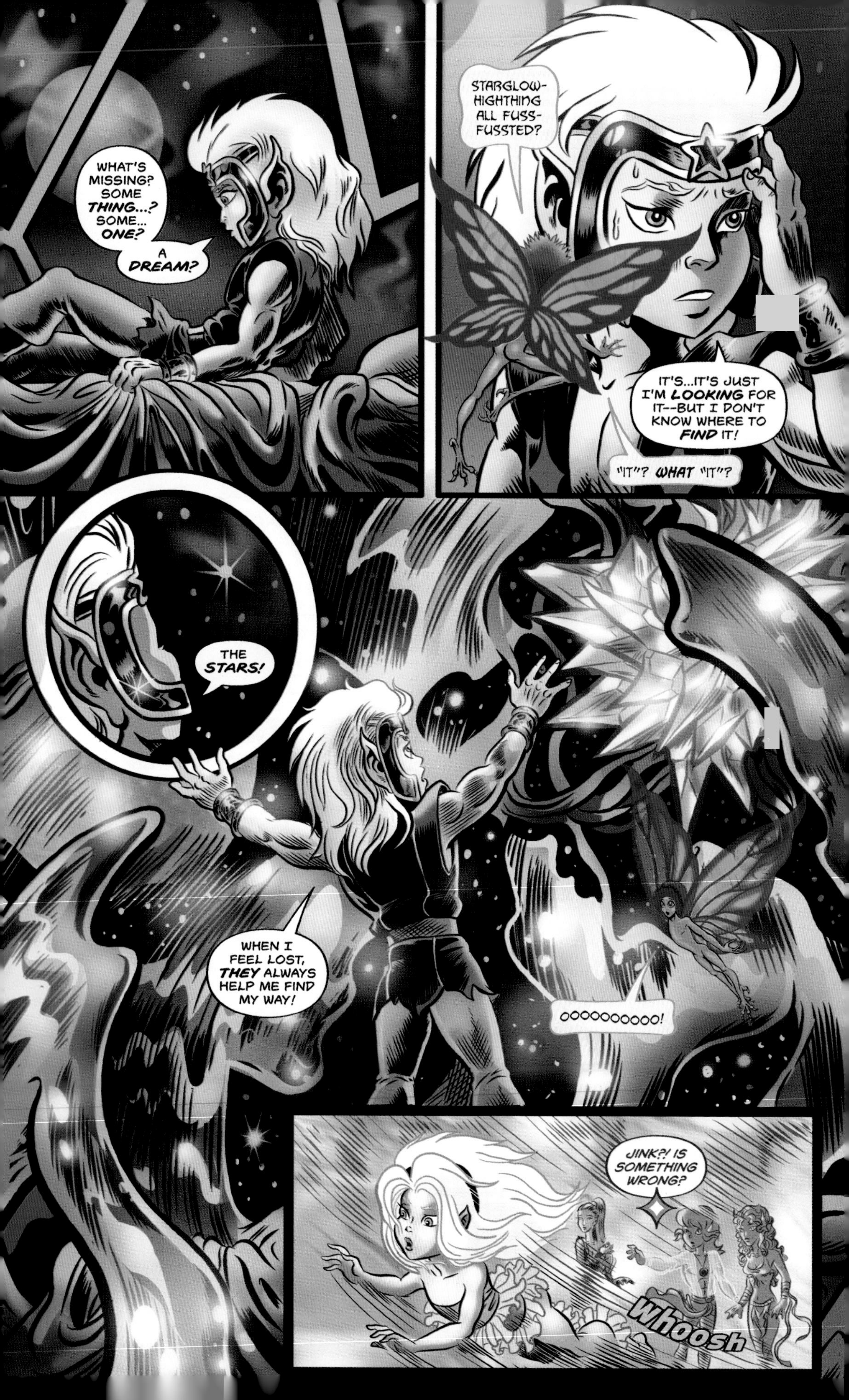
WHAT'S MISSING? SOME THING...? SOME... ONE?
A DREAM?
STARGLOW-HIGHTHING ALL FUSS-FUSSTED?
IT'S...IT'S JUST I'M LOOKING FOR IT--BUT I DON'T KNOW WHERE TO FIND IT!
"IT"? WHAT "IT"?
THE STARS!
WHEN I FEEL LOST, THEY ALWAYS HELP ME FIND MY WAY!
OOOOOOOOOO!
JINK?! IS SOMETHING WRONG?
WHOOSH

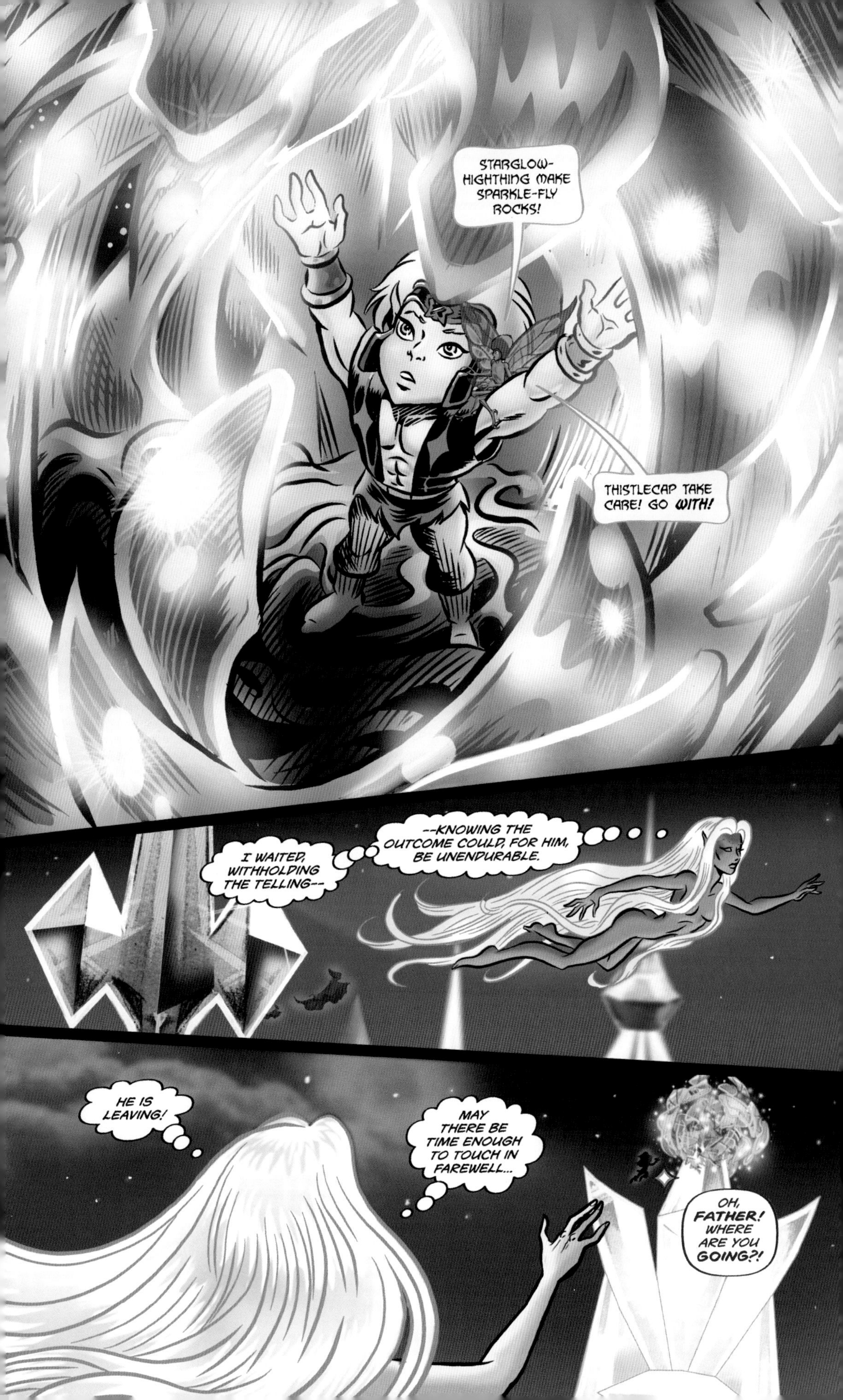
STARGLOW-HIGHTHING MAKE SPARKLE-FLY ROCKS!
THISTLECAP TAKE CARE! GO WITH!
I WAITED, WITHHOLDING THE TELLING--
--KNOWING THE OUTCOME COULD, FOR HIM, BE UNENDURABLE.
HE IS LEAVING!
MAY THERE BE TIME ENOUGH TO TOUCH IN FAREWELL...
OH, FATHER! WHERE ARE YOU GOING?!

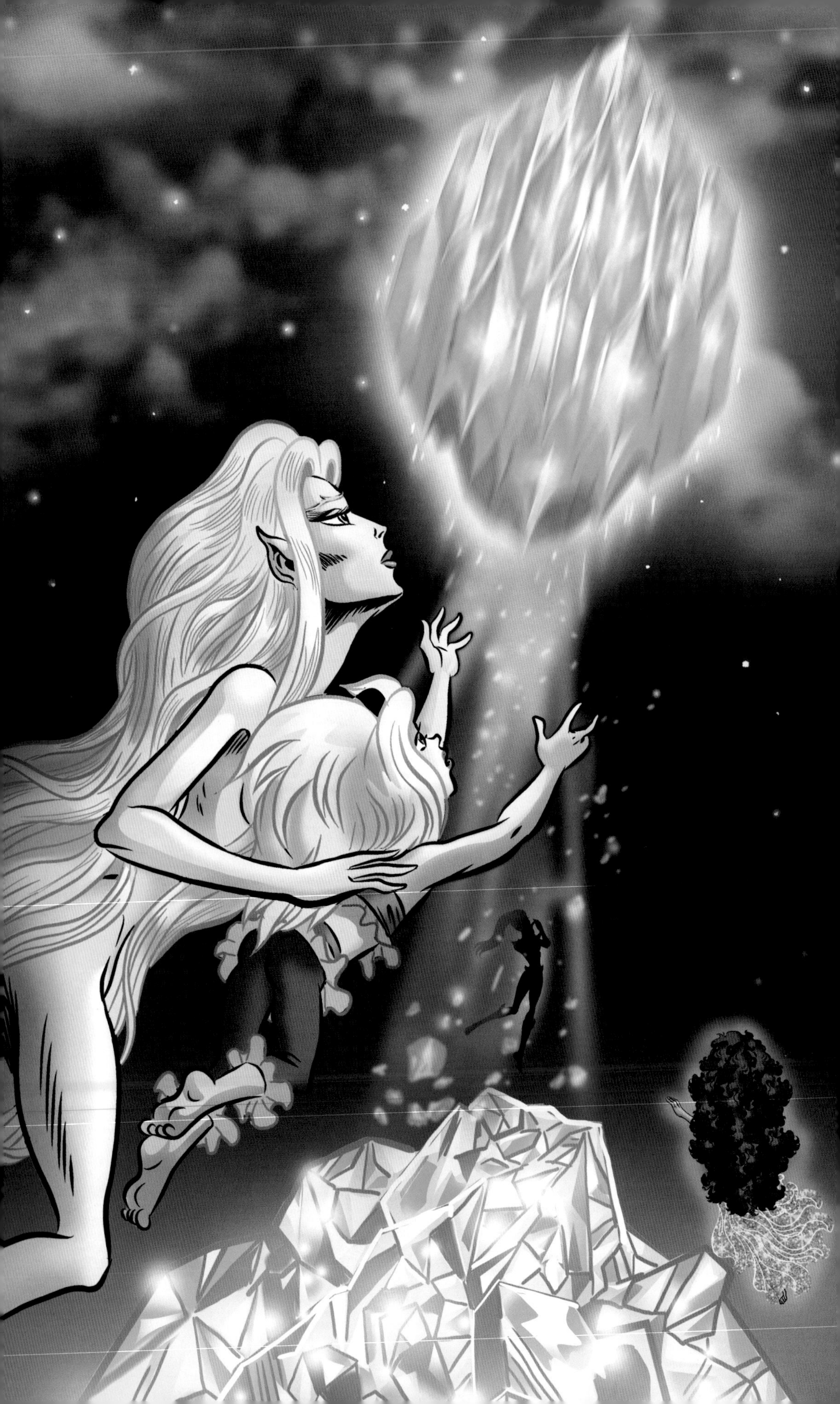

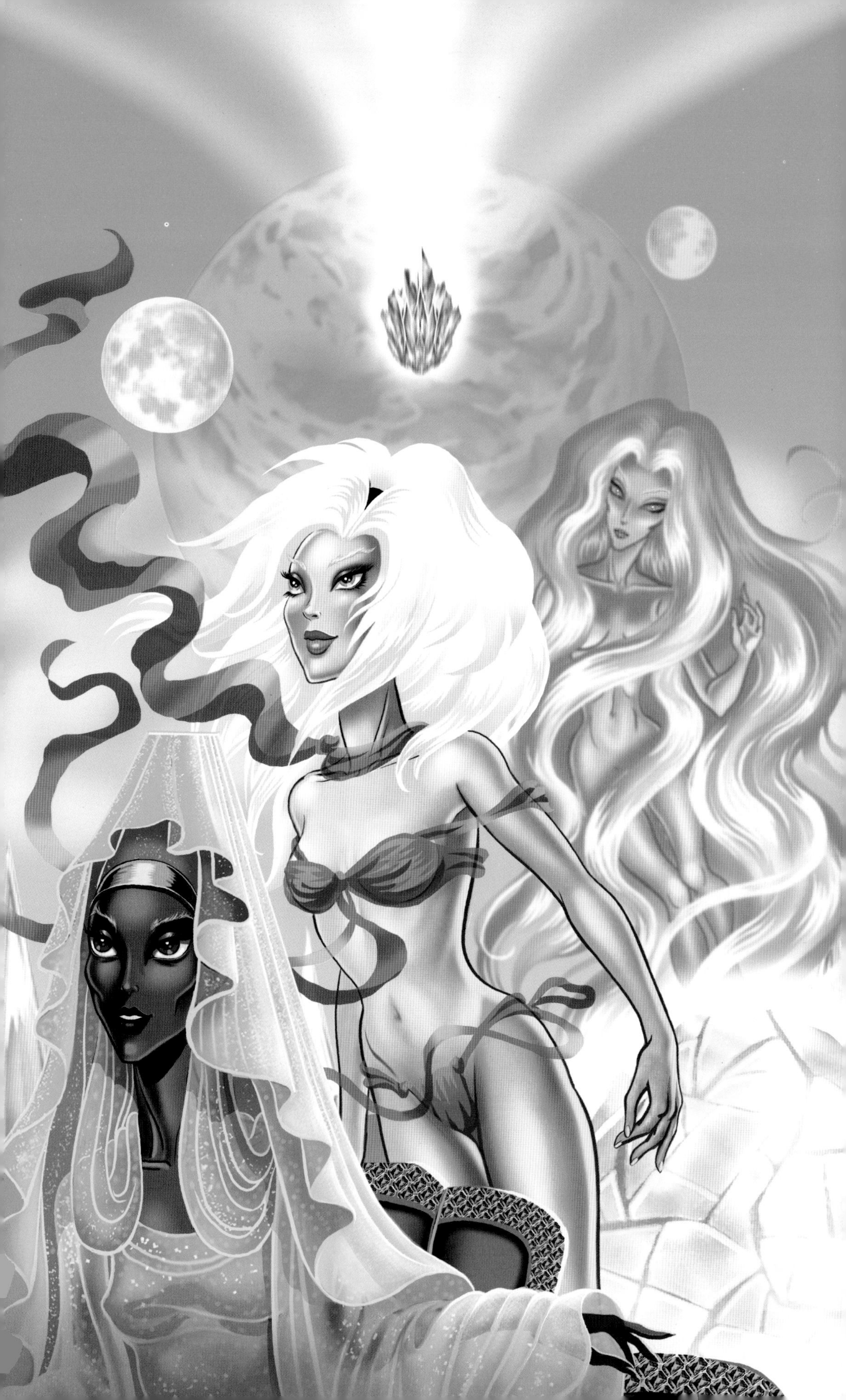

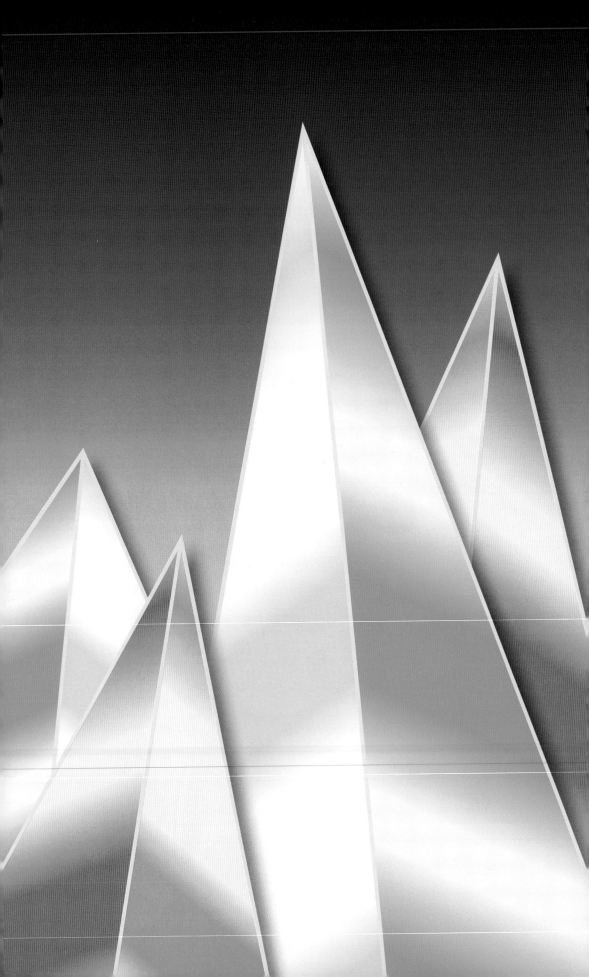

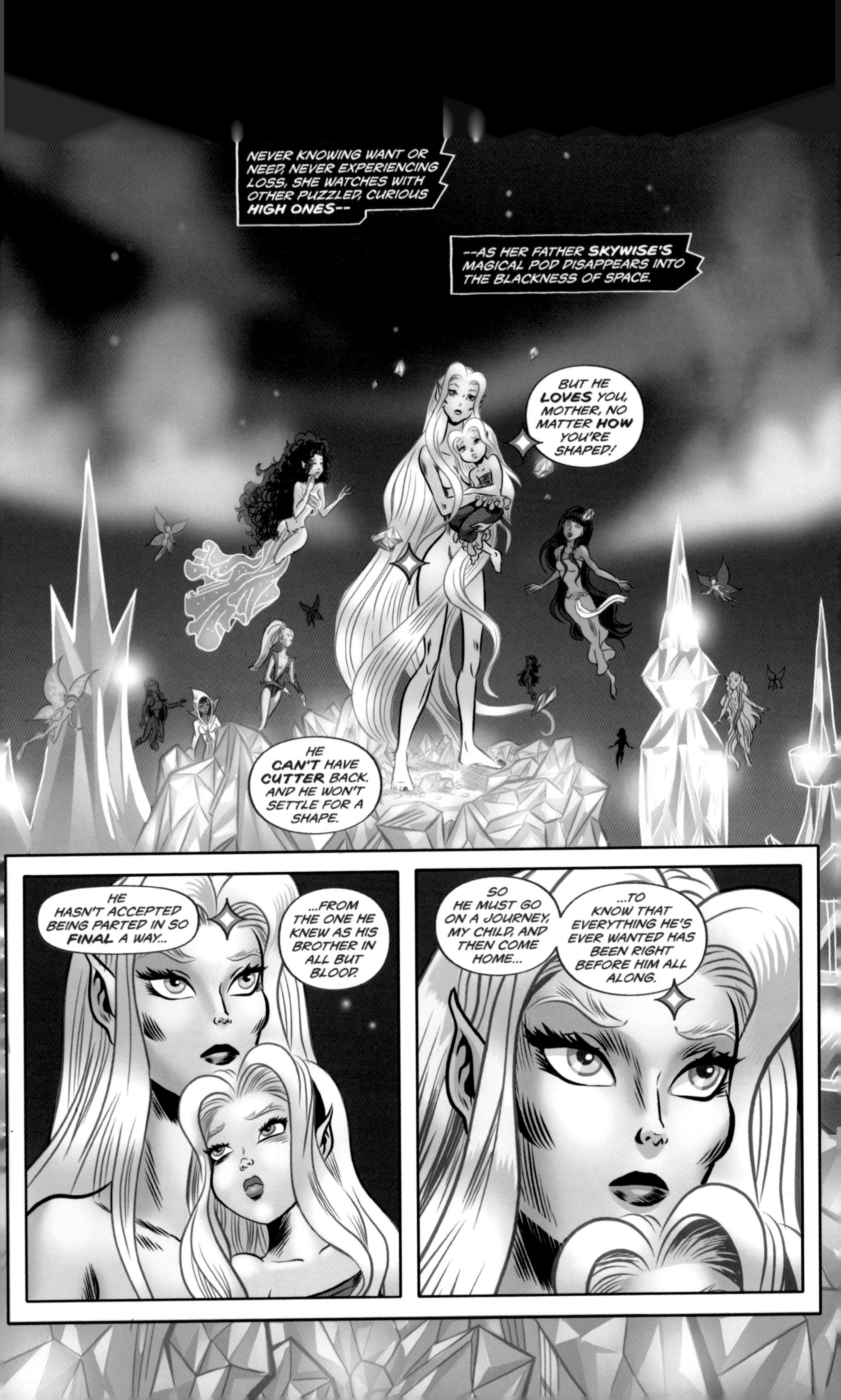
NEVER KNOWING WANT OR NEED, NEVER EXPERIENCING LOSS, SHE WATCHES WITH OTHER PUZZLED, CURIOUS HIGH ONES--
--AS HER FATHER SKYWISE'S MAGICAL POD DISAPPEARS INTO THE BLACKNESS OF SPACE.
BUT HE LOVES YOU, MOTHER, NO MATTER HOW YOU'RE SHAPED!
HE CAN'T HAVE CUTTER BACK. AND HE WON'T SETTLE FOR A SHAPE.
HE HASN'T ACCEPTED BEING PARTED IN SO FINAL A WAY...
...FROM THE ONE HE KNEW AS HIS BROTHER IN ALL BUT BLOOD.
SO HE MUST GO ON A JOURNEY, MY CHILD, AND THEN COME HOME...
...TO KNOW THAT EVERYTHING HE'S EVER WANTED HAS BEEN RIGHT BEFORE HIM ALL ALONG.

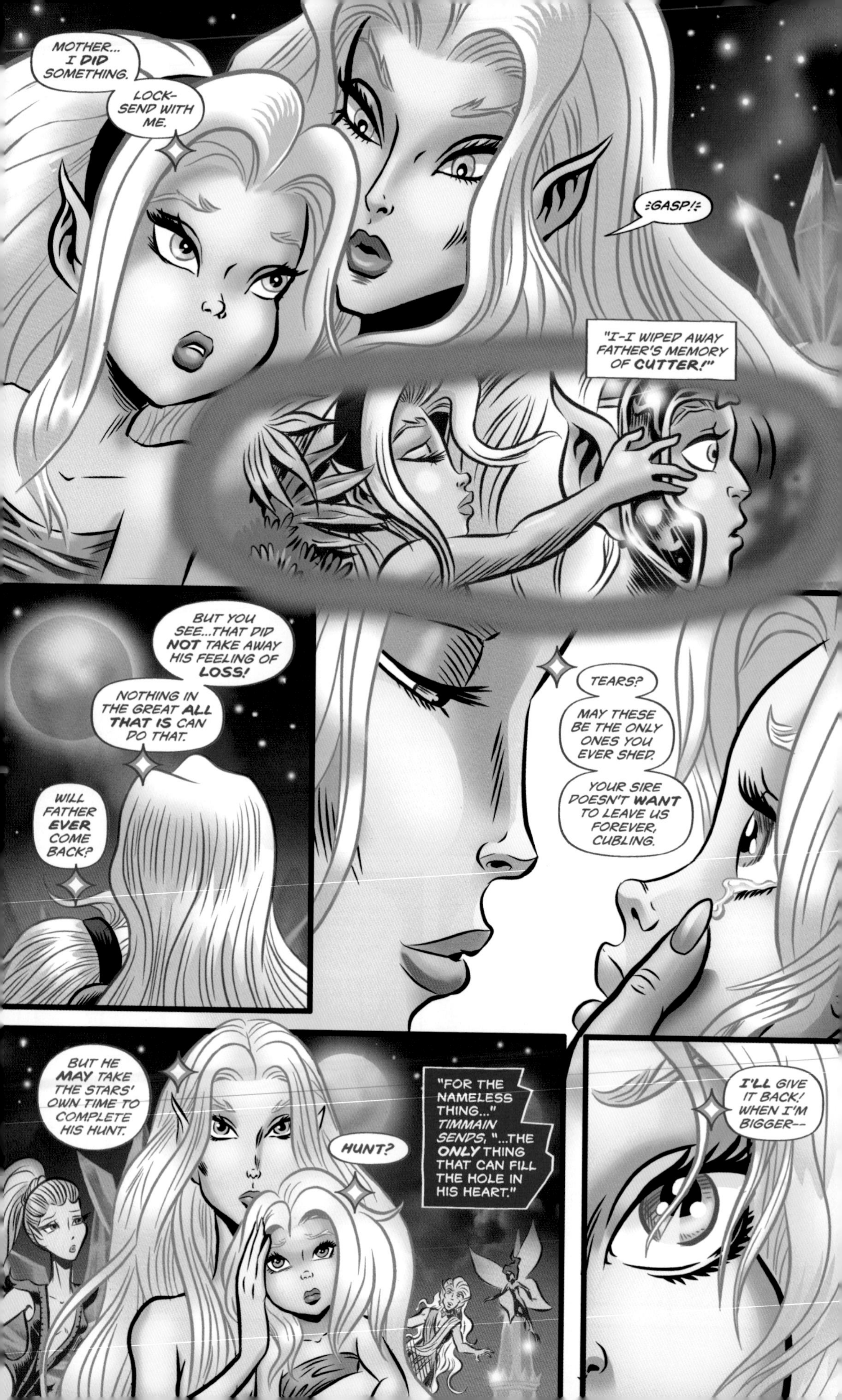
MOTHER... I DID SOMETHING.
LOCK-SEND WITH ME.
:GASP!:
"I-I WIPED AWAY FATHER'S MEMORY OF CUTTER!"
BUT YOU SEE...THAT DID NOT TAKE AWAY HIS FEELING OF LOSS!
NOTHING IN THE GREAT ALL THAT IS CAN DO THAT.
WILL FATHER EVER COME BACK?
TEARS?
MAY THESE BE THE ONLY ONES YOU EVER SHED.
YOUR SIRE DOESN'T WANT TO LEAVE US FOREVER, CUBLING.
BUT HE MAY TAKE THE STARS' OWN TIME TO COMPLETE HIS HUNT.
HUNT?
"FOR THE NAMELESS THING..." TIMMAIN SENDS, "...THE ONLY THING THAT CAN FILL THE HOLE IN HIS HEART."
I'LL GIVE IT BACK! WHEN I'M BIGGER--

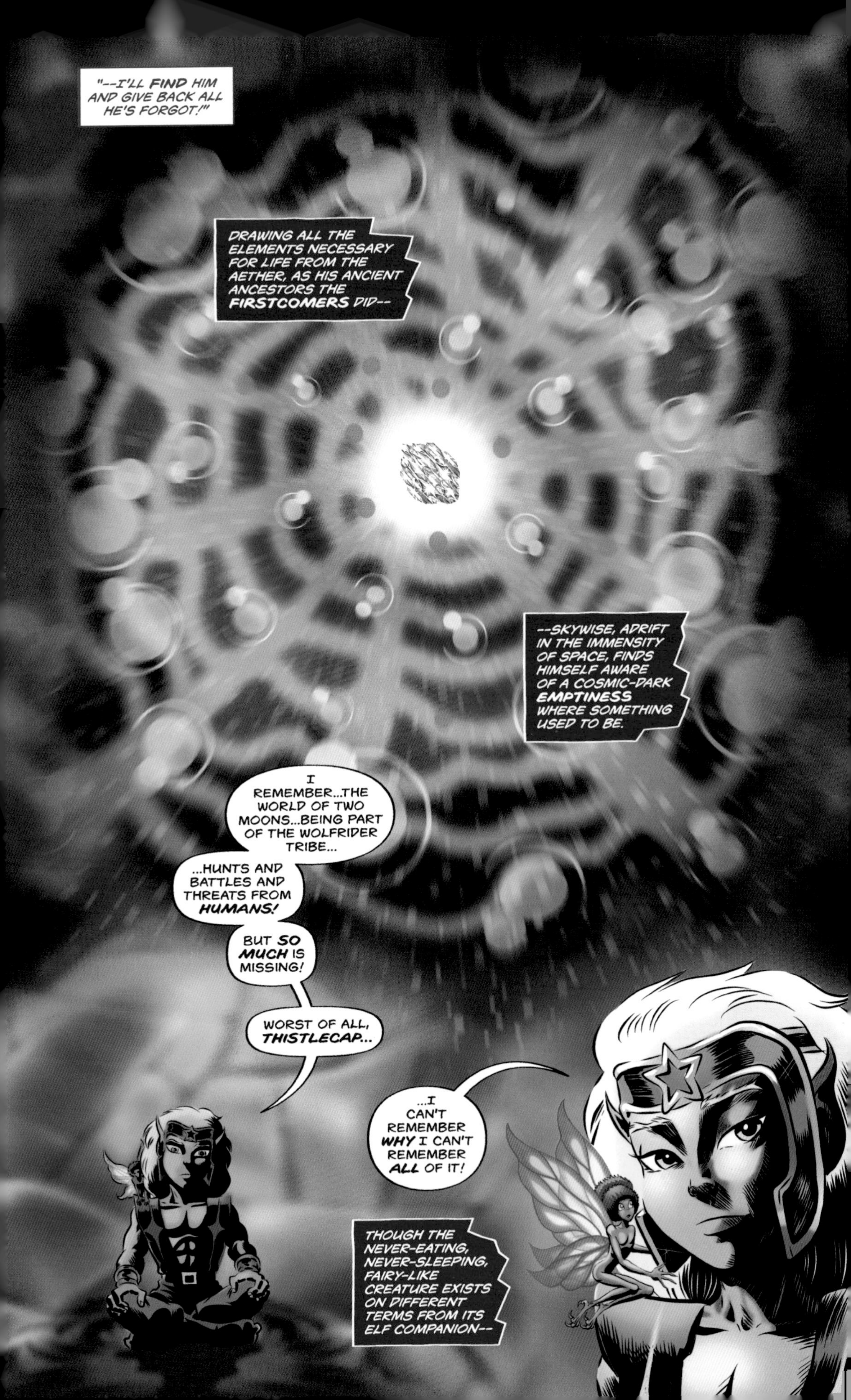
"--I'LL FIND HIM AND GIVE BACK ALL HE'S FORGOT!"
DRAWING ALL THE ELEMENTS NECESSARY FOR LIFE FROM THE AETHER, AS HIS ANCIENT ANCESTORS THE FIRSTCOMERS DID--
--SKYWISE, ADRIFT IN THE IMMENSITY OF SPACE, FINDS HIMSELF AWARE OF A COSMIC-DARK EMPTINESS WHERE SOMETHING USED TO BE.
I REMEMBER...THE WORLD OF TWO MOONS...BEING PART OF THE WOLFRIDER TRIBE...
...HUNTS AND BATTLES AND THREATS FROM HUMANS!
BUT SO MUCH IS MISSING!
WORST OF ALL, THISTLECAP...
...I CAN'T REMEMBER WHY I CAN'T REMEMBER ALL OF IT!
THOUGH THE NEVER-EATING, NEVER-SLEEPING, FAIRY-LIKE CREATURE EXISTS ON DIFFERENT TERMS FROM ITS ELF COMPANION--

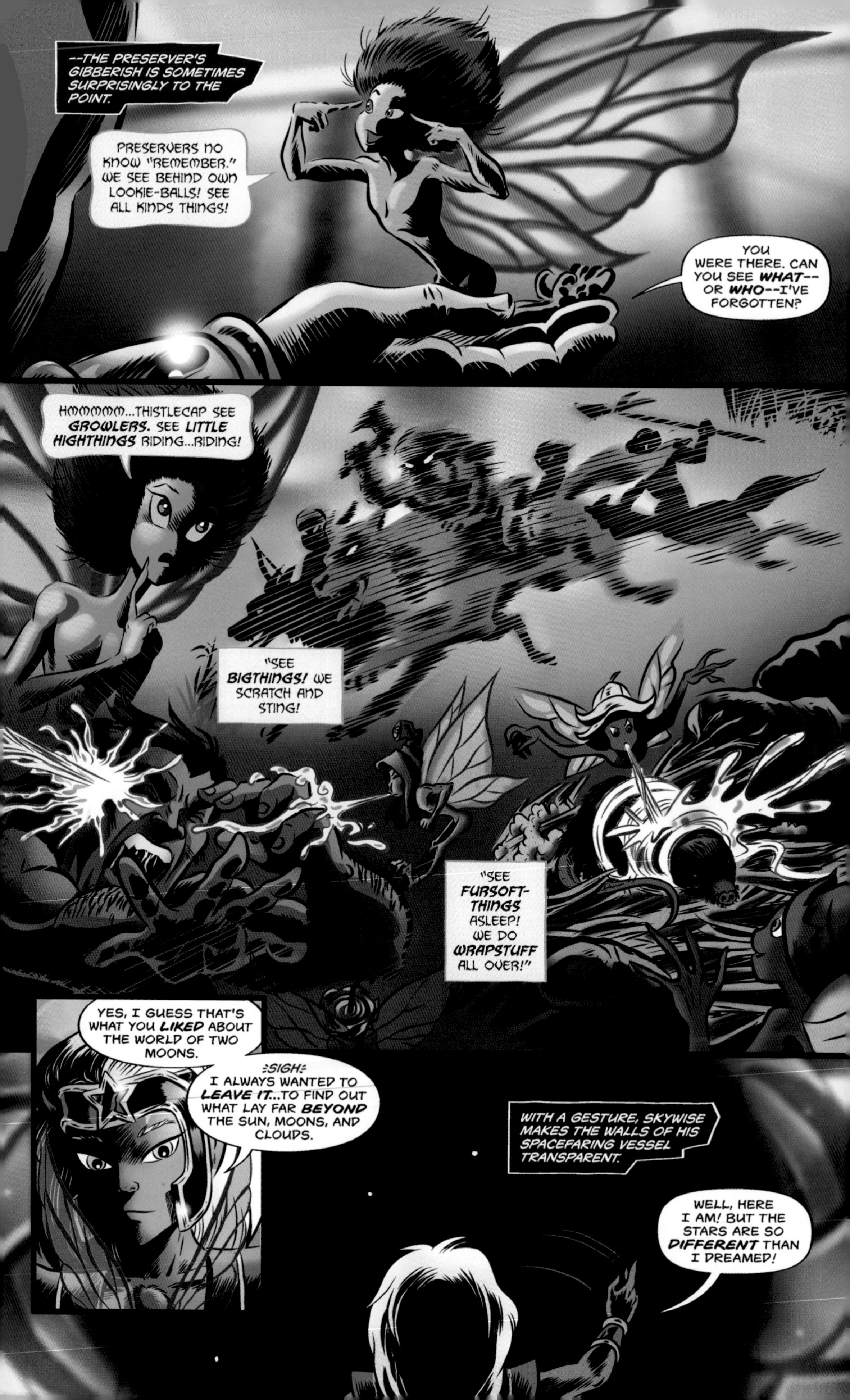
--THE PRESERVER'S GIBBERISH IS SOMETIMES SURPRISINGLY TO THE POINT.
PRESERVERS NO KNOW "REMEMBER." WE SEE BEHIND OWN LOOKIE-BALLS! SEE ALL KINDS THINGS!
YOU WERE THERE. CAN YOU SEE WHAT--OR WHO--I'VE FORGOTTEN?
HMMMMM...THISTLECAP SEE GROWLERS. SEE LITTLE HIGHTHINGS RIDING...RIDING!
"SEE BIGTHINGS! WE SCRATCH AND STING!
"SEE FURSOFT-THINGS ASLEEP! WE DO WRAPSTUFF ALL OVER!"
YES, I GUESS THAT'S WHAT YOU LIKED ABOUT THE WORLD OF TWO MOONS.
SIGH I ALWAYS WANTED TO LEAVE IT...TO FIND OUT WHAT LAY FAR BEYOND THE SUN, MOONS, AND CLOUDS.
WITH A GESTURE, SKYWISE MAKES THE WALLS OF HIS SPACEFARING VESSEL TRANSPARENT.
WELL, HERE I AM! BUT THE STARS ARE SO DIFFERENT THAN I DREAMED!

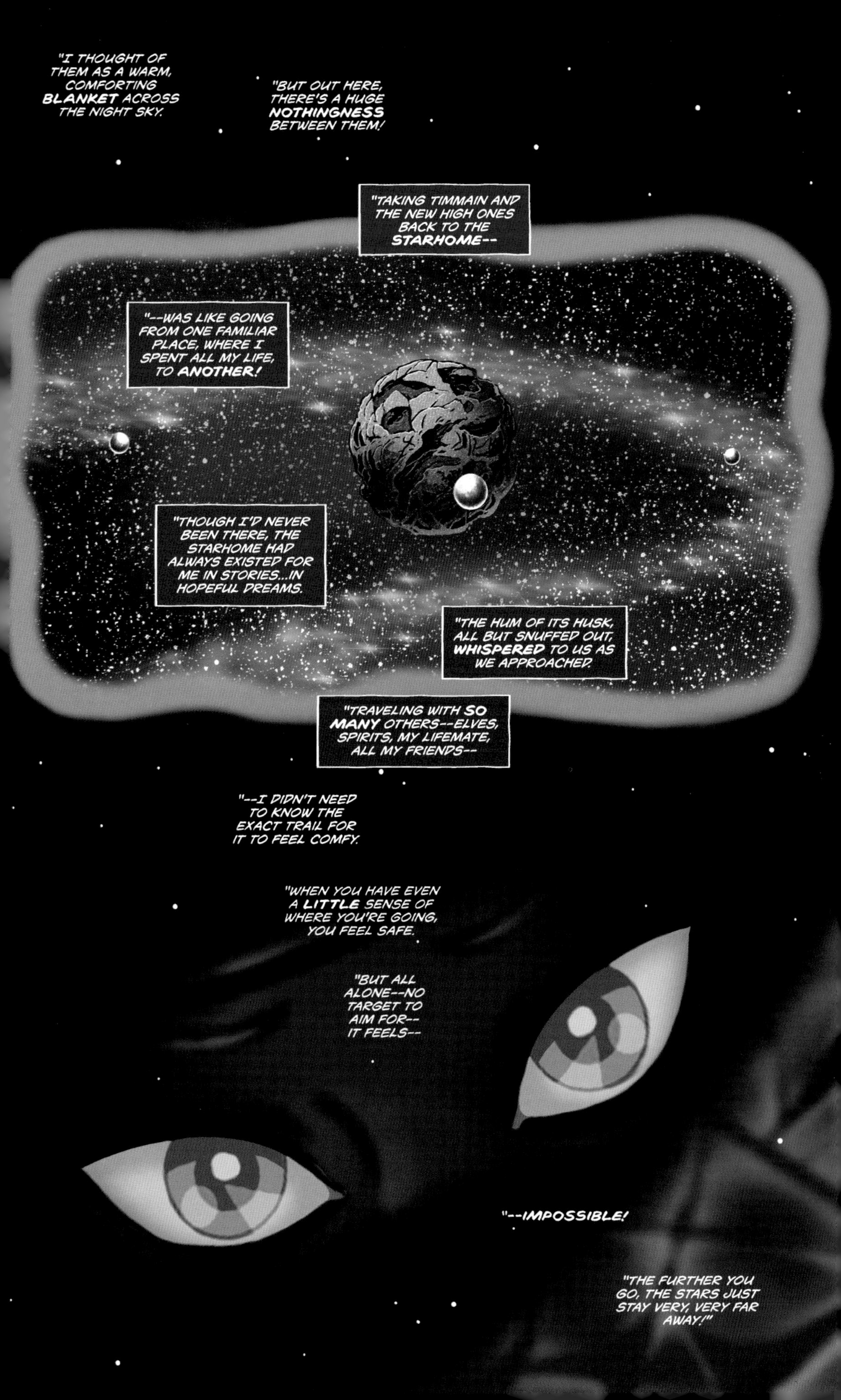
"I THOUGHT OF THEM AS A WARM, COMFORTING BLANKET ACROSS THE NIGHT SKY.
"BUT OUT HERE, THERE'S A HUGE NOTHINGNESS BETWEEN THEM!
"TAKING TIMMAIN AND THE NEW HIGH ONES BACK TO THE STARHOME--
"--WAS LIKE GOING FROM ONE FAMILIAR PLACE, WHERE I SPENT ALL MY LIFE, TO ANOTHER!
"THOUGH I'D NEVER BEEN THERE, THE STARHOME HAD ALWAYS EXISTED FOR ME IN STORIES...IN HOPEFUL DREAMS.
"THE HUM OF ITS HUSK, ALL BUT SNUFFED OUT, WHISPERED TO US AS WE APPROACHED.
"TRAVELING WITH SO MANY OTHERS--ELVES, SPIRITS, MY LIFEMATE, ALL MY FRIENDS--
"--I DIDN'T NEED TO KNOW THE EXACT TRAIL FOR IT TO FEEL COMFY.
"WHEN YOU HAVE EVEN A LITTLE SENSE OF WHERE YOU'RE GOING, YOU FEEL SAFE.
"BUT ALL ALONE--NO TARGET TO AIM FOR--IT FEELS--
"--IMPOSSIBLE!
"THE FURTHER YOU GO, THE STARS JUST STAY VERY, VERY FAR AWAY!"

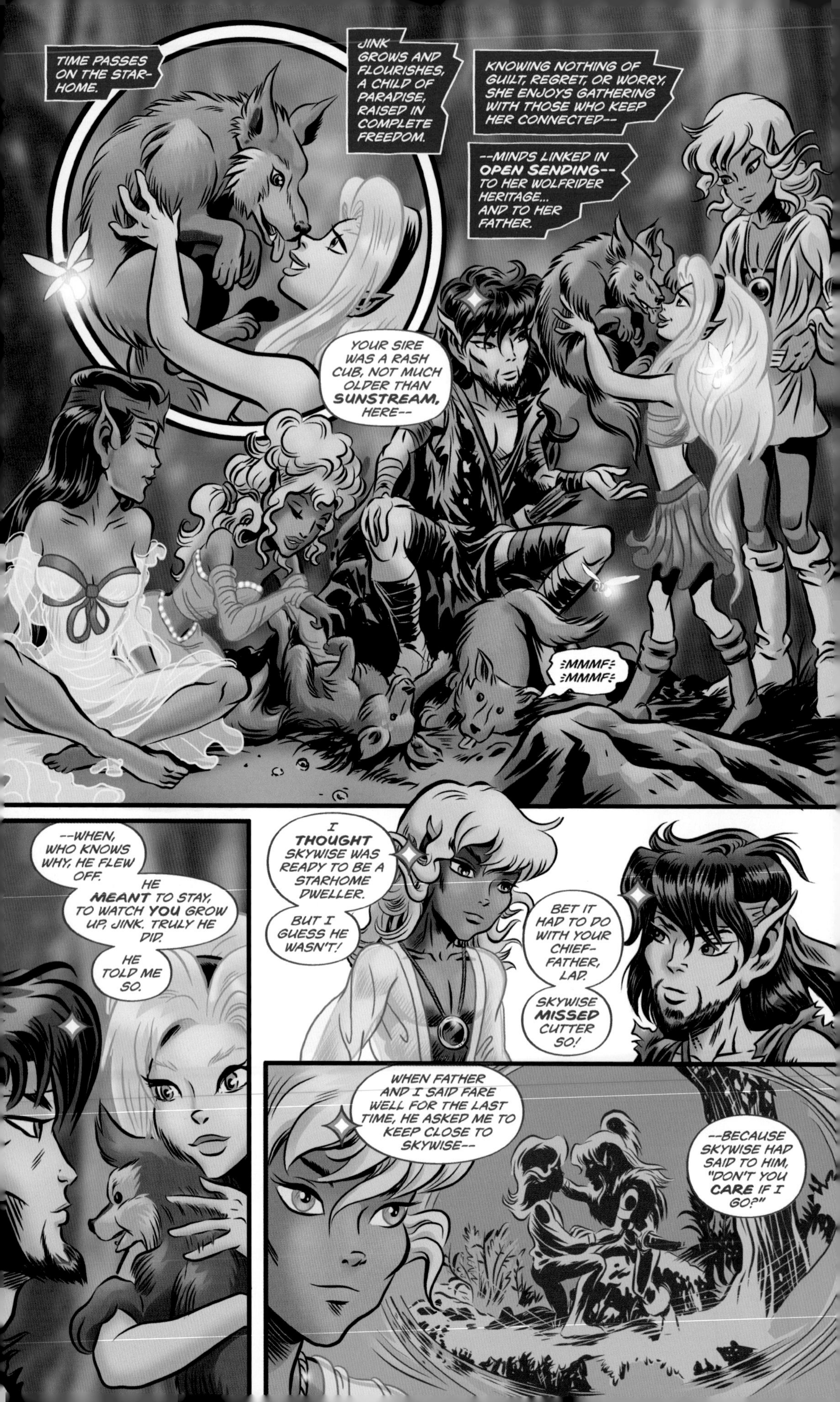
TIME PASSES ON THE STAR-HOME.
JINK GROWS AND FLOURISHES, A CHILD OF PARADISE, RAISED IN COMPLETE FREEDOM.
KNOWING NOTHING OF GUILT, REGRET, OR WORRY, SHE ENJOYS GATHERING WITH THOSE WHO KEEP HER CONNECTED--
--MINDS LINKED IN OPEN SENDING-- TO HER WOLFRIDER HERITAGE... AND TO HER FATHER.
YOUR SIRE WAS A RASH CUB, NOT MUCH OLDER THAN SUNSTREAM, HERE--
MMMF MMMF
--WHEN, WHO KNOWS WHY, HE FLEW OFF.
HE MEANT TO STAY, TO WATCH YOU GROW UP, JINK. TRULY HE DID.
HE TOLD ME SO.
I THOUGHT SKYWISE WAS READY TO BE A STARHOME DWELLER.
BUT I GUESS HE WASN'T!
BET IT HAD TO DO WITH YOUR CHIEF-FATHER, LAD.
SKYWISE MISSED CUTTER SO!
WHEN FATHER AND I SAID FARE WELL FOR THE LAST TIME, HE ASKED ME TO KEEP CLOSE TO SKYWISE--
--BECAUSE SKYWISE HAD SAID TO HIM, "DON'T YOU CARE IF I GO?"

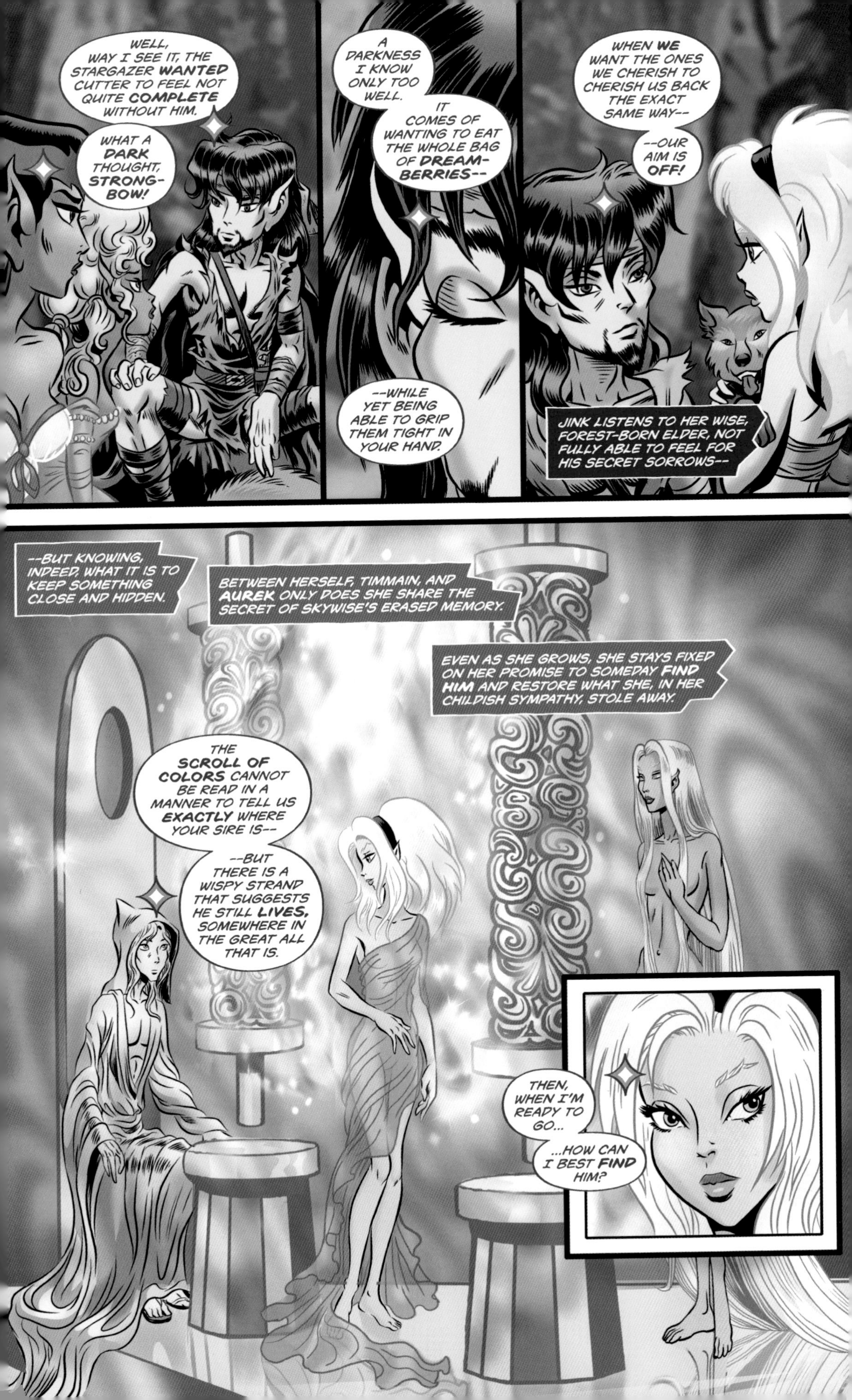
WELL, WAY I SEE IT, THE STARGAZER WANTED CUTTER TO FEEL NOT QUITE COMPLETE WITHOUT HIM.
WHAT A DARK THOUGHT, STRONG-BOW!
A DARKNESS I KNOW ONLY TOO WELL.
IT COMES OF WANTING TO EAT THE WHOLE BAG OF DREAM-BERRIES--
--WHILE YET BEING ABLE TO GRIP THEM TIGHT IN YOUR HAND.
WHEN WE WANT THE ONES WE CHERISH TO CHERISH US BACK THE EXACT SAME WAY--
--OUR AIM IS OFF!
JINK LISTENS TO HER WISE, FOREST-BORN ELDER, NOT FULLY ABLE TO FEEL FOR HIS SECRET SORROWS--
--BUT KNOWING, INDEED, WHAT IT IS TO KEEP SOMETHING CLOSE AND HIDDEN.
BETWEEN HERSELF, TIMMAIN, AND AUREK ONLY DOES SHE SHARE THE SECRET OF SKYWISE'S ERASED MEMORY.
EVEN AS SHE GROWS, SHE STAYS FIXED ON HER PROMISE TO SOMEDAY FIND HIM AND RESTORE WHAT SHE, IN HER CHILDISH SYMPATHY, STOLE AWAY.
THE SCROLL OF COLORS CANNOT BE READ IN A MANNER TO TELL US EXACTLY WHERE YOUR SIRE IS--
--BUT THERE IS A WISPY STRAND THAT SUGGESTS HE STILL LIVES, SOMEWHERE IN THE GREAT ALL THAT IS.
THEN, WHEN I'M READY TO GO...
...HOW CAN I BEST FIND HIM?

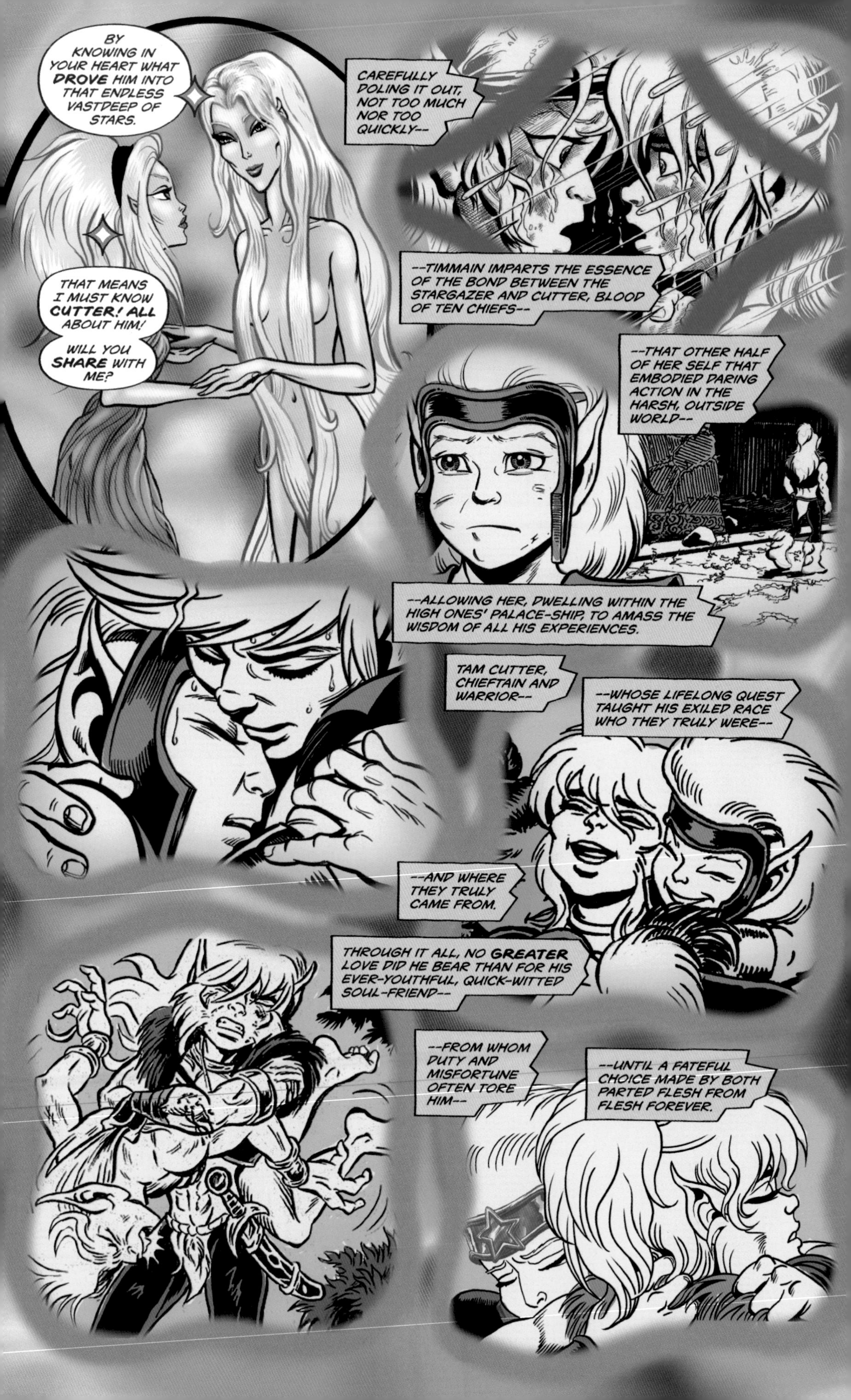

BY KNOWING IN YOUR HEART WHAT DROVE HIM INTO THAT ENDLESS VASTDEEP OF STARS.
THAT MEANS I MUST KNOW CUTTER! ALL ABOUT HIM!
WILL YOU SHARE WITH ME?
CAREFULLY DOLING IT OUT, NOT TOO MUCH NOR TOO QUICKLY--
--TIMMAIN IMPARTS THE ESSENCE OF THE BOND BETWEEN THE STARGAZER AND CUTTER, BLOOD OF TEN CHIEFS--
--THAT OTHER HALF OF HER SELF THAT EMBODIED DARING ACTION IN THE HARSH, OUTSIDE WORLD--
--ALLOWING HER, DWELLING WITHIN THE HIGH ONES' PALACE-SHIP, TO AMASS THE WISDOM OF ALL HIS EXPERIENCES.
TAM CUTTER, CHIEFTAIN AND WARRIOR--
--WHOSE LIFELONG QUEST TAUGHT HIS EXILED RACE WHO THEY TRULY WERE--
--AND WHERE THEY TRULY CAME FROM.
THROUGH IT ALL, NO GREATER LOVE DID HE BEAR THAN FOR HIS EVER-YOUTHFUL, QUICK-WITTED SOUL-FRIEND--
--FROM WHOM DUTY AND MISFORTUNE OFTEN TORE HIM--
--UNTIL A FATEFUL CHOICE MADE BY BOTH PARTED FLESH FROM FLESH FOREVER.

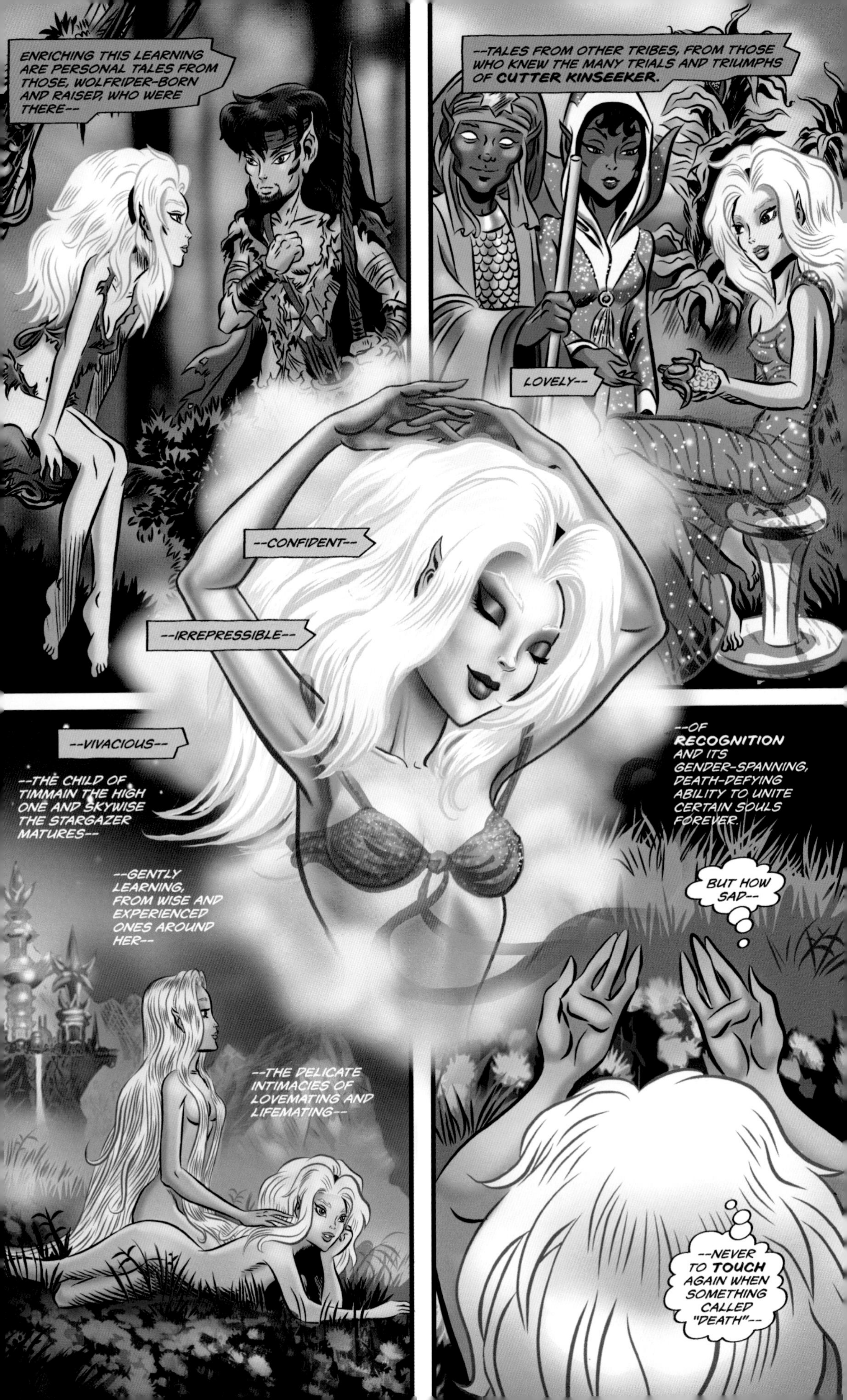

ENRICHING THIS LEARNING ARE PERSONAL TALES FROM THOSE, WOLFRIDER-BORN AND RAISED, WHO WERE THERE--
--TALES FROM OTHER TRIBES, FROM THOSE WHO KNEW THE MANY TRIALS AND TRIUMPHS OF CUTTER KINSEEKER.
LOVELY--
--CONFIDENT--
--IRREPRESSIBLE--
--VIVACIOUS--
--THE CHILD OF TIMMAIN THE HIGH ONE AND SKYWISE THE STARGAZER MATURES--
--GENTLY LEARNING, FROM WISE AND EXPERIENCED ONES AROUND HER--
--THE DELICATE INTIMACIES OF LOVEMATING AND LIFEMATING--
--OF RECOGNITION AND ITS GENDER-SPANNING, DEATH-DEFYING ABILITY TO UNITE CERTAIN SOULS FOREVER.
BUT HOW SAD--
--NEVER TO TOUCH AGAIN WHEN SOMETHING CALLED "DEATH"--

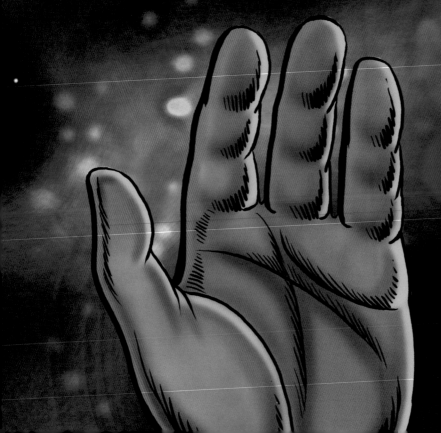

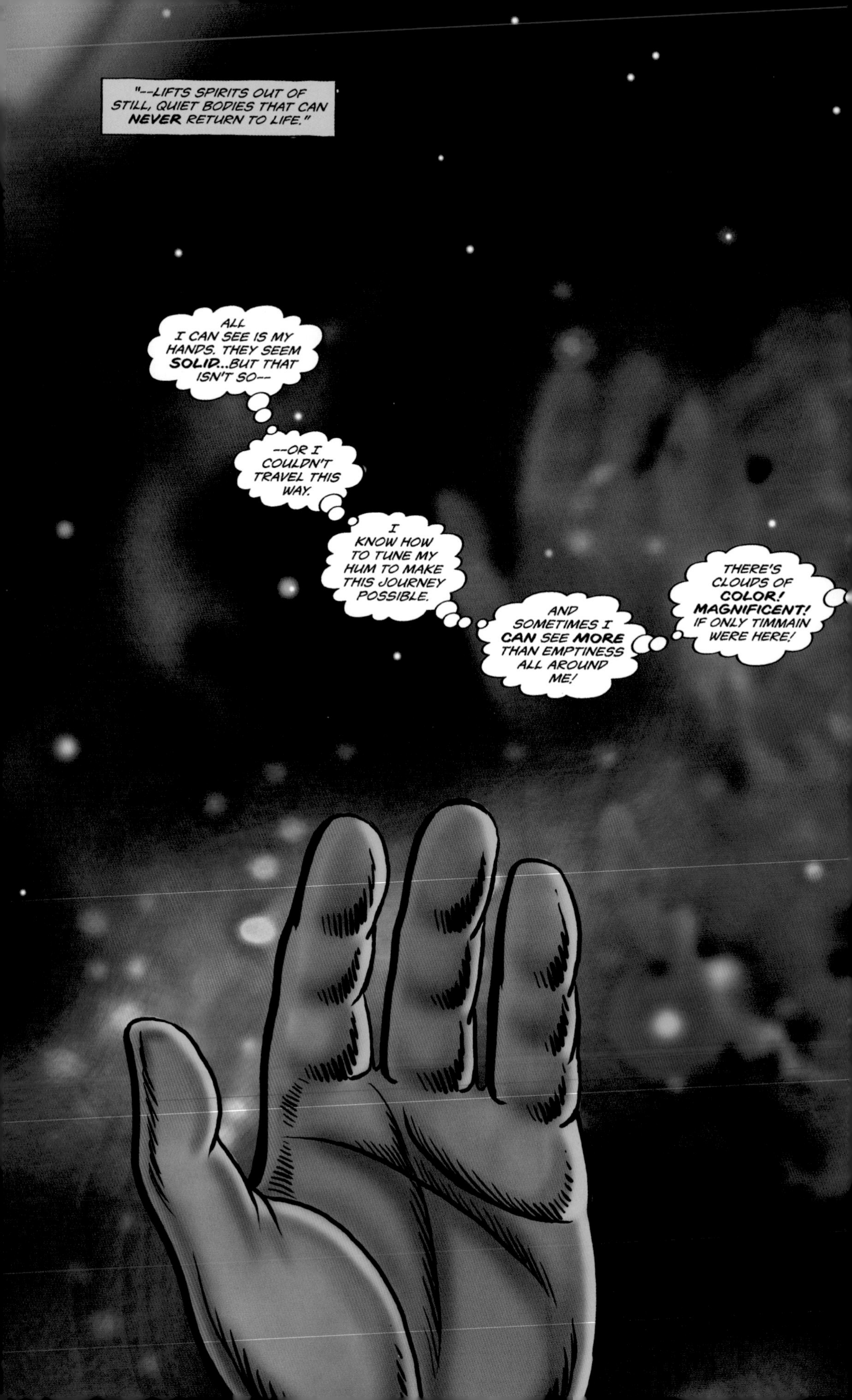

"--LIFTS SPIRITS OUT OF STILL, QUIET BODIES THAT CAN **NEVER** RETURN TO LIFE."

ALL I CAN SEE IS MY HANDS. THEY SEEM **SOLID**...BUT THAT ISN'T SO--

--OR I COULDN'T TRAVEL THIS WAY.

I KNOW HOW TO TUNE MY HUM TO MAKE THIS JOURNEY POSSIBLE.

AND SOMETIMES I **CAN** SEE **MORE** THAN EMPTINESS ALL AROUND ME!

THERE'S CLOUDS OF **COLOR!** **MAGNIFICENT!** IF ONLY TIMMAIN WERE HERE!

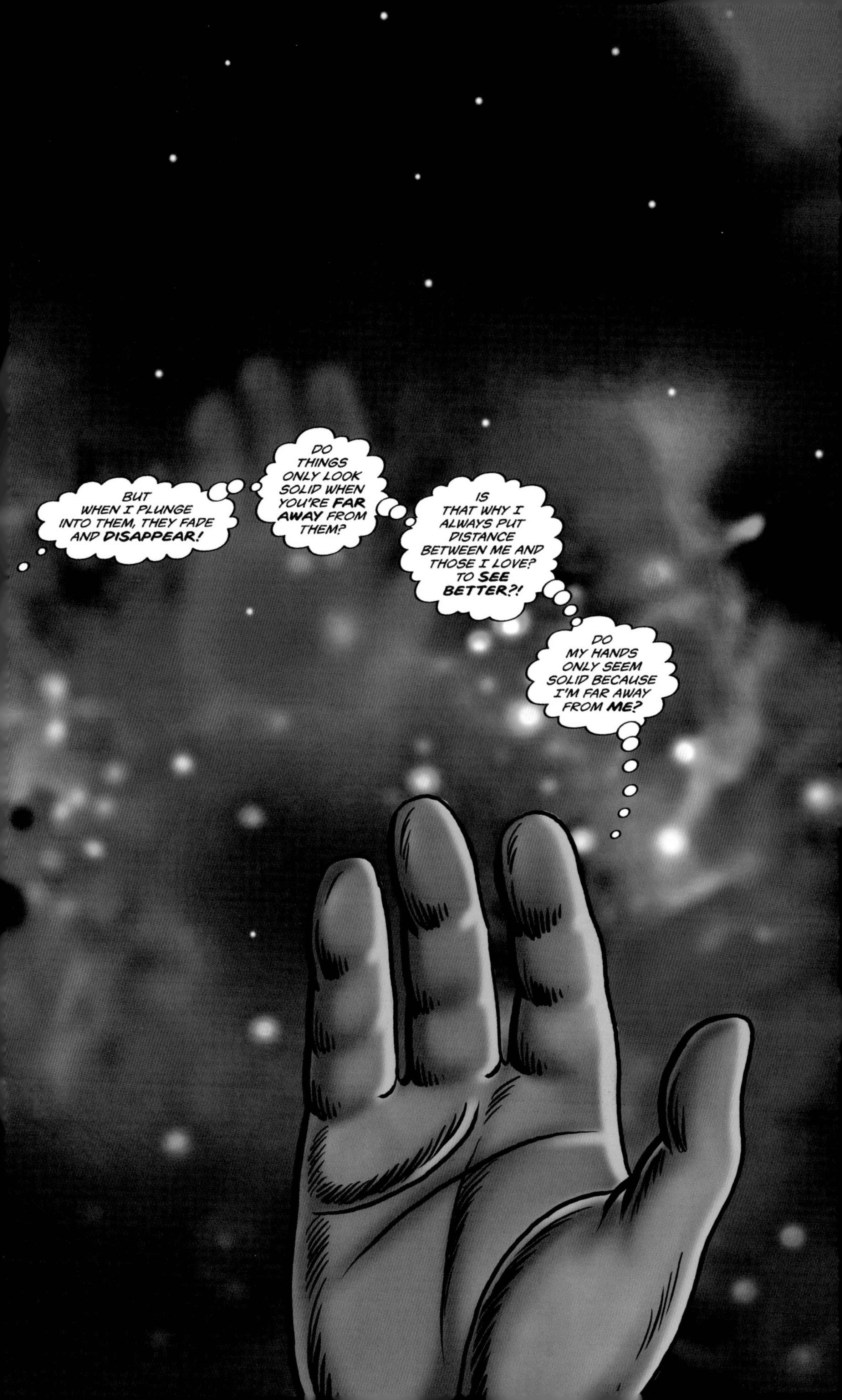
BUT WHEN I PLUNGE INTO THEM, THEY FADE AND DISAPPEAR!
DO THINGS ONLY LOOK SOLID WHEN YOU'RE FAR AWAY FROM THEM?
IS THAT WHY I ALWAYS PUT DISTANCE BETWEEN ME AND THOSE I LOVE? TO SEE BETTER?!
DO MY HANDS ONLY SEEM SOLID BECAUSE I'M FAR AWAY FROM ME?

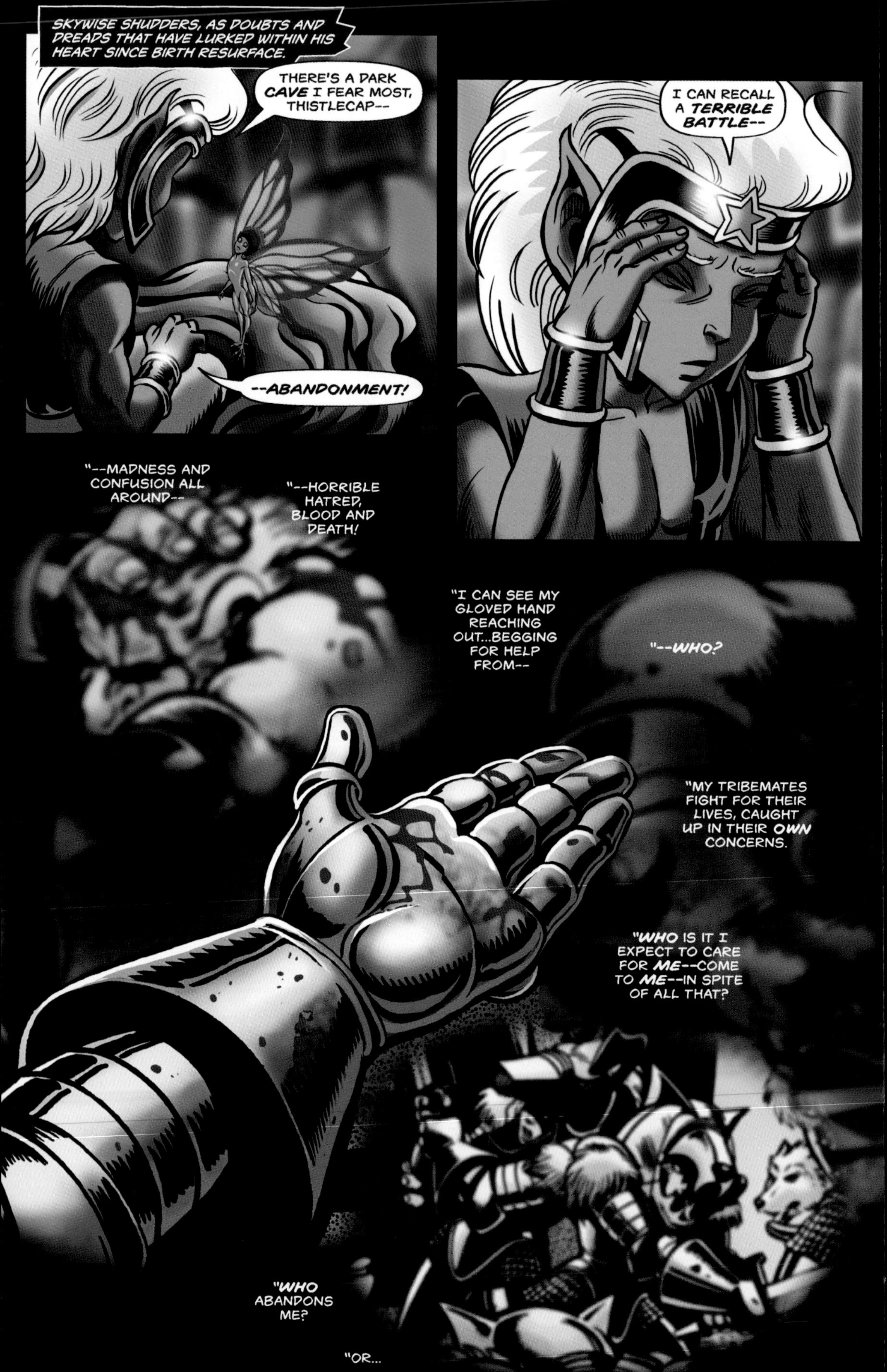
SKYWISE SHUDDERS, AS DOUBTS AND DREADS THAT HAVE LURKED WITHIN HIS HEART SINCE BIRTH RESURFACE.
THERE'S A DARK CAVE I FEAR MOST, THISTLECAP--
--ABANDONMENT!
I CAN RECALL A TERRIBLE BATTLE--
"--MADNESS AND CONFUSION ALL AROUND--
"--HORRIBLE HATRED, BLOOD AND DEATH!
"I CAN SEE MY GLOVED HAND REACHING OUT...BEGGING FOR HELP FROM--
"--WHO?
"MY TRIBEMATES FIGHT FOR THEIR LIVES, CAUGHT UP IN THEIR OWN CONCERNS.
"WHO IS IT I EXPECT TO CARE FOR ME--COME TO ME--IN SPITE OF ALL THAT?
"WHO ABANDONS ME?
"OR...

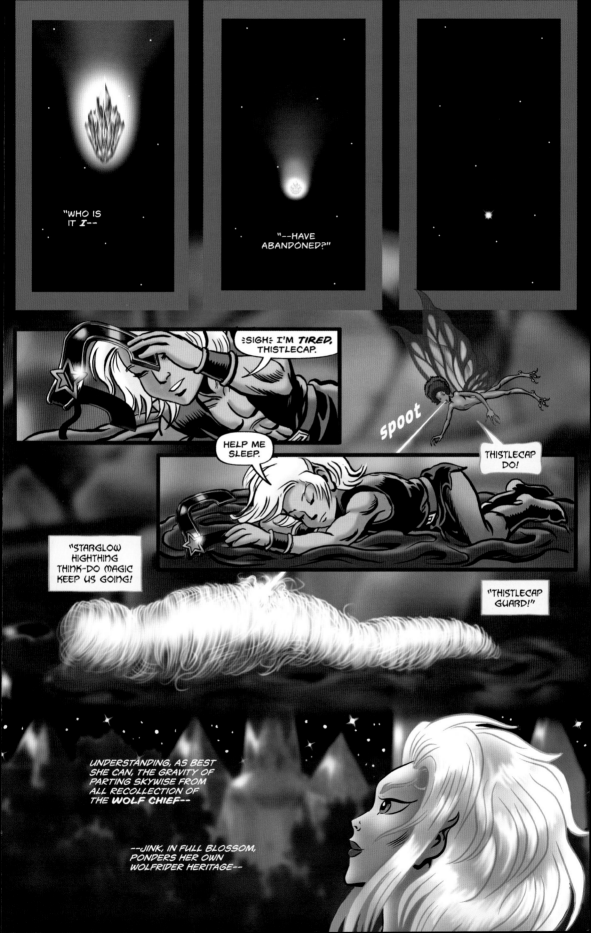

"WHO IS IT *I*--

"--HAVE ABANDONED?"

‡SIGH‡ I'M *TIRED*, THISTLECAP.

HELP ME SLEEP.

spoot

THISTLECAP *DO!*

"STARGLOW HIGHTHING THINK-DO MAGIC KEEP US GOING!

"THISTLECAP GUARD!"

UNDERSTANDING, AS BEST SHE CAN, THE GRAVITY OF PARTING SKYWISE FROM ALL RECOLLECTION OF THE *WOLF CHIEF*--

--JINK, IN FULL BLOSSOM, PONDERS HER OWN WOLFRIDER HERITAGE--

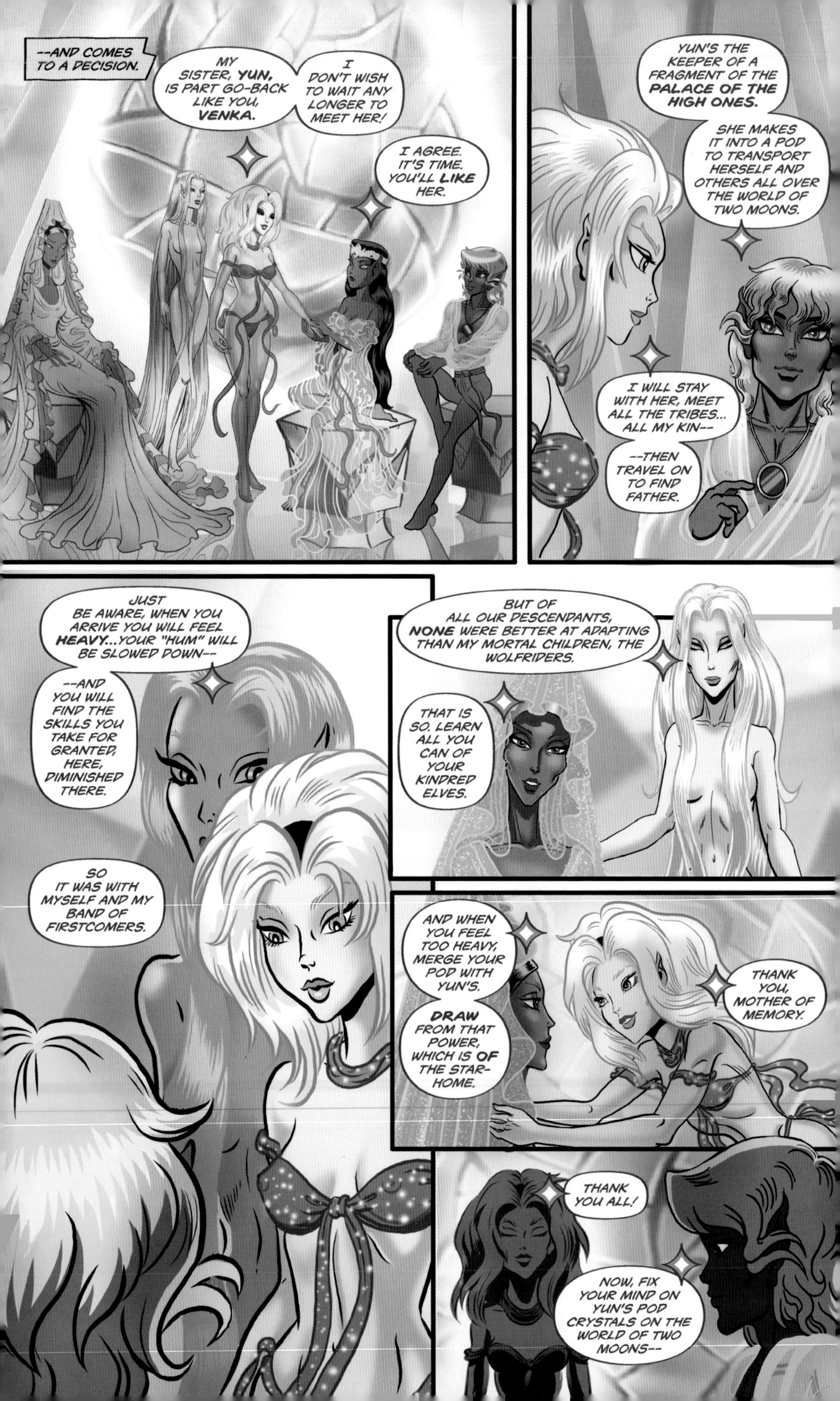
--AND COMES TO A DECISION.
MY SISTER, YUN, IS PART GO-BACK LIKE YOU, VENKA.
I DON'T WISH TO WAIT ANY LONGER TO MEET HER!
I AGREE. IT'S TIME. YOU'LL LIKE HER.
YUN'S THE KEEPER OF A FRAGMENT OF THE PALACE OF THE HIGH ONES.
SHE MAKES IT INTO A POD TO TRANSPORT HERSELF AND OTHERS ALL OVER THE WORLD OF TWO MOONS.
I WILL STAY WITH HER, MEET ALL THE TRIBES... ALL MY KIN--
--THEN TRAVEL ON TO FIND FATHER.
JUST BE AWARE, WHEN YOU ARRIVE YOU WILL FEEL HEAVY...YOUR "HUM" WILL BE SLOWED DOWN--
--AND YOU WILL FIND THE SKILLS YOU TAKE FOR GRANTED, HERE, DIMINISHED THERE.
SO IT WAS WITH MYSELF AND MY BAND OF FIRSTCOMERS.
BUT OF ALL OUR DESCENDANTS, NONE WERE BETTER AT ADAPTING THAN MY MORTAL CHILDREN, THE WOLFRIDERS.
THAT IS SO. LEARN ALL YOU CAN OF YOUR KINDRED ELVES.
AND WHEN YOU FEEL TOO HEAVY, MERGE YOUR POD WITH YUN'S.
DRAW FROM THAT POWER, WHICH IS OF THE STAR-HOME.
THANK YOU, MOTHER OF MEMORY.
THANK YOU ALL!
NOW, FIX YOUR MIND ON YUN'S POD CRYSTALS ON THE WORLD OF TWO MOONS--

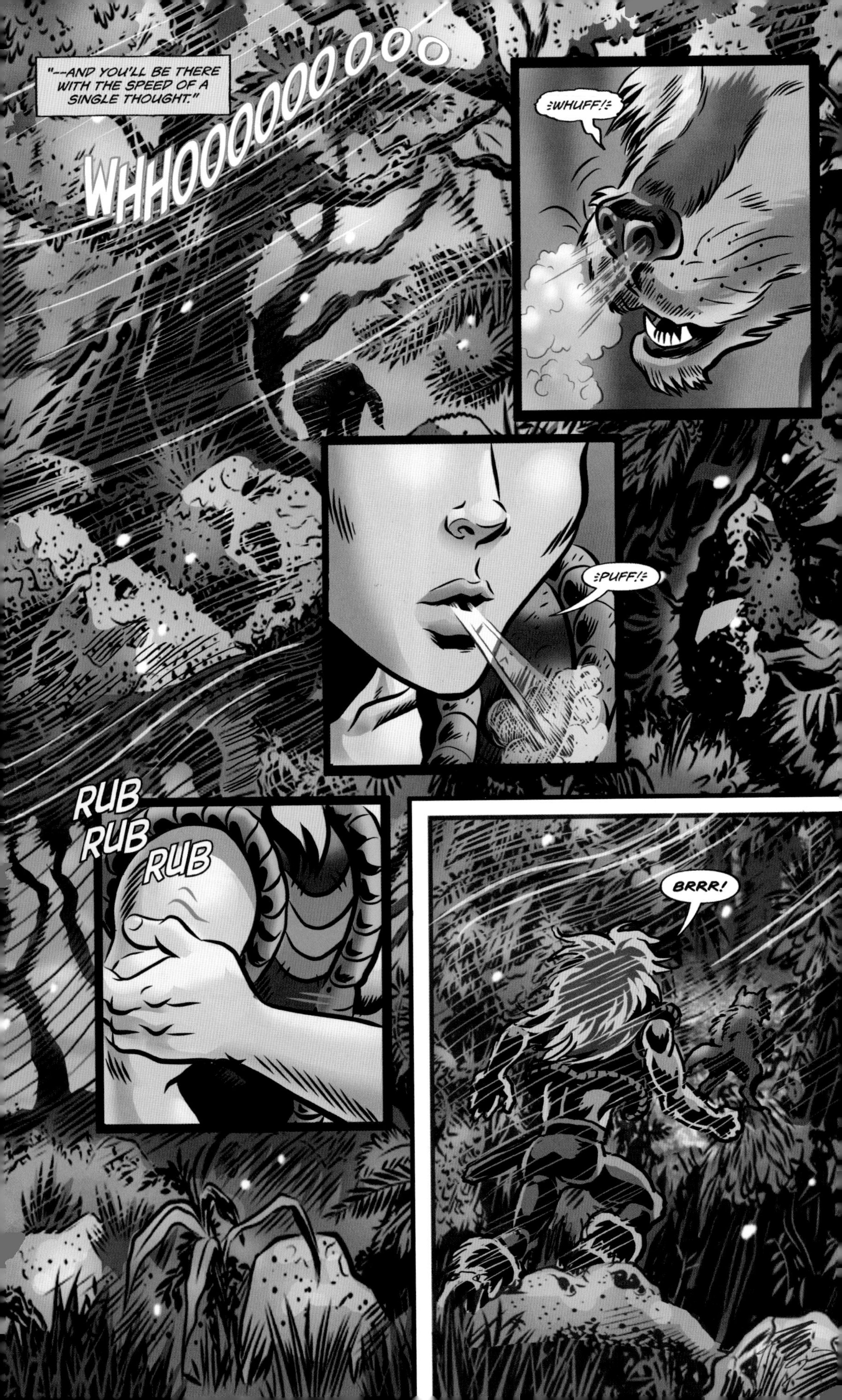
"--AND YOU'LL BE THERE WITH THE SPEED OF A SINGLE THOUGHT."
WHHOOOOOOOOOO
WHUFF!
PUFF!
RUB RUB RUB
BRRR!

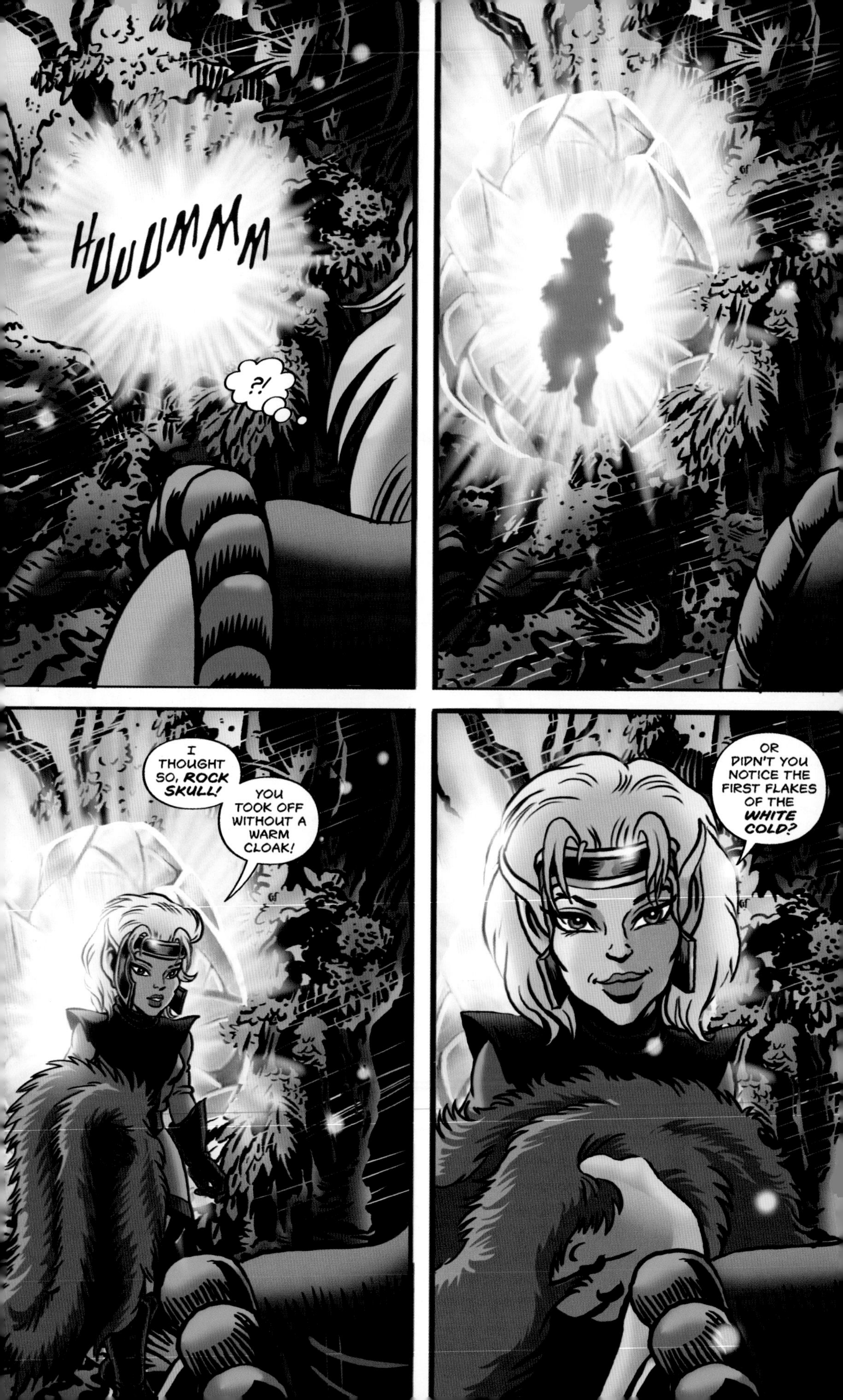

HUUUMMMM
?!
I THOUGHT SO, ROCK SKULL!
YOU TOOK OFF WITHOUT A WARM CLOAK!
OR DIDN'T YOU NOTICE THE FIRST FLAKES OF THE WHITE COLD?

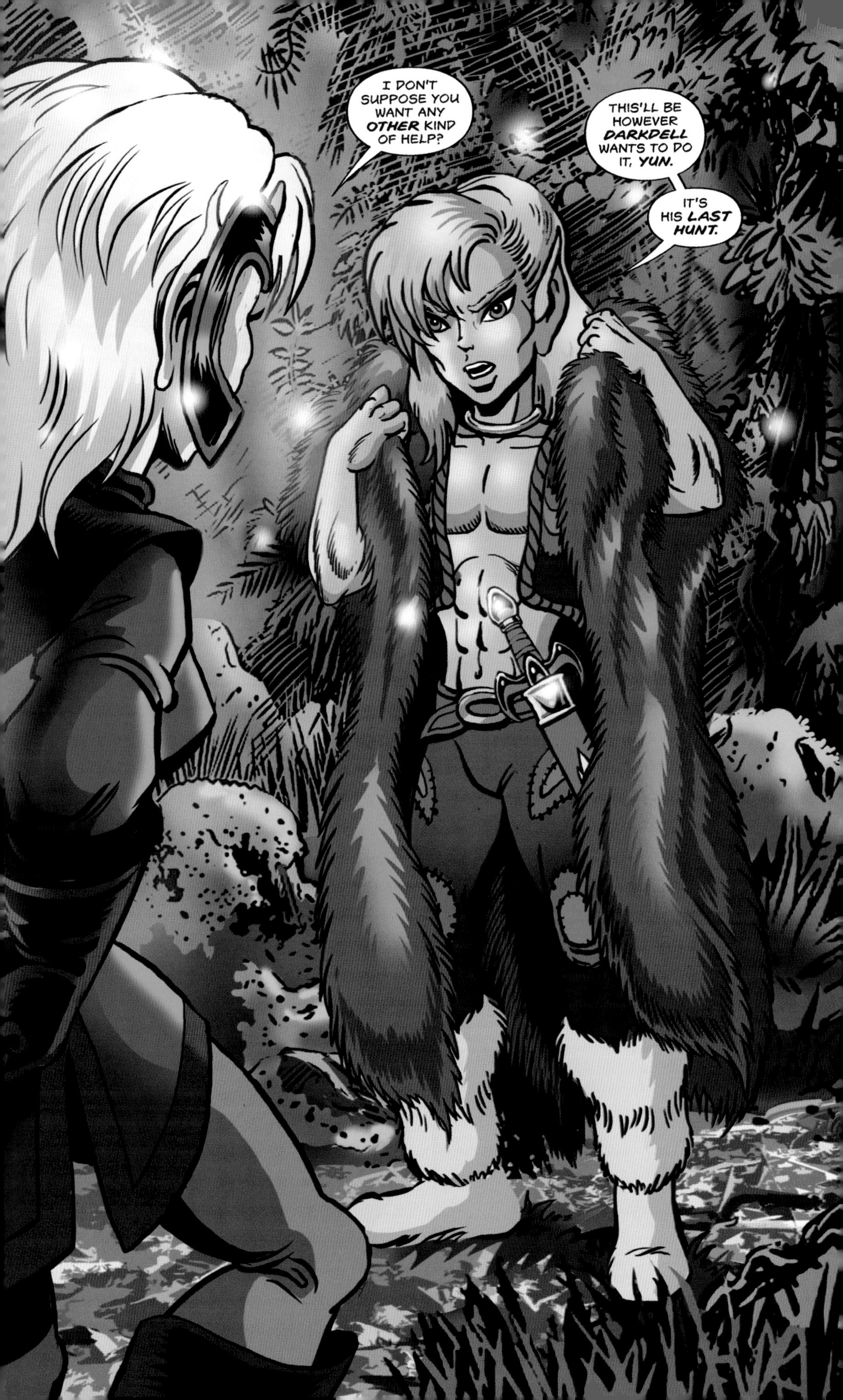
I DON'T SUPPOSE YOU WANT ANY OTHER KIND OF HELP?
THIS'LL BE HOWEVER DARKDELL WANTS TO DO IT, YUN.
IT'S HIS LAST HUNT.

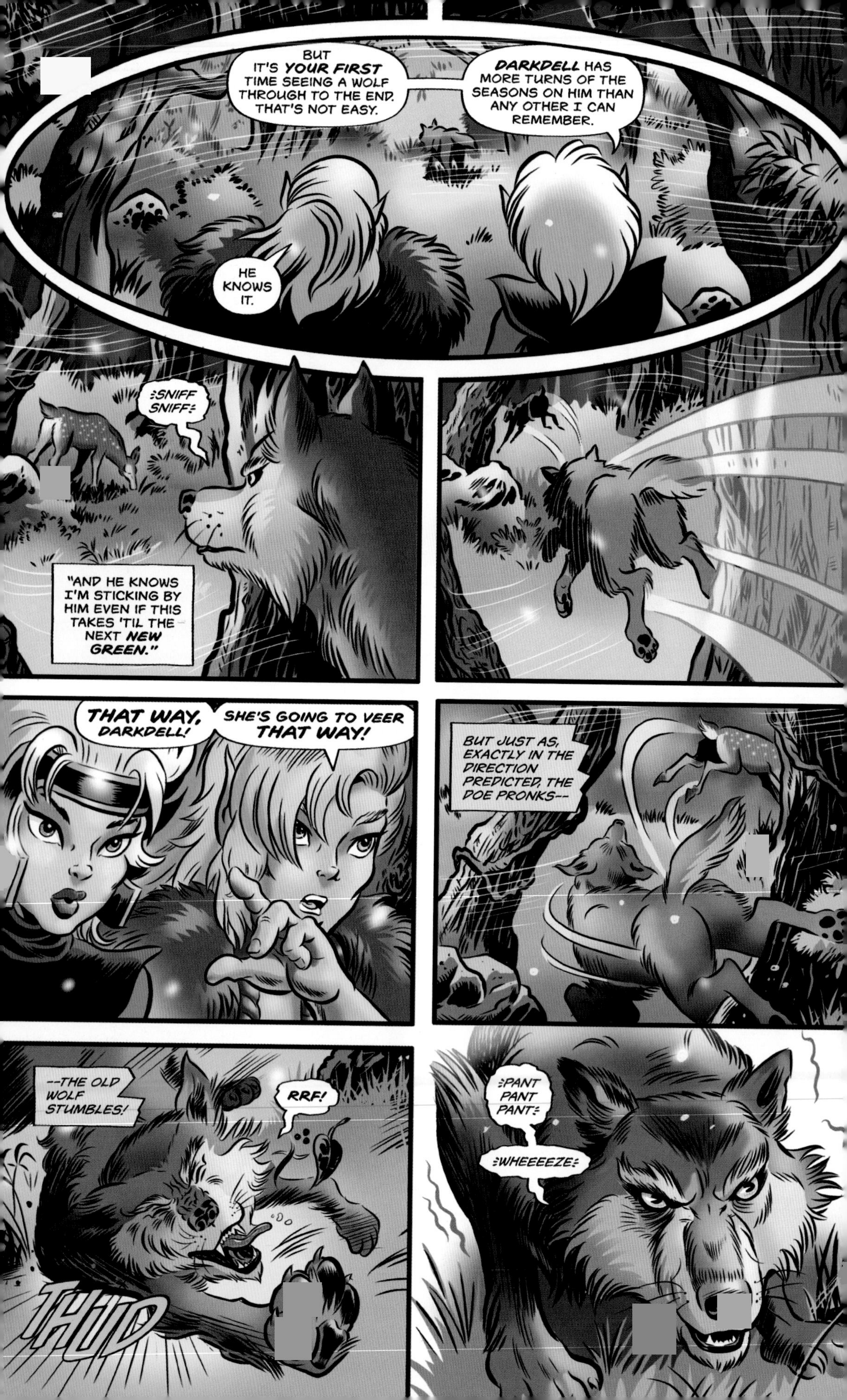
BUT IT'S YOUR FIRST TIME SEEING A WOLF THROUGH TO THE END. THAT'S NOT EASY.
DARKDELL HAS MORE TURNS OF THE SEASONS ON HIM THAN ANY OTHER I CAN REMEMBER.
HE KNOWS IT.
SNIFF SNIFF
"AND HE KNOWS I'M STICKING BY HIM EVEN IF THIS TAKES 'TIL THE NEXT NEW GREEN."
THAT WAY, DARKDELL!
SHE'S GOING TO VEER THAT WAY!
BUT JUST AS, EXACTLY IN THE DIRECTION PREDICTED, THE DOE PRONKS--
--THE OLD WOLF STUMBLES!
RRF!
THUD
PANT PANT PANT
WHEEEEEZE

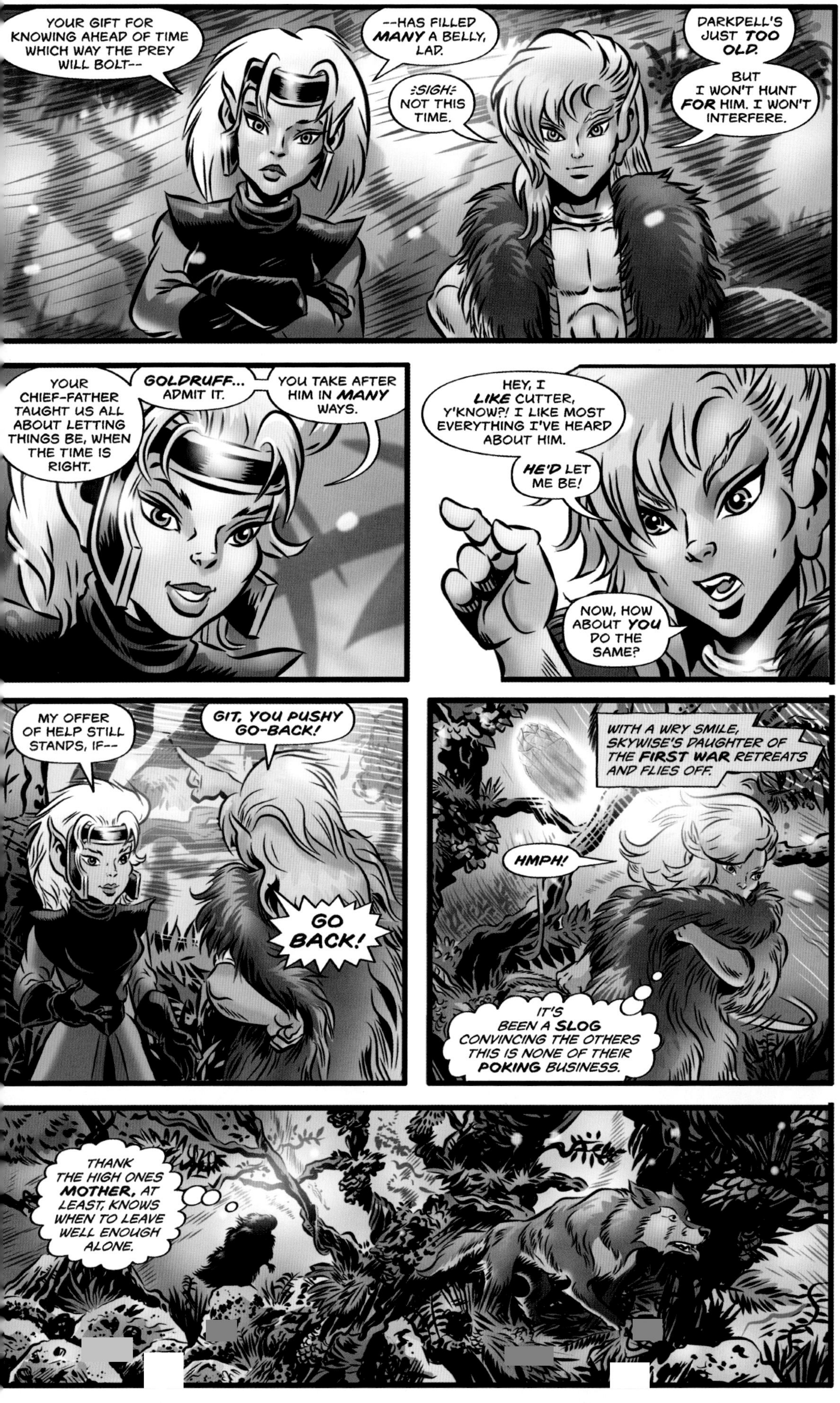
YOUR GIFT FOR KNOWING AHEAD OF TIME WHICH WAY THE PREY WILL BOLT--
--HAS FILLED MANY A BELLY, LAD.
:SIGH: NOT THIS TIME.
DARKDELL'S JUST TOO OLD.
BUT I WON'T HUNT FOR HIM. I WON'T INTERFERE.
YOUR CHIEF-FATHER TAUGHT US ALL ABOUT LETTING THINGS BE, WHEN THE TIME IS RIGHT.
GOLDRUFF... ADMIT IT.
YOU TAKE AFTER HIM IN MANY WAYS.
HEY, I LIKE CUTTER, Y'KNOW?! I LIKE MOST EVERYTHING I'VE HEARD ABOUT HIM.
HE'D LET ME BE!
NOW, HOW ABOUT YOU DO THE SAME?
MY OFFER OF HELP STILL STANDS, IF--
GIT, YOU PUSHY GO-BACK!
GO BACK!
WITH A WRY SMILE, SKYWISE'S DAUGHTER OF THE FIRST WAR RETREATS AND FLIES OFF.
HMPH!
IT'S BEEN A SLOG CONVINCING THE OTHERS THIS IS NONE OF THEIR POKING BUSINESS.
THANK THE HIGH ONES MOTHER, AT LEAST, KNOWS WHEN TO LEAVE WELL ENOUGH ALONE.

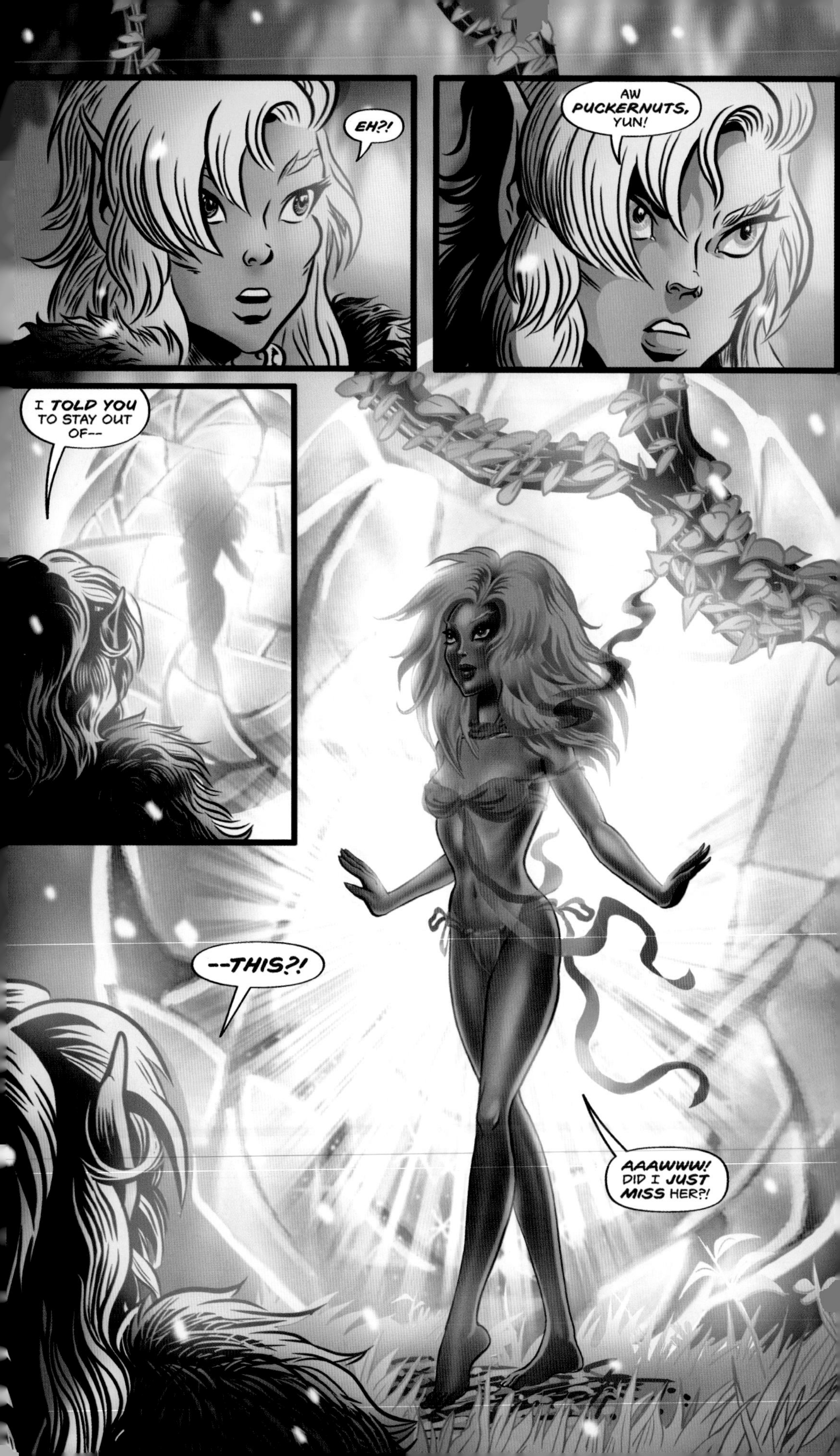
EH?!
AW PUCKERNUTS, YUN!
I TOLD YOU TO STAY OUT OF--
--THIS?!
AAAWWW! DID I JUST MISS HER?!

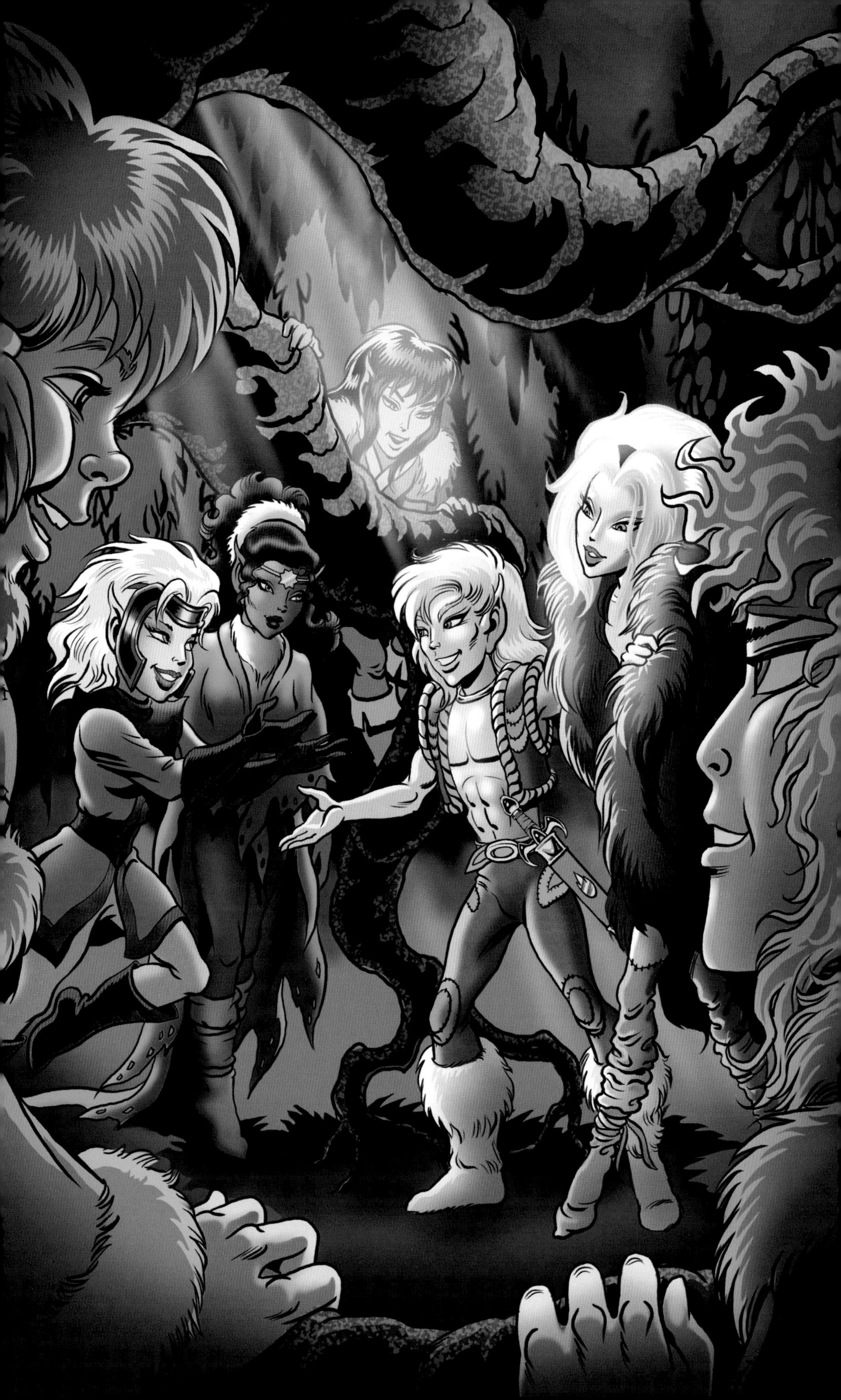

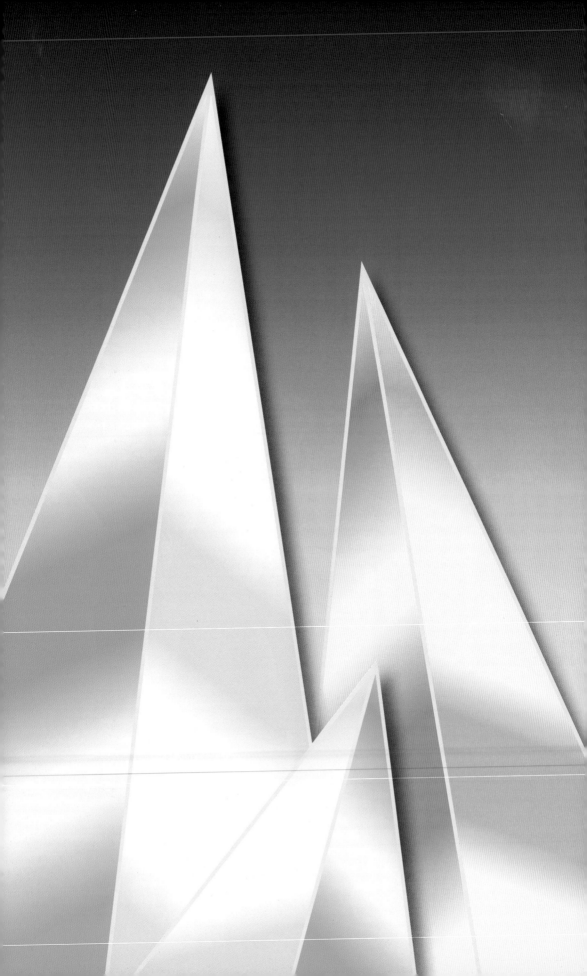

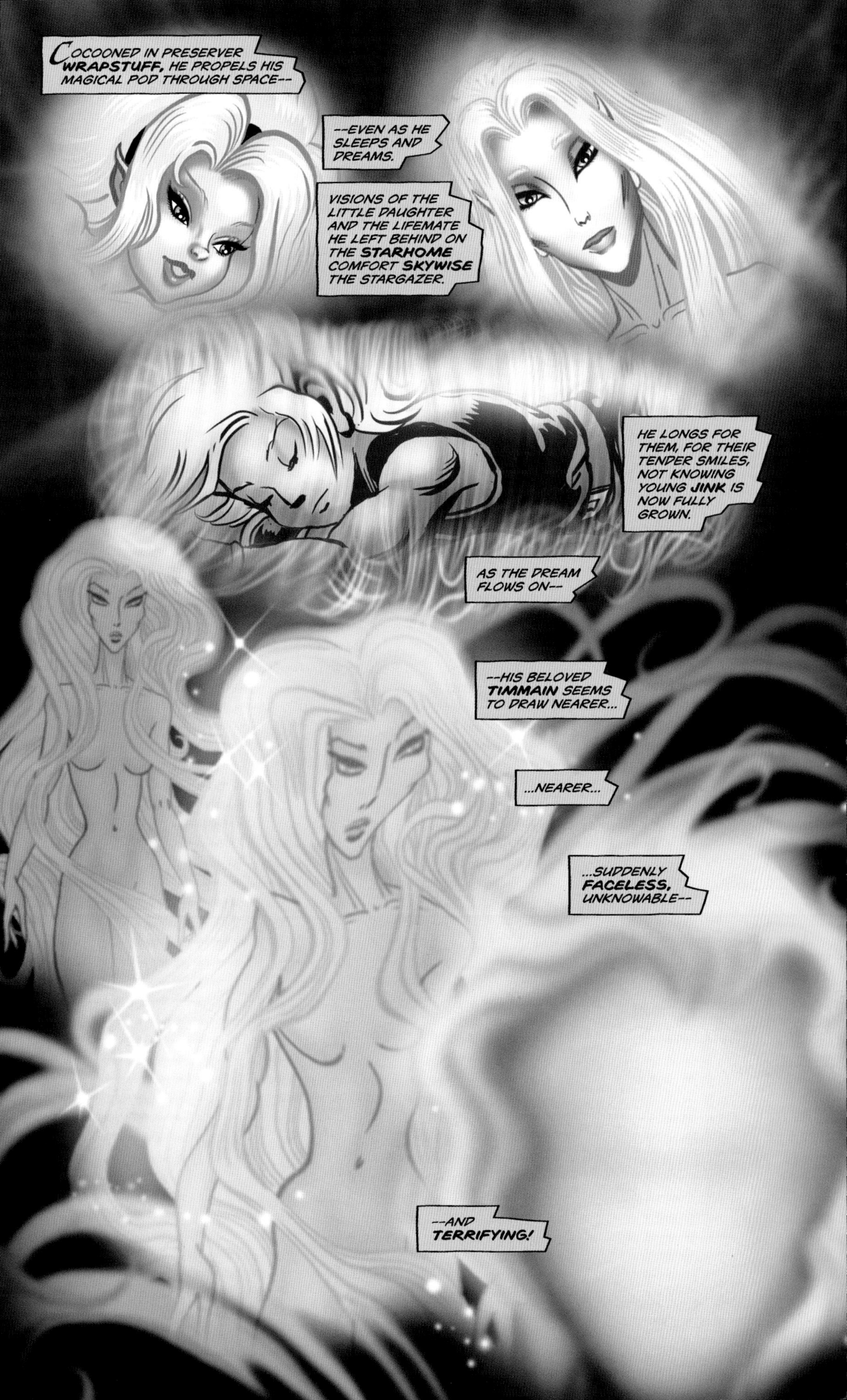
COCOONED IN PRESERVER WRAPSTUFF, HE PROPELS HIS MAGICAL POD THROUGH SPACE--
--EVEN AS HE SLEEPS AND DREAMS.
VISIONS OF THE LITTLE DAUGHTER AND THE LIFEMATE HE LEFT BEHIND ON THE STARHOME COMFORT SKYWISE THE STARGAZER.
HE LONGS FOR THEM, FOR THEIR TENDER SMILES, NOT KNOWING YOUNG JINK IS NOW FULLY GROWN.
AS THE DREAM FLOWS ON--
--HIS BELOVED TIMMAIN SEEMS TO DRAW NEARER...
...NEARER...
...SUDDENLY FACELESS, UNKNOWABLE--
--AND TERRIFYING!

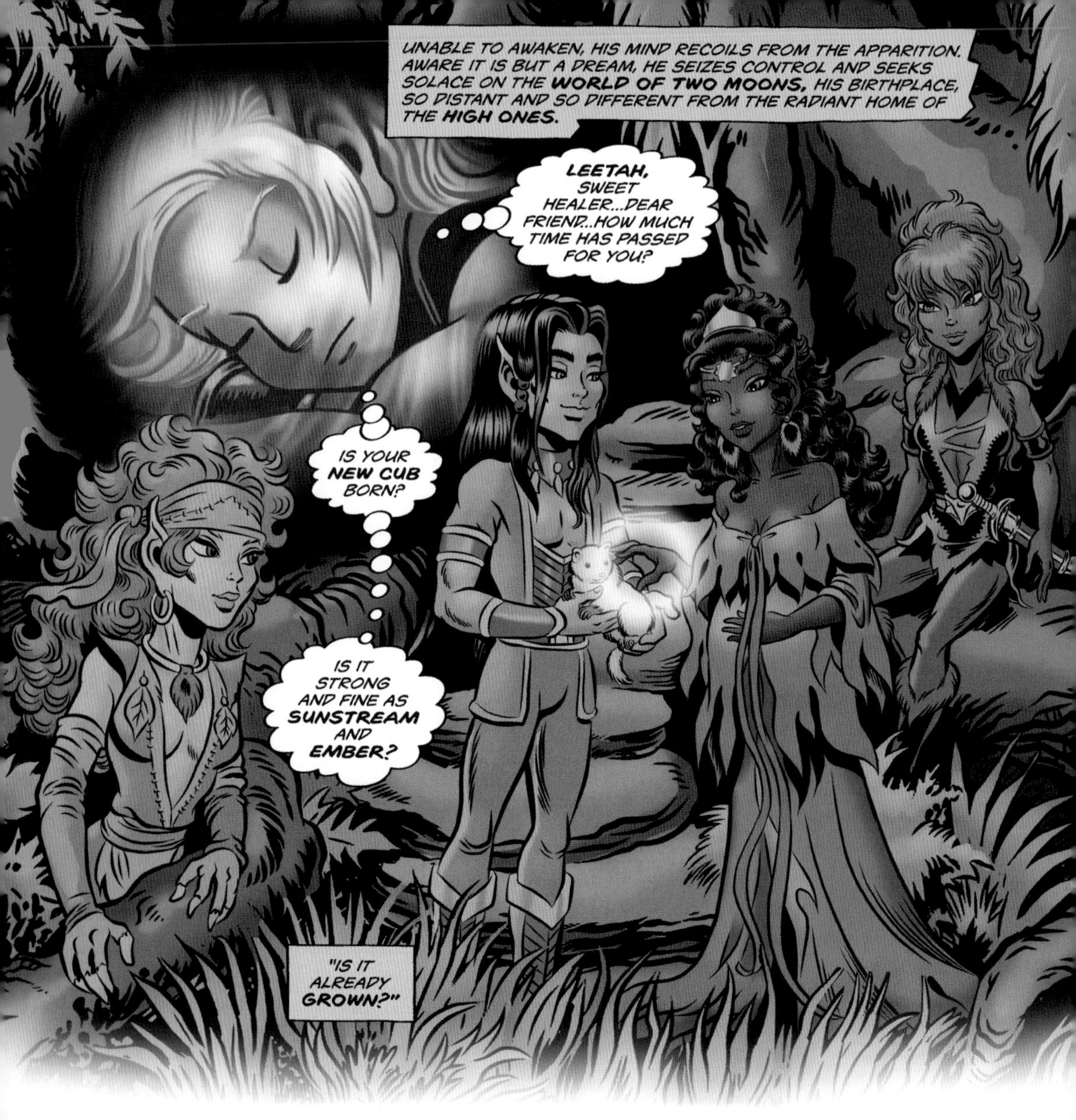
UNABLE TO AWAKEN, HIS MIND RECOILS FROM THE APPARITION. AWARE IT IS BUT A DREAM, HE SEIZES CONTROL AND SEEKS SOLACE ON THE **WORLD OF TWO MOONS,** HIS BIRTHPLACE, SO DISTANT AND SO DIFFERENT FROM THE RADIANT HOME OF THE **HIGH ONES.**
LEETAH, SWEET HEALER...DEAR FRIEND...HOW MUCH TIME HAS PASSED FOR YOU?
IS YOUR **NEW CUB** BORN?
IS IT STRONG AND FINE AS **SUNSTREAM** AND **EMBER?**
"IS IT ALREADY **GROWN?"**

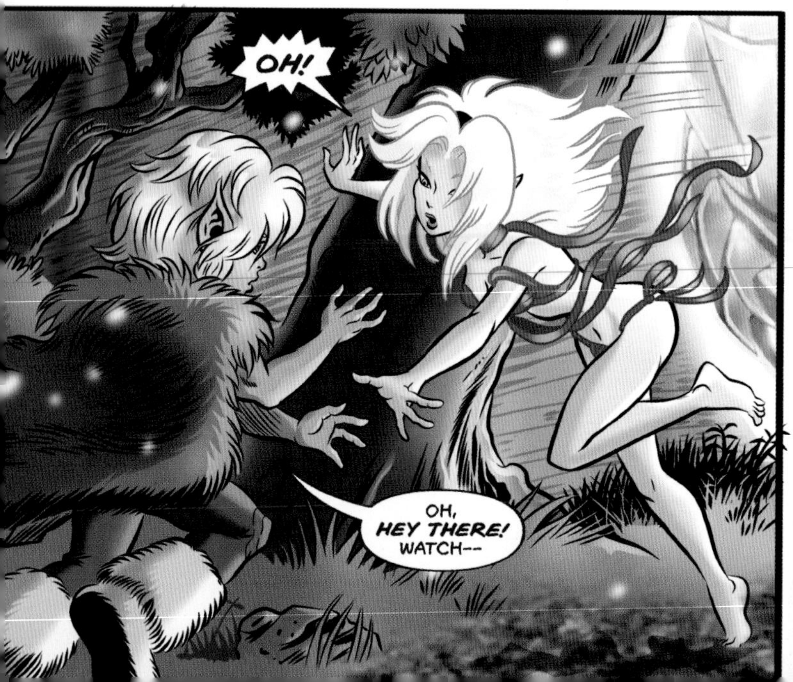
OH!
OH, **HEY THERE!** WATCH--

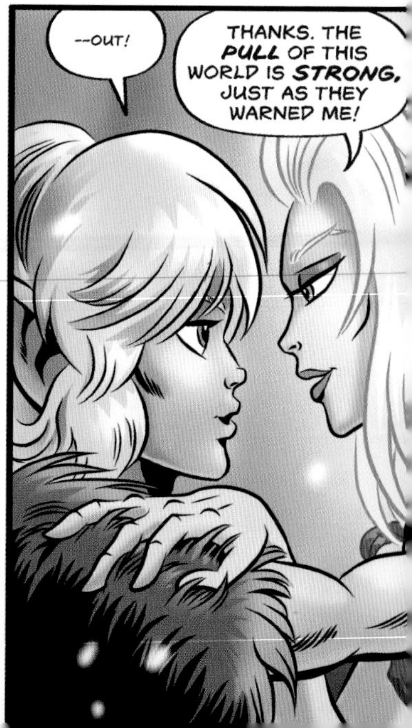
--OUT!
THANKS. THE **PULL** OF THIS WORLD IS **STRONG,** JUST AS THEY WARNED ME!

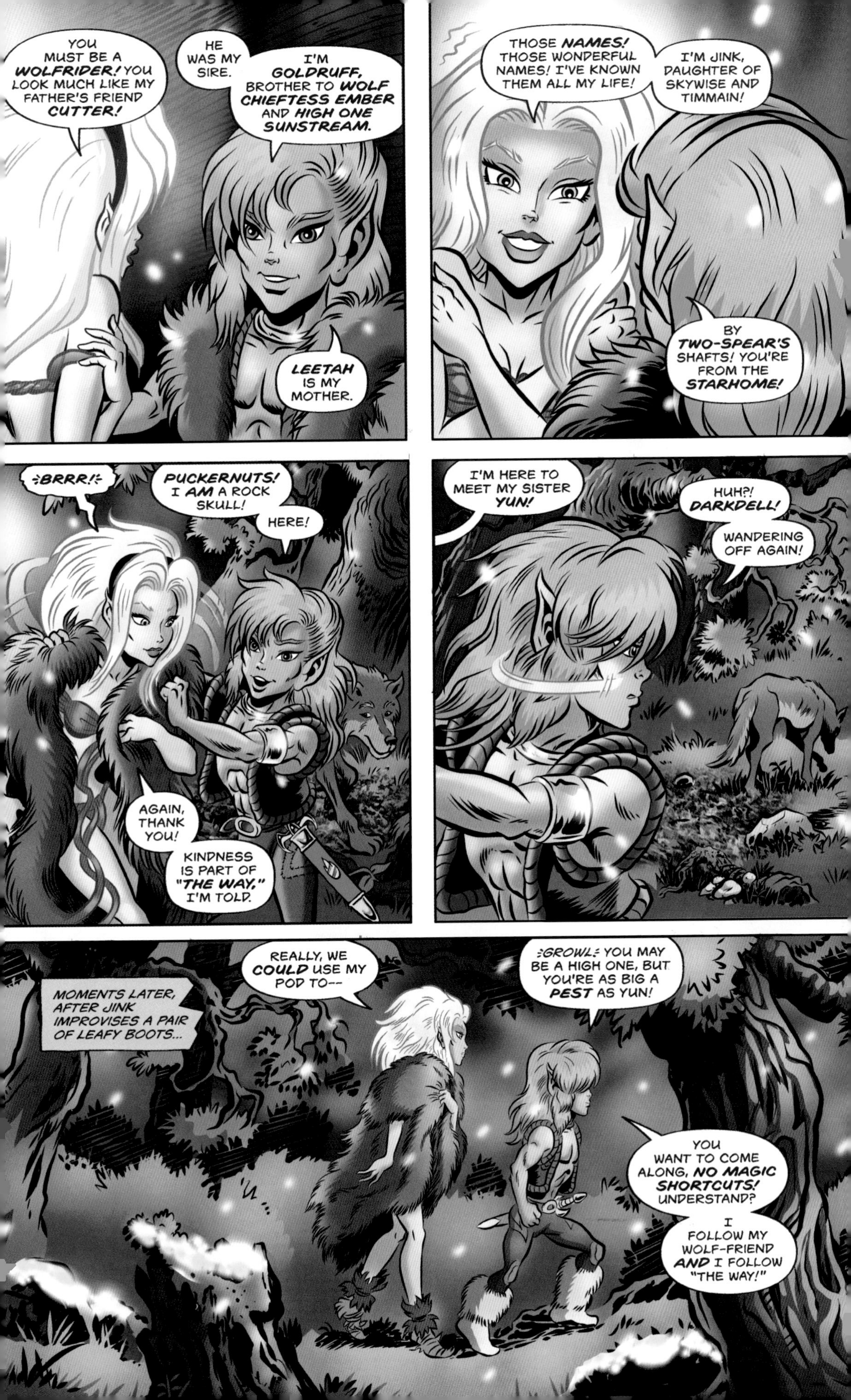
YOU MUST BE A WOLFRIDER! YOU LOOK MUCH LIKE MY FATHER'S FRIEND CUTTER!
HE WAS MY SIRE.
I'M GOLDRUFF, BROTHER TO WOLF CHIEFTESS EMBER AND HIGH ONE SUNSTREAM.
LEETAH IS MY MOTHER.
THOSE NAMES! THOSE WONDERFUL NAMES! I'VE KNOWN THEM ALL MY LIFE!
I'M JINK, DAUGHTER OF SKYWISE AND TIMMAIN!
BY TWO-SPEAR'S SHAFTS! YOU'RE FROM THE STARHOME!
BRRR!
PUCKERNUTS! I AM A ROCK SKULL!
HERE!
AGAIN, THANK YOU!
KINDNESS IS PART OF "THE WAY," I'M TOLD.
I'M HERE TO MEET MY SISTER YUN!
HUH?! DARKDELL!
WANDERING OFF AGAIN!
MOMENTS LATER, AFTER JINK IMPROVISES A PAIR OF LEAFY BOOTS...
REALLY, WE COULD USE MY POD TO--
GROWL: YOU MAY BE A HIGH ONE, BUT YOU'RE AS BIG A PEST AS YUN!
YOU WANT TO COME ALONG, NO MAGIC SHORTCUTS! UNDERSTAND?
I FOLLOW MY WOLF-FRIEND AND I FOLLOW "THE WAY!"

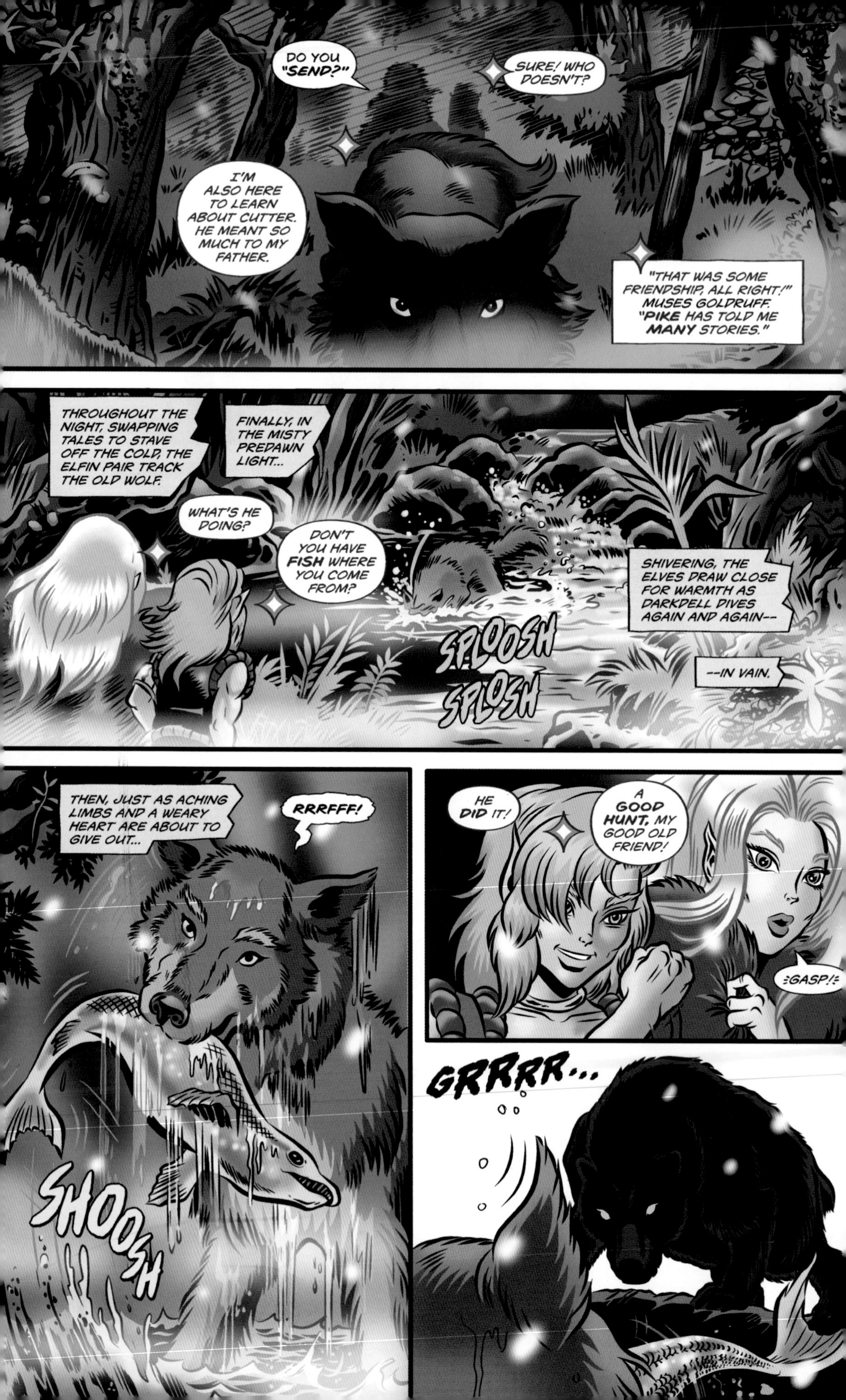
DO YOU "SEND?"
SURE! WHO DOESN'T?
I'M ALSO HERE TO LEARN ABOUT CUTTER. HE MEANT SO MUCH TO MY FATHER.
"THAT WAS SOME FRIENDSHIP, ALL RIGHT!" MUSES GOLDRUFF. "PIKE HAS TOLD ME MANY STORIES."
THROUGHOUT THE NIGHT, SWAPPING TALES TO STAVE OFF THE COLD, THE ELFIN PAIR TRACK THE OLD WOLF.
FINALLY, IN THE MISTY PREDAWN LIGHT...
WHAT'S HE DOING?
DON'T YOU HAVE FISH WHERE YOU COME FROM?
SPLOOSH
SPLOSH
SHIVERING, THE ELVES DRAW CLOSE FOR WARMTH AS DARKDELL DIVES AGAIN AND AGAIN--
--IN VAIN.
THEN, JUST AS ACHING LIMBS AND A WEARY HEART ARE ABOUT TO GIVE OUT...
RRRFFF!
SHOOOSH
HE DID IT!
A GOOD HUNT, MY GOOD OLD FRIEND!
GASP!
GRRRR...

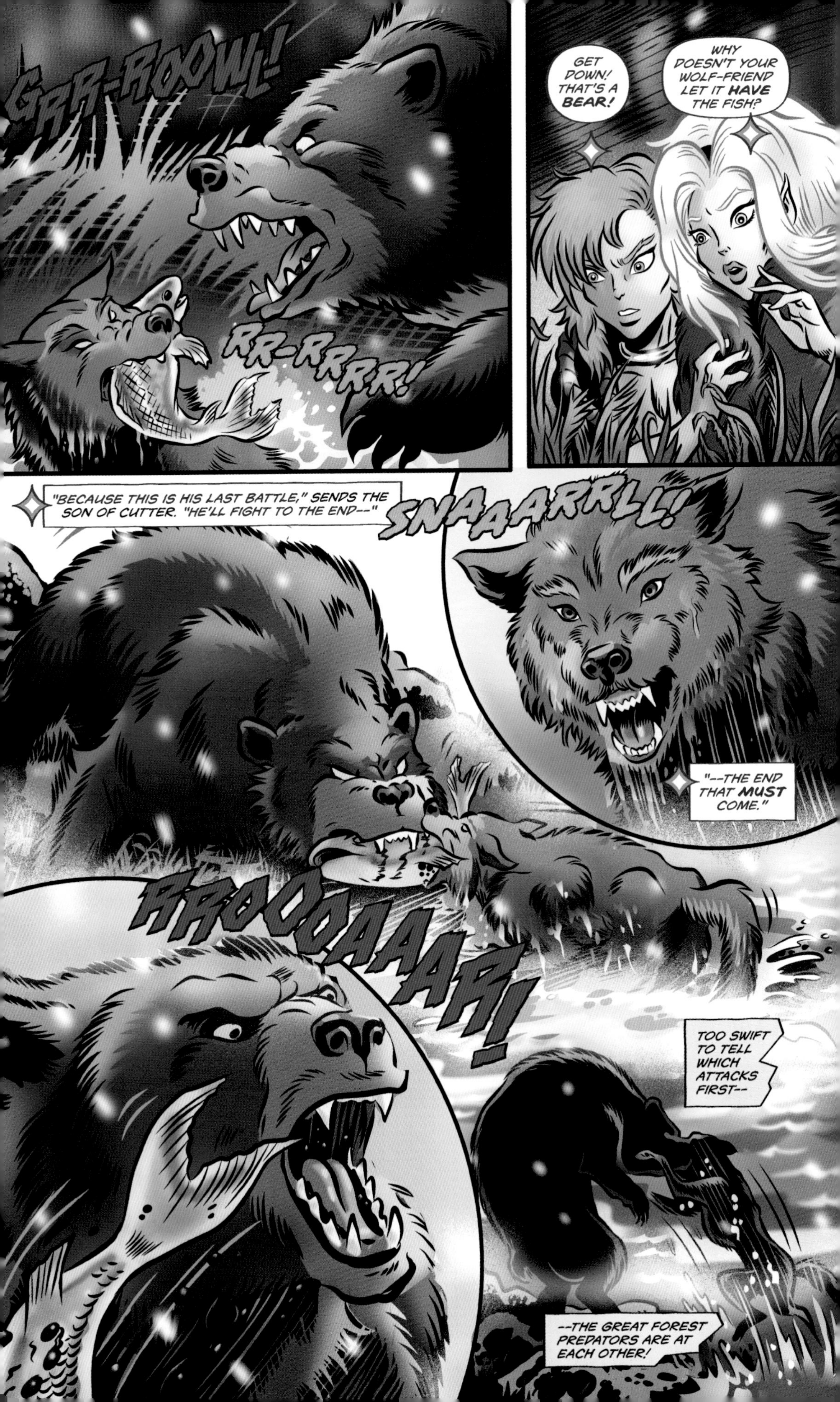
GRR-ROOWL!
RR-RRRRR!
GET DOWN! THAT'S A BEAR!
WHY DOESN'T YOUR WOLF-FRIEND LET IT HAVE THE FISH?
"BECAUSE THIS IS HIS LAST BATTLE," SENDS THE SON OF CUTTER. "HE'LL FIGHT TO THE END--"
SNAAARRLL!
"--THE END THAT MUST COME."
RROOOAAAR!
TOO SWIFT TO TELL WHICH ATTACKS FIRST--
--THE GREAT FOREST PREDATORS ARE AT EACH OTHER!

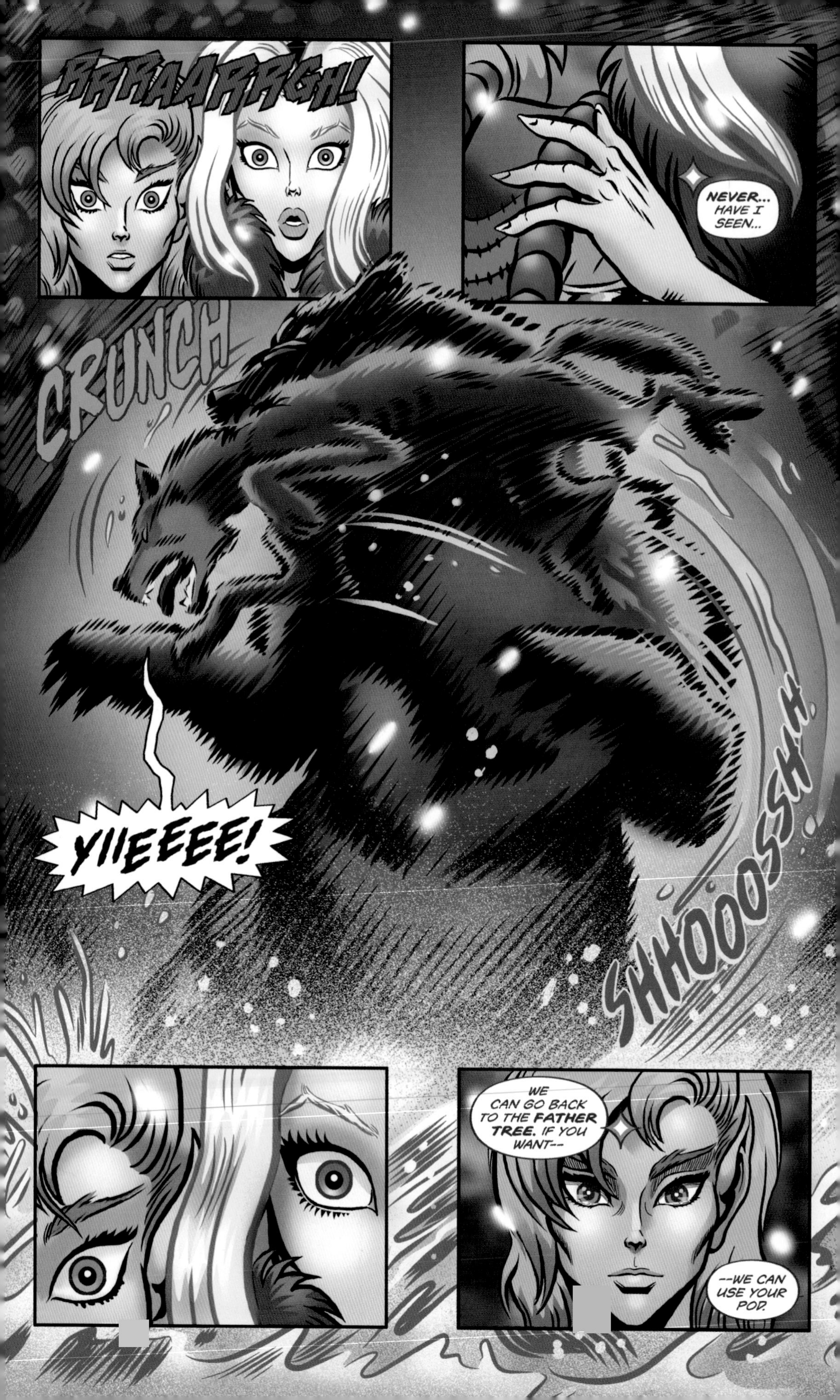

KRRAARRGH!
NEVER... HAVE I SEEN...
CRUNCH
YIIEEEE!
SHHOOOSSHH
WE CAN GO BACK TO THE FATHER TREE. IF YOU WANT--
--WE CAN USE YOUR POD.

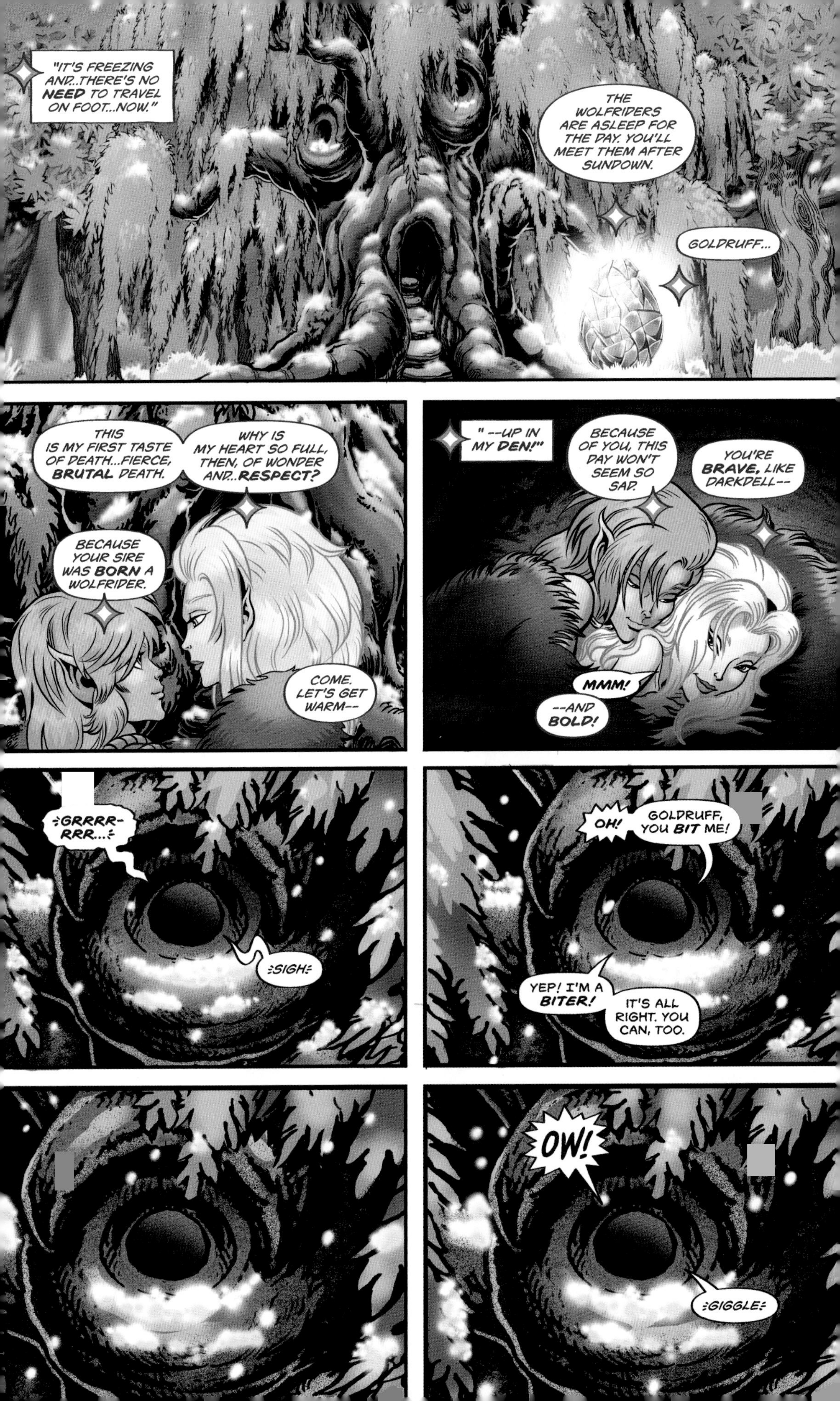

"IT'S FREEZING AND...THERE'S NO NEED TO TRAVEL ON FOOT...NOW."
THE WOLFRIDERS ARE ASLEEP FOR THE DAY. YOU'LL MEET THEM AFTER SUNDOWN.
GOLDRUFF...
THIS IS MY FIRST TASTE OF DEATH...FIERCE, BRUTAL DEATH.
WHY IS MY HEART SO FULL, THEN, OF WONDER AND...RESPECT?
BECAUSE YOUR SIRE WAS BORN A WOLFRIDER.
COME. LET'S GET WARM--
" --UP IN MY DEN!"
BECAUSE OF YOU, THIS DAY WON'T SEEM SO SAD.
YOU'RE BRAVE, LIKE DARKDELL--
MMM!
--AND BOLD!
GRRRR-RRR...
SIGH
OH!
GOLDRUFF, YOU BIT ME!
YEP! I'M A BITER!
IT'S ALL RIGHT. YOU CAN, TOO.
OW!
GIGGLE

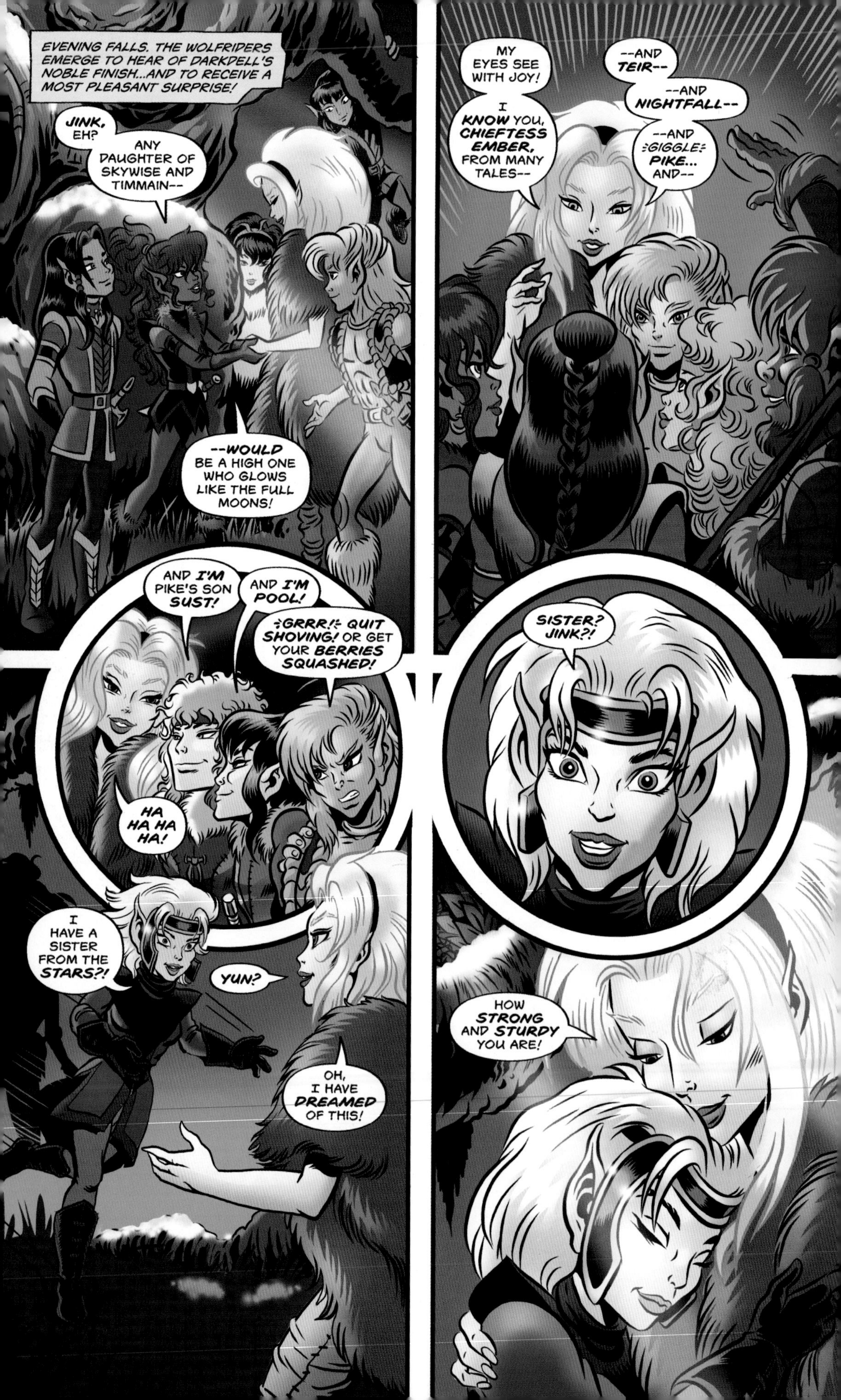
EVENING FALLS. THE WOLFRIDERS EMERGE TO HEAR OF DARKDELL'S NOBLE FINISH...AND TO RECEIVE A MOST PLEASANT SURPRISE!
JINK, EH?
ANY DAUGHTER OF SKYWISE AND TIMMAIN--
--WOULD BE A HIGH ONE WHO GLOWS LIKE THE FULL MOONS!
MY EYES SEE WITH JOY!
I KNOW YOU, CHIEFTESS EMBER, FROM MANY TALES--
--AND TEIR--
--AND NIGHTFALL--
--AND GIGGLE PIKE... AND--
AND I'M PIKE'S SON SUST!
AND I'M POOL!
GRRR! QUIT SHOVING! OR GET YOUR BERRIES SQUASHED!
HA HA HA HA!
SISTER? JINK?!
I HAVE A SISTER FROM THE STARS?!
YUN?
OH, I HAVE DREAMED OF THIS!
HOW STRONG AND STURDY YOU ARE!

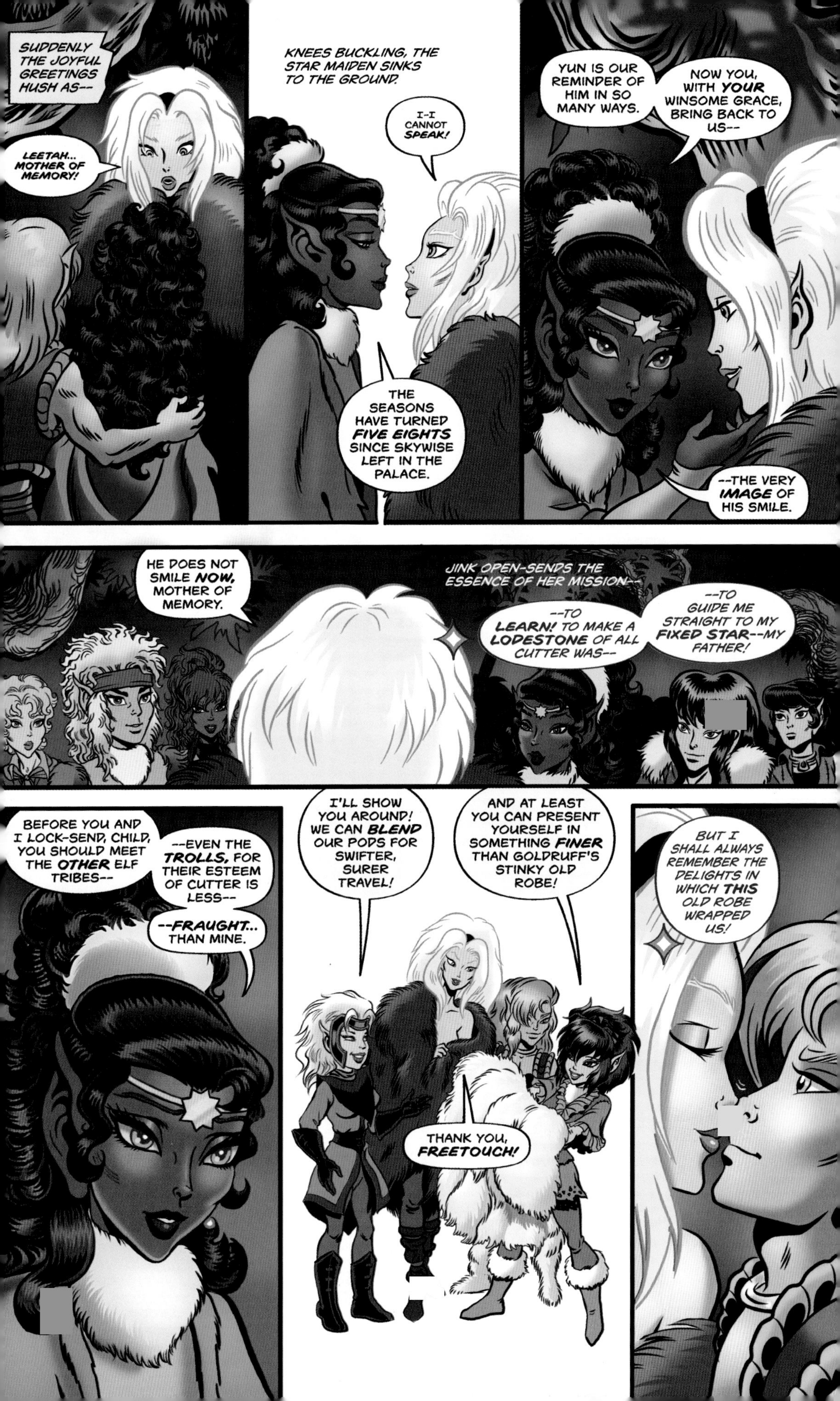

SUDDENLY THE JOYFUL GREETINGS HUSH AS--
LEETAH... MOTHER OF MEMORY!
KNEES BUCKLING, THE STAR MAIDEN SINKS TO THE GROUND.
I-I CANNOT SPEAK!
THE SEASONS HAVE TURNED FIVE EIGHTS SINCE SKYWISE LEFT IN THE PALACE.
YUN IS OUR REMINDER OF HIM IN SO MANY WAYS.
NOW YOU, WITH YOUR WINSOME GRACE, BRING BACK TO US--
--THE VERY IMAGE OF HIS SMILE.
HE DOES NOT SMILE NOW, MOTHER OF MEMORY.
JINK OPEN-SENDS THE ESSENCE OF HER MISSION--
--TO LEARN! TO MAKE A LODESTONE OF ALL CUTTER WAS--
--TO GUIDE ME STRAIGHT TO MY FIXED STAR--MY FATHER!
BEFORE YOU AND I LOCK-SEND, CHILD, YOU SHOULD MEET THE OTHER ELF TRIBES--
--EVEN THE TROLLS, FOR THEIR ESTEEM OF CUTTER IS LESS--
--FRAUGHT... THAN MINE.
I'LL SHOW YOU AROUND! WE CAN BLEND OUR PODS FOR SWIFTER, SURER TRAVEL!
AND AT LEAST YOU CAN PRESENT YOURSELF IN SOMETHING FINER THAN GOLDRUFF'S STINKY OLD ROBE!
THANK YOU, FREETOUCH!
BUT I SHALL ALWAYS REMEMBER THE DELIGHTS IN WHICH THIS OLD ROBE WRAPPED US!

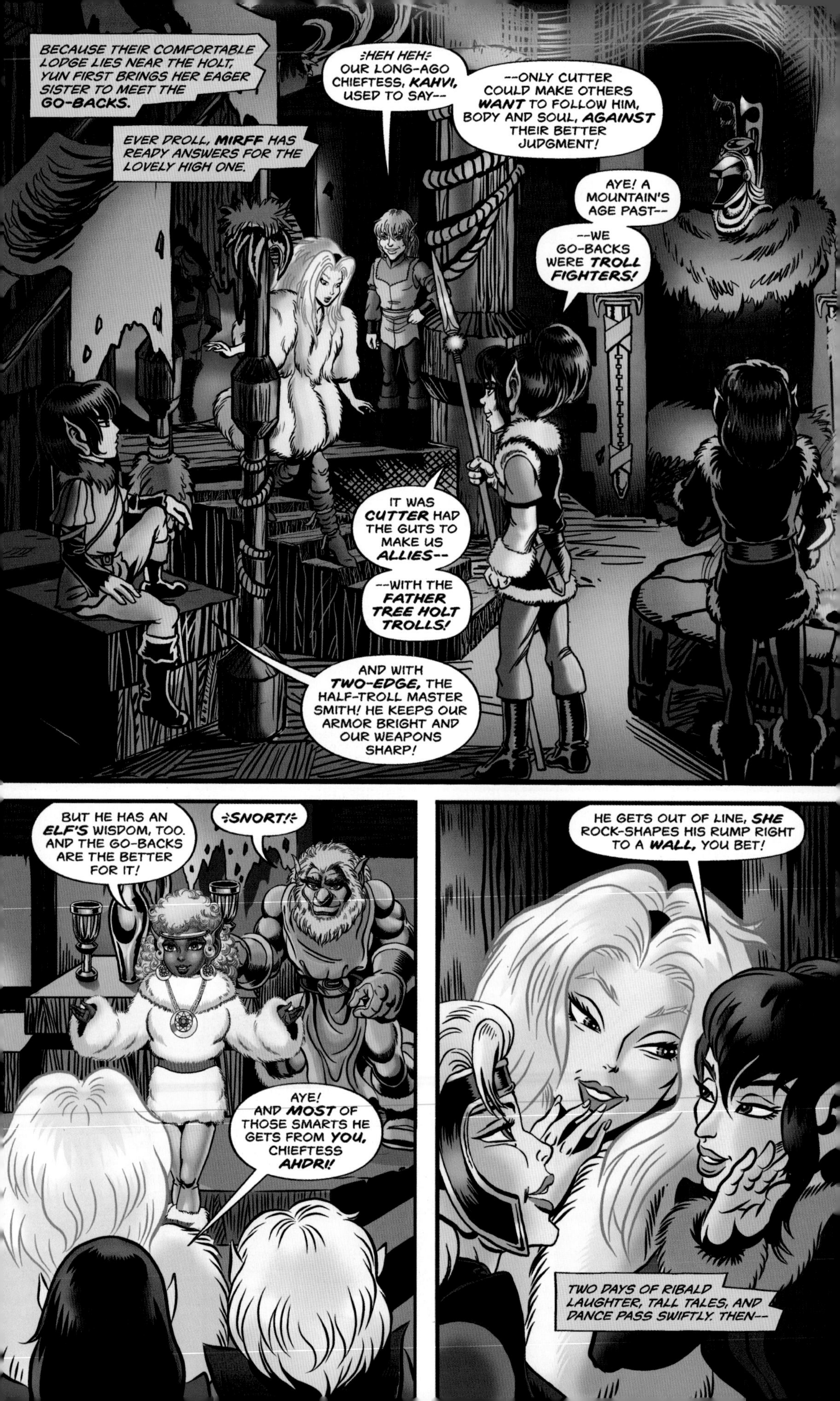

BECAUSE THEIR COMFORTABLE LODGE LIES NEAR THE HOLT, YUN FIRST BRINGS HER EAGER SISTER TO MEET THE GO-BACKS.
EVER DROLL, MIRFF HAS READY ANSWERS FOR THE LOVELY HIGH ONE.
:HEH HEH: OUR LONG-AGO CHIEFTESS, KAHVI, USED TO SAY--
--ONLY CUTTER COULD MAKE OTHERS WANT TO FOLLOW HIM, BODY AND SOUL, AGAINST THEIR BETTER JUDGMENT!
AYE! A MOUNTAIN'S AGE PAST--
--WE GO-BACKS WERE TROLL FIGHTERS!
IT WAS CUTTER HAD THE GUTS TO MAKE US ALLIES--
--WITH THE FATHER TREE HOLT TROLLS!
AND WITH TWO-EDGE, THE HALF-TROLL MASTER SMITH! HE KEEPS OUR ARMOR BRIGHT AND OUR WEAPONS SHARP!
BUT HE HAS AN ELF'S WISDOM, TOO. AND THE GO-BACKS ARE THE BETTER FOR IT!
:SNORT!:
AYE! AND MOST OF THOSE SMARTS HE GETS FROM YOU, CHIEFTESS AHDRI!
HE GETS OUT OF LINE, SHE ROCK-SHAPES HIS RUMP RIGHT TO A WALL, YOU BET!
TWO DAYS OF RIBALD LAUGHTER, TALL TALES, AND DANCE PASS SWIFTLY. THEN--

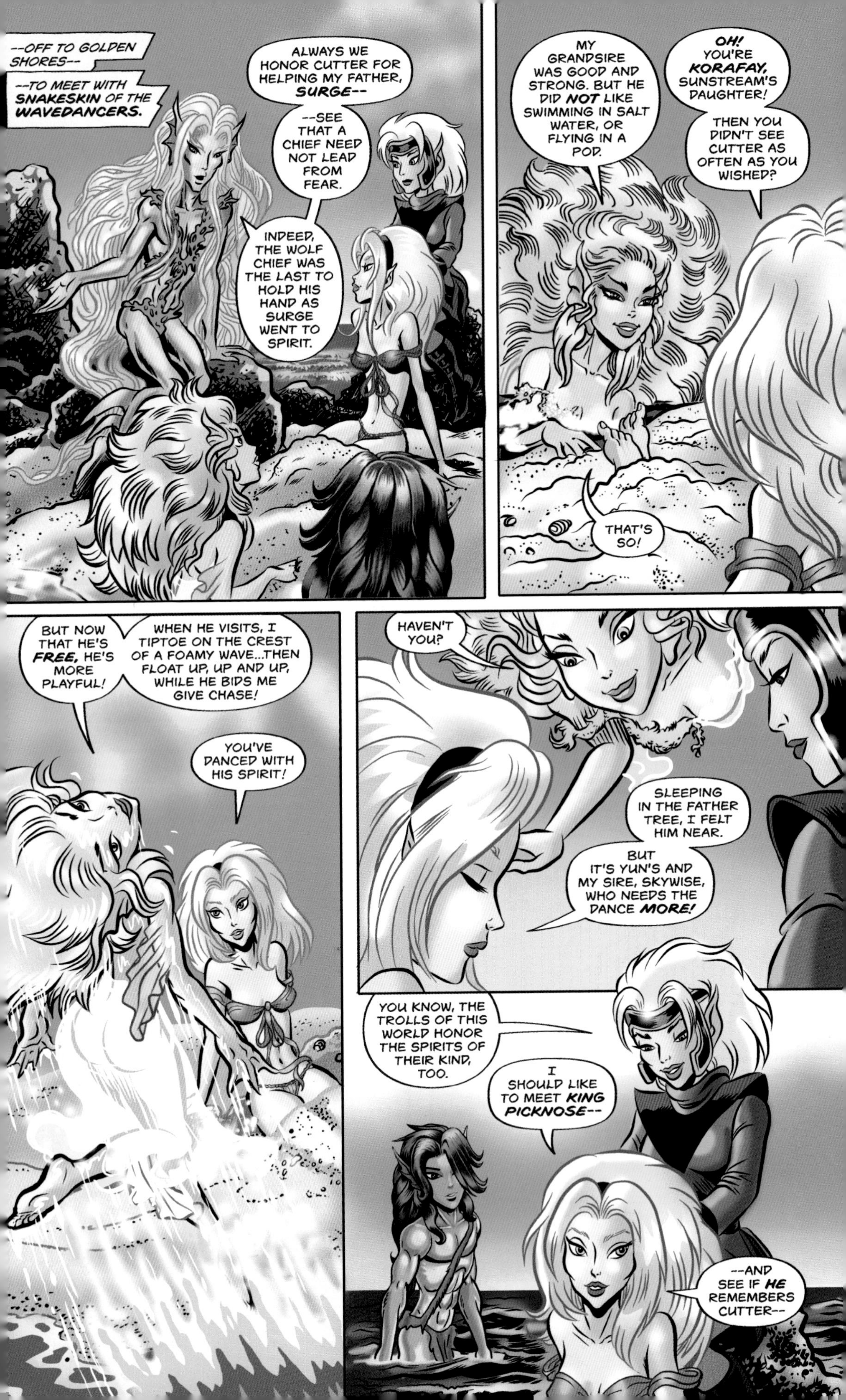
--OFF TO GOLDEN SHORES--
--TO MEET WITH SNAKESKIN OF THE WAVEDANCERS.
ALWAYS WE HONOR CUTTER FOR HELPING MY FATHER, SURGE--
--SEE THAT A CHIEF NEED NOT LEAD FROM FEAR.
INDEED, THE WOLF CHIEF WAS THE LAST TO HOLD HIS HAND AS SURGE WENT TO SPIRIT.
MY GRANDSIRE WAS GOOD AND STRONG. BUT HE DID NOT LIKE SWIMMING IN SALT WATER, OR FLYING IN A POD.
OH! YOU'RE KORAFAY, SUNSTREAM'S DAUGHTER!
THEN YOU DIDN'T SEE CUTTER AS OFTEN AS YOU WISHED?
THAT'S SO!
BUT NOW THAT HE'S FREE, HE'S MORE PLAYFUL!
WHEN HE VISITS, I TIPTOE ON THE CREST OF A FOAMY WAVE...THEN FLOAT UP, UP AND UP, WHILE HE BIDS ME GIVE CHASE!
YOU'VE DANCED WITH HIS SPIRIT!
HAVEN'T YOU?
SLEEPING IN THE FATHER TREE, I FELT HIM NEAR.
BUT IT'S YUN'S AND MY SIRE, SKYWISE, WHO NEEDS THE DANCE MORE!
YOU KNOW, THE TROLLS OF THIS WORLD HONOR THE SPIRITS OF THEIR KIND, TOO.
I SHOULD LIKE TO MEET KING PICKNOSE--
--AND SEE IF HE REMEMBERS CUTTER--

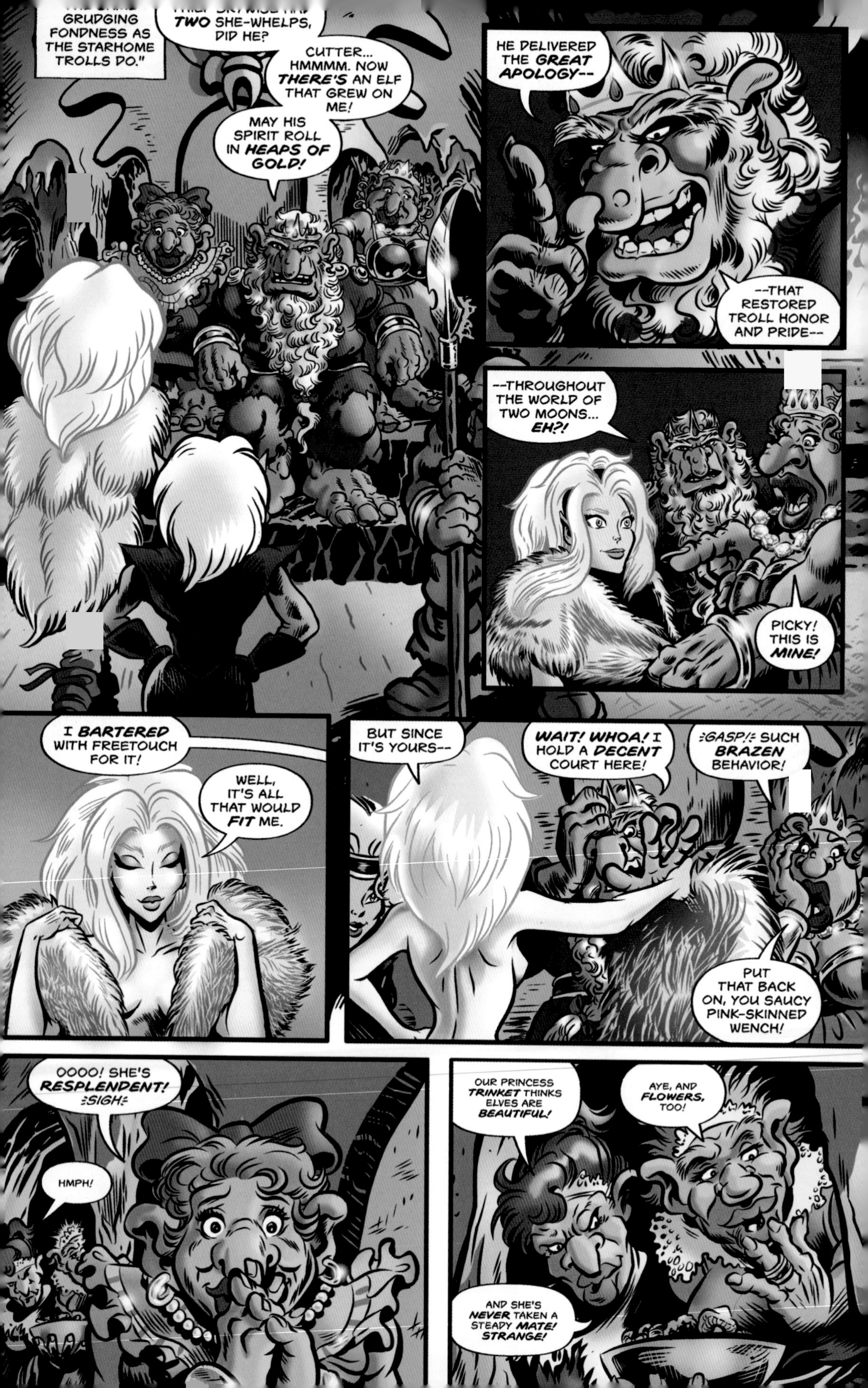

GRUDGING FONDNESS AS THE STARHOME TROLLS DO."
TWO SHE-WHELPS, DID HE?
CUTTER... HMMMM. NOW THERE'S AN ELF THAT GREW ON ME!
MAY HIS SPIRIT ROLL IN HEAPS OF GOLD!
HE DELIVERED THE GREAT APOLOGY--
--THAT RESTORED TROLL HONOR AND PRIDE--
--THROUGHOUT THE WORLD OF TWO MOONS... EH?!
PICKY! THIS IS MINE!
I BARTERED WITH FREETOUCH FOR IT!
WELL, IT'S ALL THAT WOULD FIT ME.
BUT SINCE IT'S YOURS--
WAIT! WHOA! I HOLD A DECENT COURT HERE!
:GASP!: SUCH BRAZEN BEHAVIOR!
PUT THAT BACK ON, YOU SAUCY PINK-SKINNED WENCH!
OOOO! SHE'S RESPLENDENT! :SIGH:
HMPH!
OUR PRINCESS TRINKET THINKS ELVES ARE BEAUTIFUL!
AYE, AND FLOWERS, TOO!
AND SHE'S NEVER TAKEN A STEADY MATE! STRANGE!

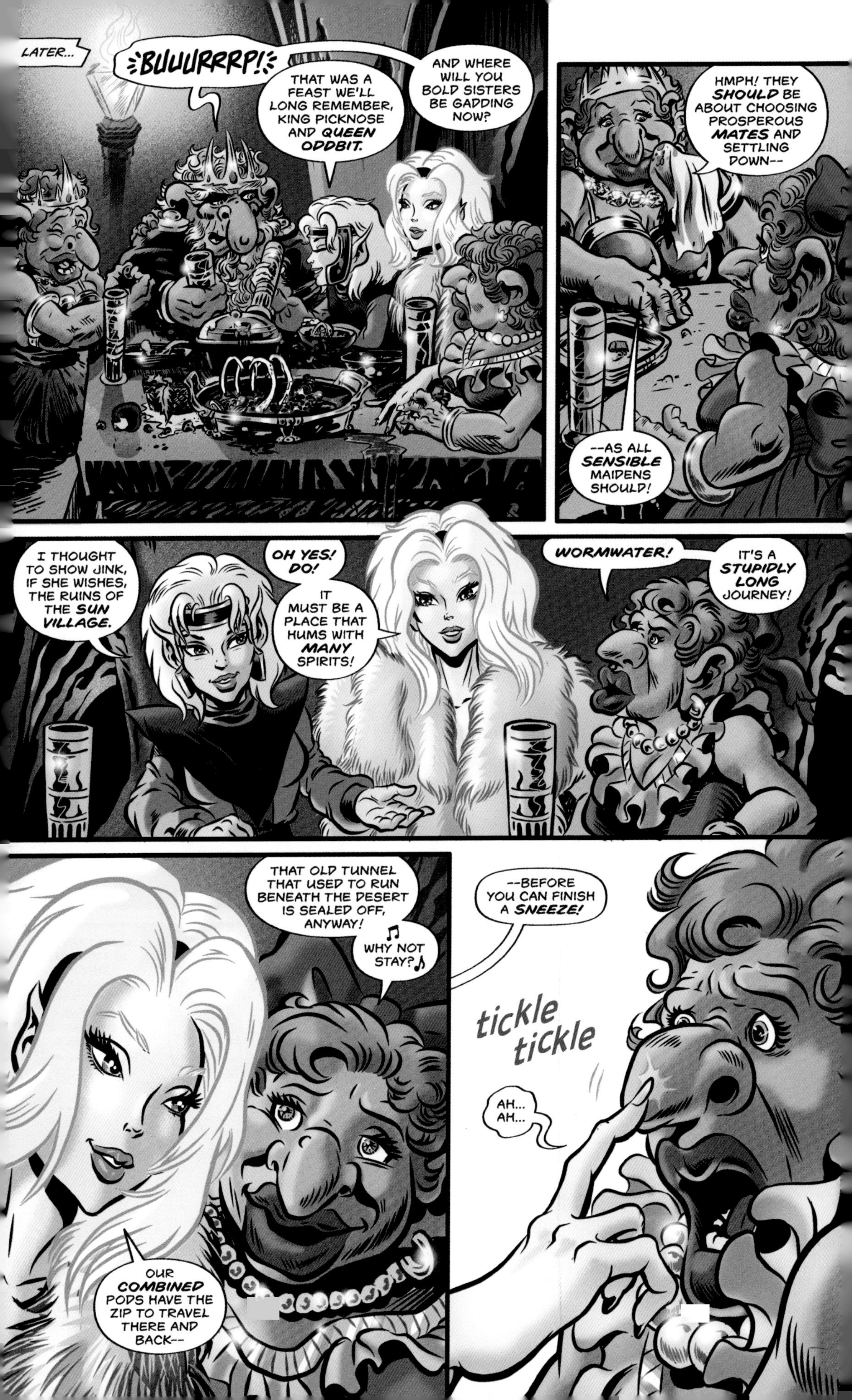

LATER...
BUUURRRP!
THAT WAS A FEAST WE'LL LONG REMEMBER, KING PICKNOSE AND QUEEN ODDBIT.
AND WHERE WILL YOU BOLD SISTERS BE GADDING NOW?
HMPH! THEY SHOULD BE ABOUT CHOOSING PROSPEROUS MATES AND SETTLING DOWN--
--AS ALL SENSIBLE MAIDENS SHOULD!
I THOUGHT TO SHOW JINK, IF SHE WISHES, THE RUINS OF THE SUN VILLAGE.
OH YES! DO!
IT MUST BE A PLACE THAT HUMS WITH MANY SPIRITS!
WORMWATER!
IT'S A STUPIDLY LONG JOURNEY!
THAT OLD TUNNEL THAT USED TO RUN BENEATH THE DESERT IS SEALED OFF, ANYWAY!
♫ WHY NOT STAY? ♪
OUR COMBINED PODS HAVE THE ZIP TO TRAVEL THERE AND BACK--
--BEFORE YOU CAN FINISH A SNEEZE!
tickle tickle
AH... AH...

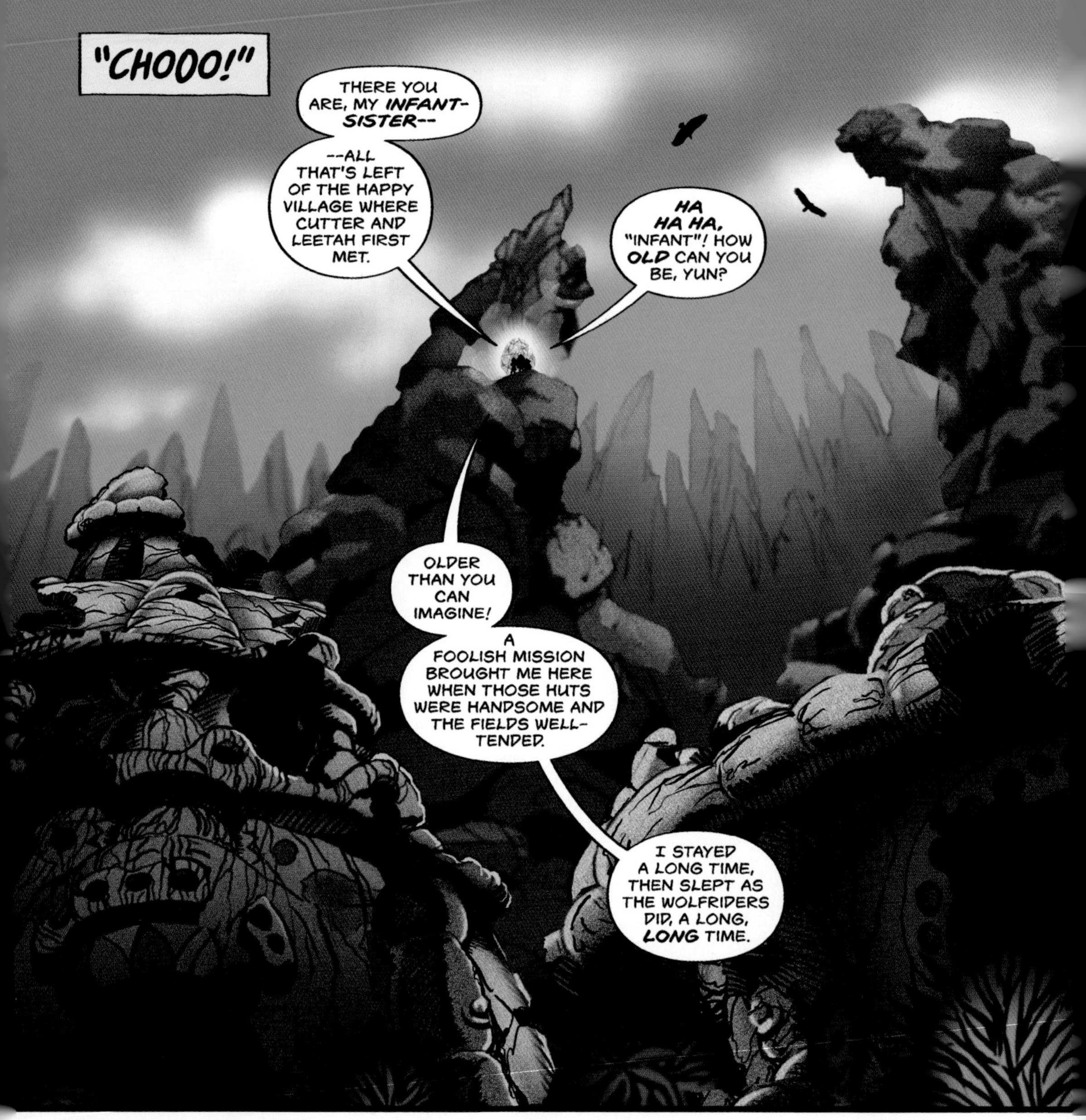
"CHOOO!"
THERE YOU ARE, MY INFANT-SISTER--
--ALL THAT'S LEFT OF THE HAPPY VILLAGE WHERE CUTTER AND LEETAH FIRST MET.
HA HA HA, "INFANT"! HOW OLD CAN YOU BE, YUN?
OLDER THAN YOU CAN IMAGINE!
A FOOLISH MISSION BROUGHT ME HERE WHEN THOSE HUTS WERE HANDSOME AND THE FIELDS WELL-TENDED.
I STAYED A LONG TIME, THEN SLEPT AS THE WOLFRIDERS DID, A LONG, LONG TIME.

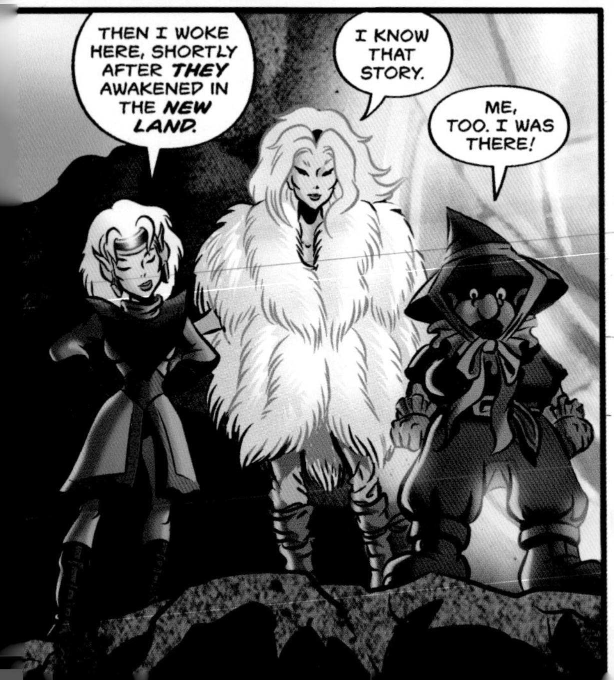
THEN I WOKE HERE, SHORTLY AFTER THEY AWAKENED IN THE NEW LAND.
I KNOW THAT STORY.
ME, TOO. I WAS THERE!

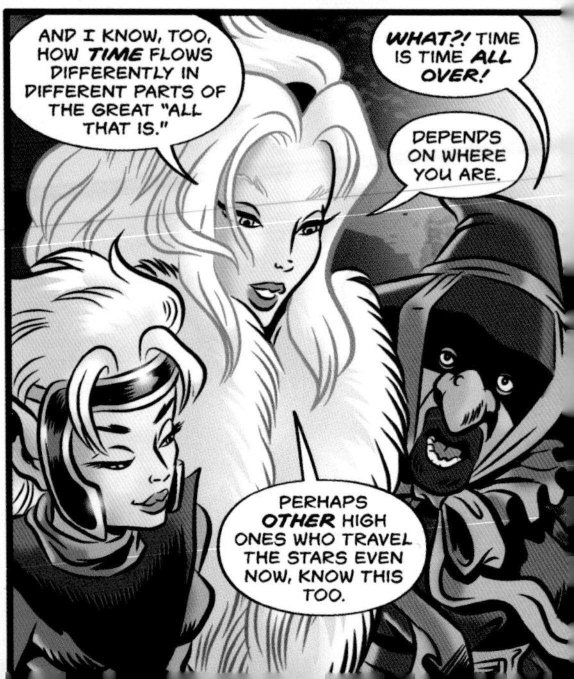
AND I KNOW, TOO, HOW TIME FLOWS DIFFERENTLY IN DIFFERENT PARTS OF THE GREAT "ALL THAT IS."
WHAT?! TIME IS TIME ALL OVER!
DEPENDS ON WHERE YOU ARE.
PERHAPS OTHER HIGH ONES WHO TRAVEL THE STARS EVEN NOW, KNOW THIS TOO.

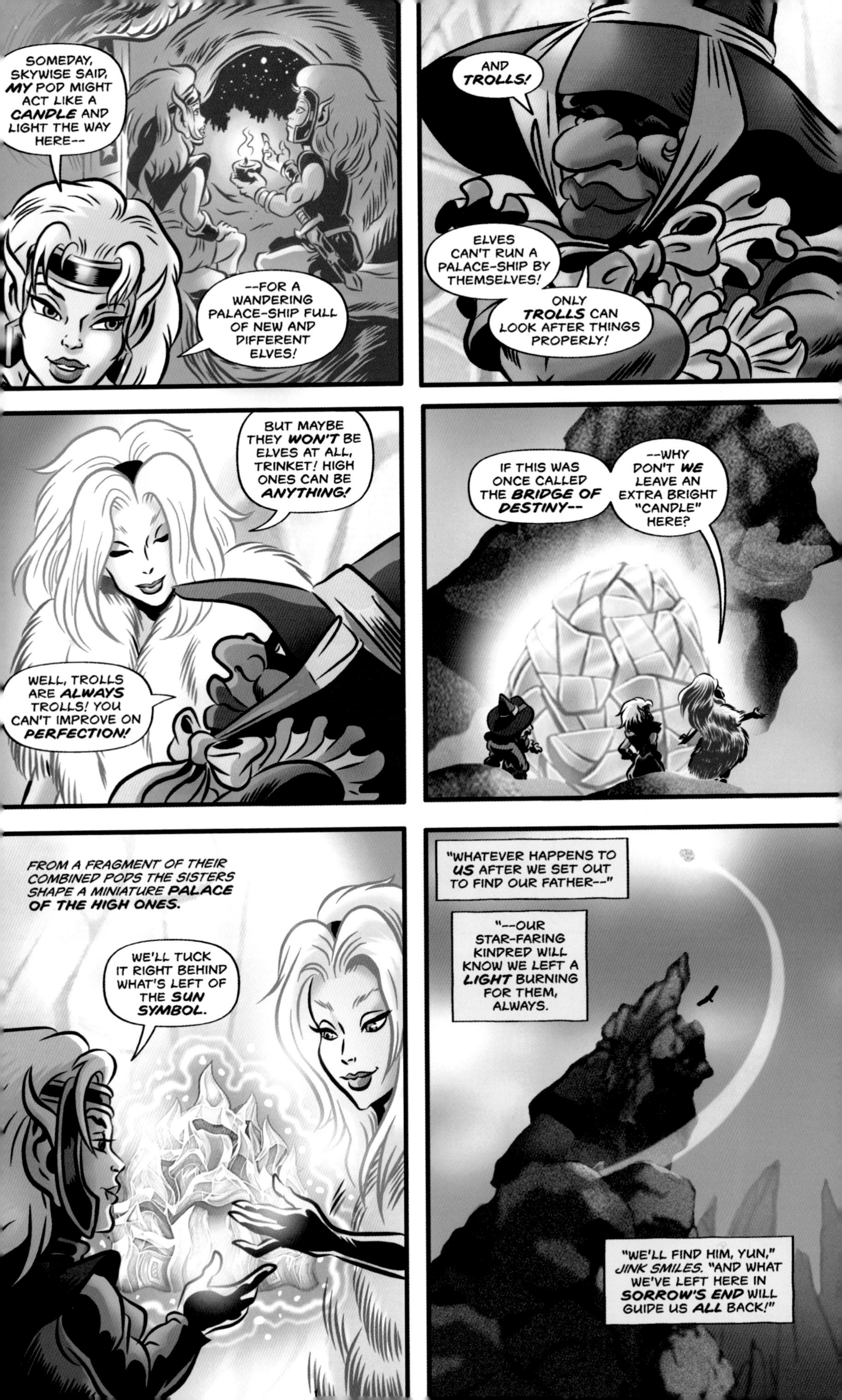

SOMEDAY, SKYWISE SAID, MY POD MIGHT ACT LIKE A CANDLE AND LIGHT THE WAY HERE--
--FOR A WANDERING PALACE-SHIP FULL OF NEW AND DIFFERENT ELVES!
AND TROLLS!
ELVES CAN'T RUN A PALACE-SHIP BY THEMSELVES!
ONLY TROLLS CAN LOOK AFTER THINGS PROPERLY!
BUT MAYBE THEY WON'T BE ELVES AT ALL, TRINKET! HIGH ONES CAN BE ANYTHING!
WELL, TROLLS ARE ALWAYS TROLLS! YOU CAN'T IMPROVE ON PERFECTION!
IF THIS WAS ONCE CALLED THE BRIDGE OF DESTINY--
--WHY DON'T WE LEAVE AN EXTRA BRIGHT "CANDLE" HERE?
FROM A FRAGMENT OF THEIR COMBINED PODS THE SISTERS SHAPE A MINIATURE PALACE OF THE HIGH ONES.
WE'LL TUCK IT RIGHT BEHIND WHAT'S LEFT OF THE SUN SYMBOL.
"WHATEVER HAPPENS TO US AFTER WE SET OUT TO FIND OUR FATHER--"
"--OUR STAR-FARING KINDRED WILL KNOW WE LEFT A LIGHT BURNING FOR THEM, ALWAYS.
"WE'LL FIND HIM, YUN," JINK SMILES. "AND WHAT WE'VE LEFT HERE IN SORROW'S END WILL GUIDE US ALL BACK!"

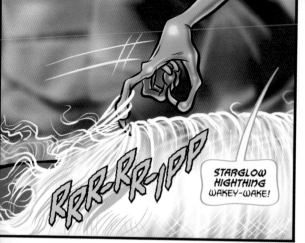

RRR·RR·IPP

STARGLOW
HIGHTHING
WAKEY-WAKE!

EVER SO SLOWLY, SKYWISE THE STARGAZER SWIMS BACK TO CONSCIOUSNESS...

TH-THISTLECAP?
WHY DID YOU W--

PRESERVER ALWAYS KNOWS *PALACE CALL!* MUST *ANSWER* PALACE CALL!

WH-WHAT?

PALACE CALL! SAME AS STARHOME! BUT *VERY PUNY!*

OUT THERE! OUT THERE!

A WAVE OF HIS HAND AND THE BEJEWELED BLACKNESS COMES INTO VIEW.

I DON'T KNOW WHERE WE ARE, BUT IT'S *FAR* FROM THE STARHOME.

SO HOW CAN THERE BE...?

GROGGILY HE BECOMES AWARE OF THE FAINTEST OF "HUMS."

BY THE THREE MOONS!

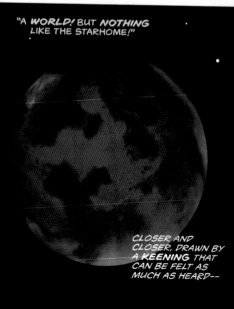

"A *WORLD!* BUT *NOTHING* LIKE THE STARHOME!"

CLOSER AND CLOSER, DRAWN BY A *KEENING* THAT CAN BE FELT AS MUCH AS HEARD--

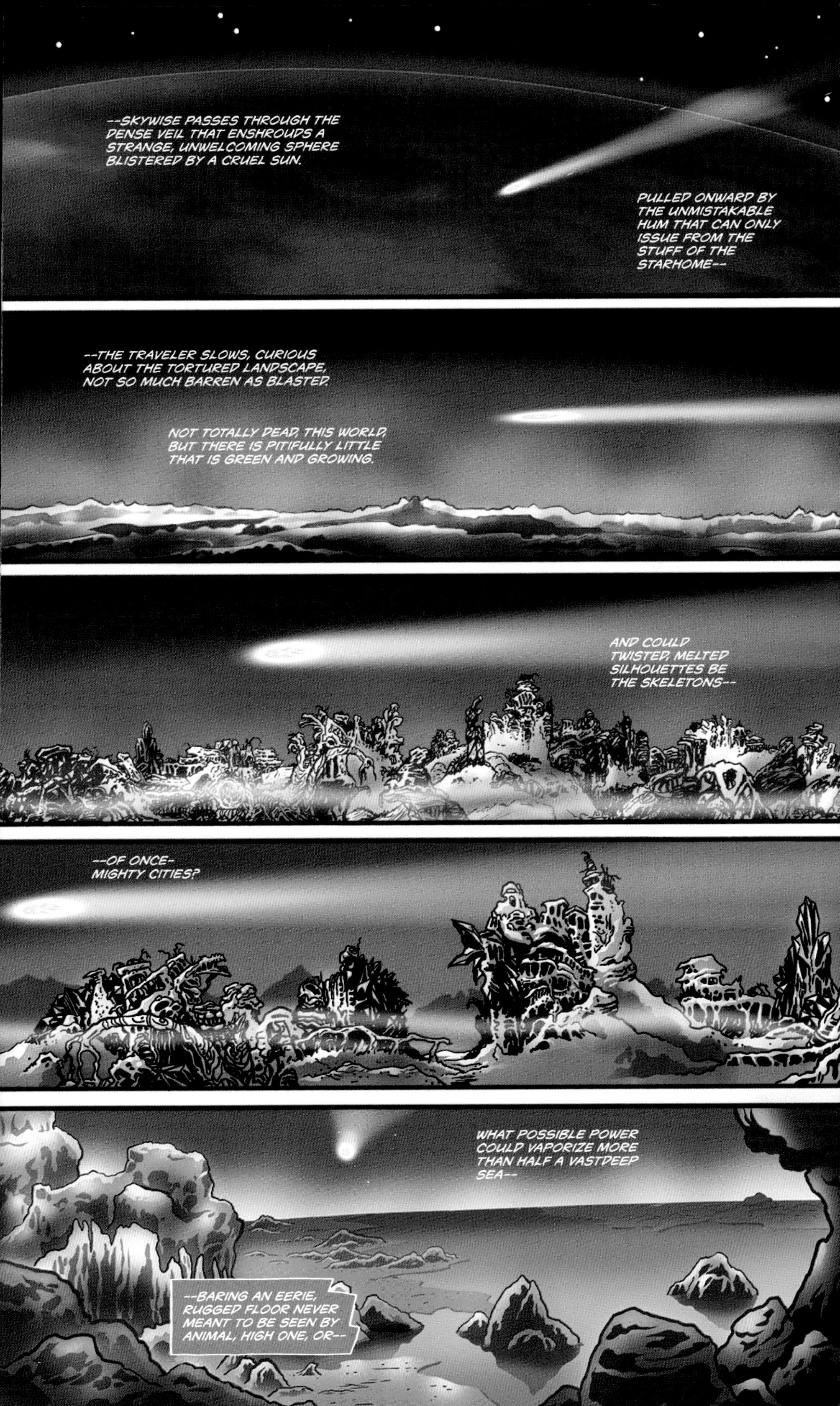
--SKYWISE PASSES THROUGH THE DENSE VEIL THAT ENSHROUDS A STRANGE, UNWELCOMING SPHERE BLISTERED BY A CRUEL SUN.
PULLED ONWARD BY THE UNMISTAKABLE HUM THAT CAN ONLY ISSUE FROM THE STUFF OF THE STARHOME--
--THE TRAVELER SLOWS, CURIOUS ABOUT THE TORTURED LANDSCAPE, NOT SO MUCH BARREN AS BLASTED.
NOT TOTALLY DEAD, THIS WORLD, BUT THERE IS PITIFULLY LITTLE THAT IS GREEN AND GROWING.
AND COULD TWISTED, MELTED SILHOUETTES BE THE SKELETONS--
--OF ONCE-MIGHTY CITIES?
WHAT POSSIBLE POWER COULD VAPORIZE MORE THAN HALF A VASTDEEP SEA--
--BARING AN EERIE, RUGGED FLOOR NEVER MEANT TO BE SEEN BY ANIMAL, HIGH ONE, OR--

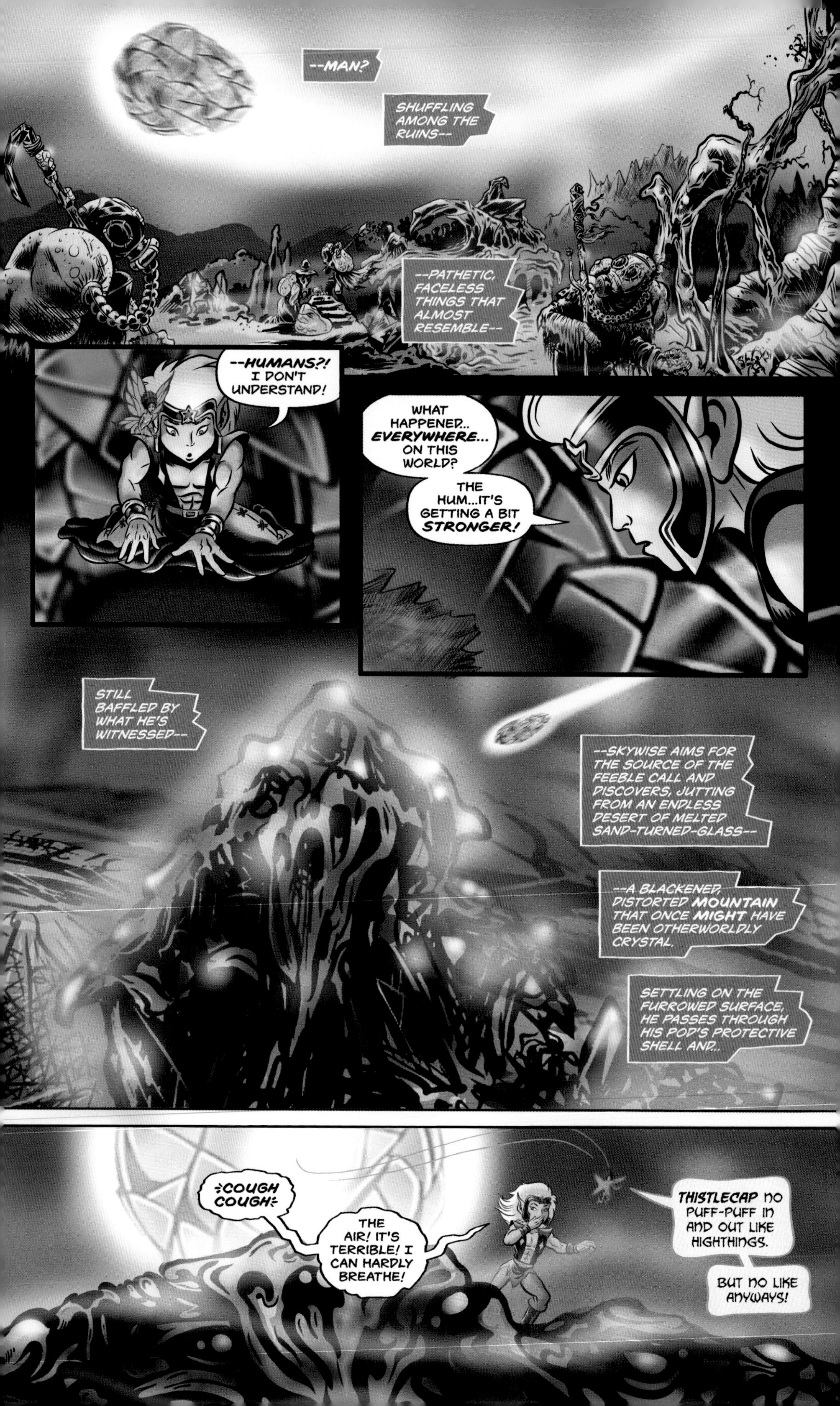
--MAN?
SHUFFLING AMONG THE RUINS--
--PATHETIC, FACELESS THINGS THAT ALMOST RESEMBLE--
--HUMANS?! I DON'T UNDERSTAND!
WHAT HAPPENED.. EVERYWHERE... ON THIS WORLD?
THE HUM...IT'S GETTING A BIT STRONGER!
STILL BAFFLED BY WHAT HE'S WITNESSED--
--SKYWISE AIMS FOR THE SOURCE OF THE FEEBLE CALL AND DISCOVERS, JUTTING FROM AN ENDLESS DESERT OF MELTED SAND-TURNED-GLASS--
--A BLACKENED, DISTORTED MOUNTAIN THAT ONCE MIGHT HAVE BEEN OTHERWORLDLY CRYSTAL.
SETTLING ON THE FURROWED SURFACE, HE PASSES THROUGH HIS POD'S PROTECTIVE SHELL AND..
COUGH COUGH
THE AIR! IT'S TERRIBLE! I CAN HARDLY BREATHE!
THISTLECAP NO PUFF-PUFF IN AND OUT LIKE HIGHTHINGS.
BUT NO LIKE ANYWAYS!

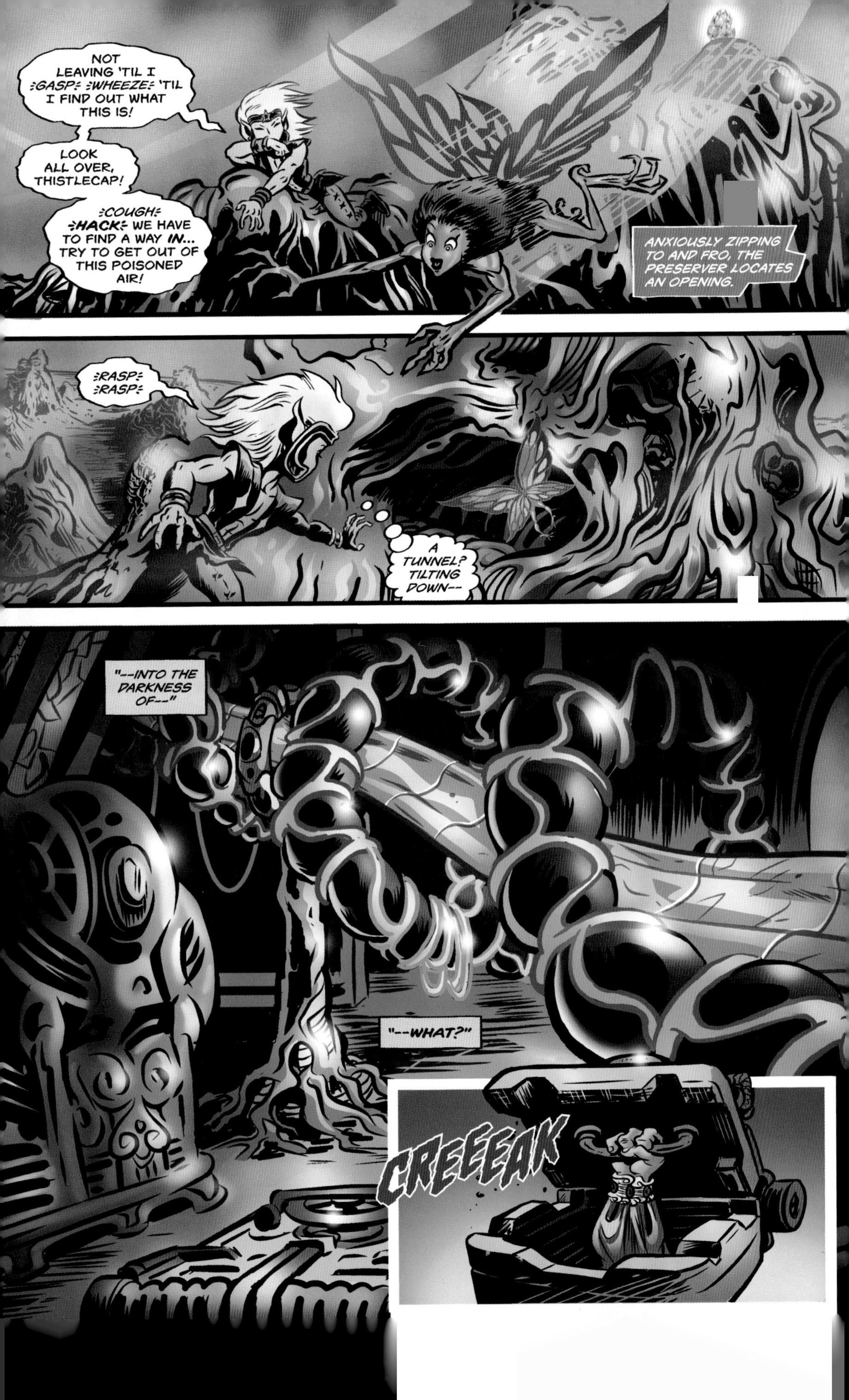
NOT LEAVING 'TIL I -GASP- -WHEEZE- 'TIL I FIND OUT WHAT THIS IS!
LOOK ALL OVER, THISTLECAP!
-COUGH- -HACK- WE HAVE TO FIND A WAY IN... TRY TO GET OUT OF THIS POISONED AIR!
ANXIOUSLY ZIPPING TO AND FRO, THE PRESERVER LOCATES AN OPENING.
-RASP- -RASP-
A TUNNEL? TILTING DOWN--
"--INTO THE DARKNESS OF--"
"--WHAT?"
CREEEAK

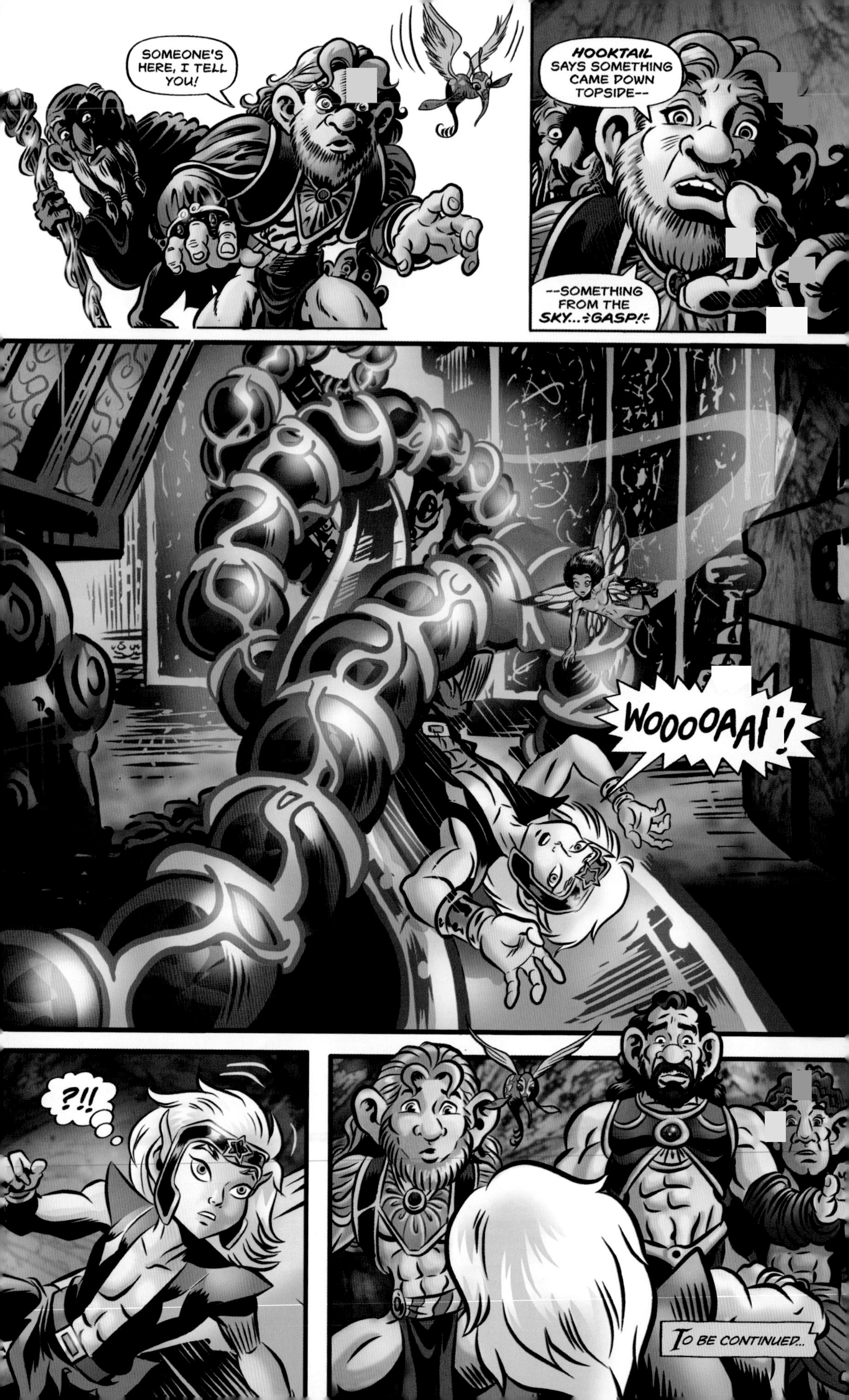

SOMEONE'S HERE, I TELL YOU!
HOOKTAIL SAYS SOMETHING CAME DOWN TOPSIDE--
--SOMETHING FROM THE SKY... ÷GASP!÷
WOOOOAAI!
?!!
TO BE CONTINUED...

FROM THE DRAWING BOARD

Sketchbook Commentary by Richard Pini

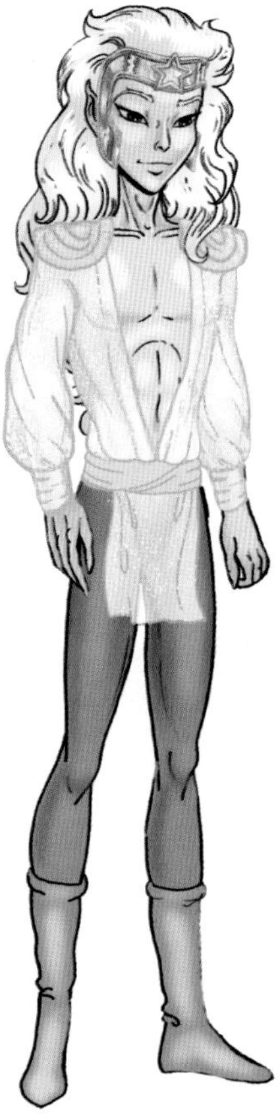

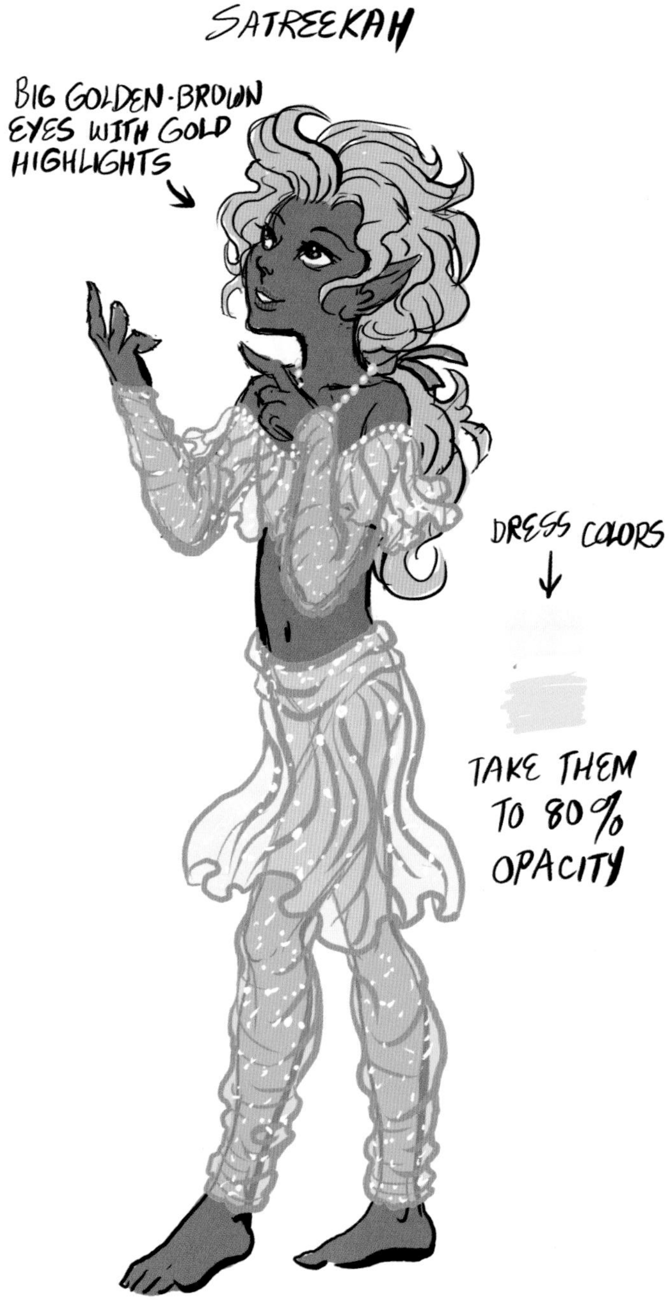

SATREEKAH
BIG GOLDEN-BROWN EYES WITH GOLD HIGHLIGHTS
DRESS COLORS
TAKE THEM TO 80% OPACITY

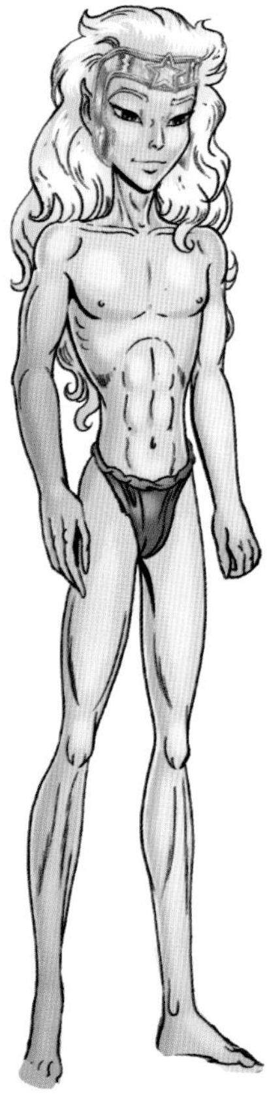

The look of *ElfQuest: Stargazer's Hunt* is a true collaboration between Wendy (as designer and layout artist) and Sonny (who provides the finished art and colors). Wendy has long had a love of designing costumes that "work"—that can, and have, been realized by cosplayers for decades. Here (and on the following page) are some of Wendy's ideas and color notes.

On the new world of the restored Starhome, the elves evolve to look more and more like the ancestral High Ones, and their garb becomes more ethereal as well. **Clockwise from upper left:** Aroree, Spray, and Savah.

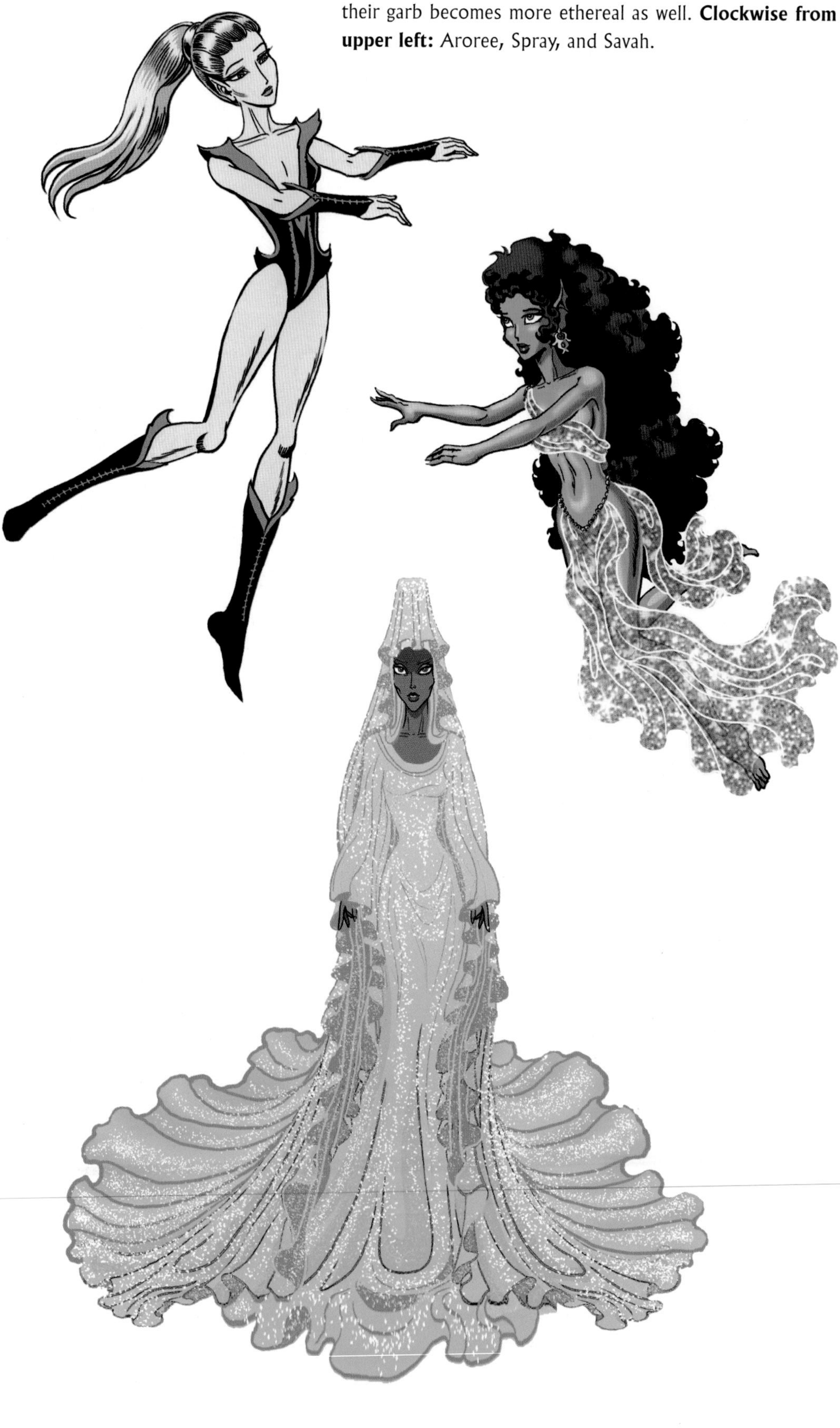

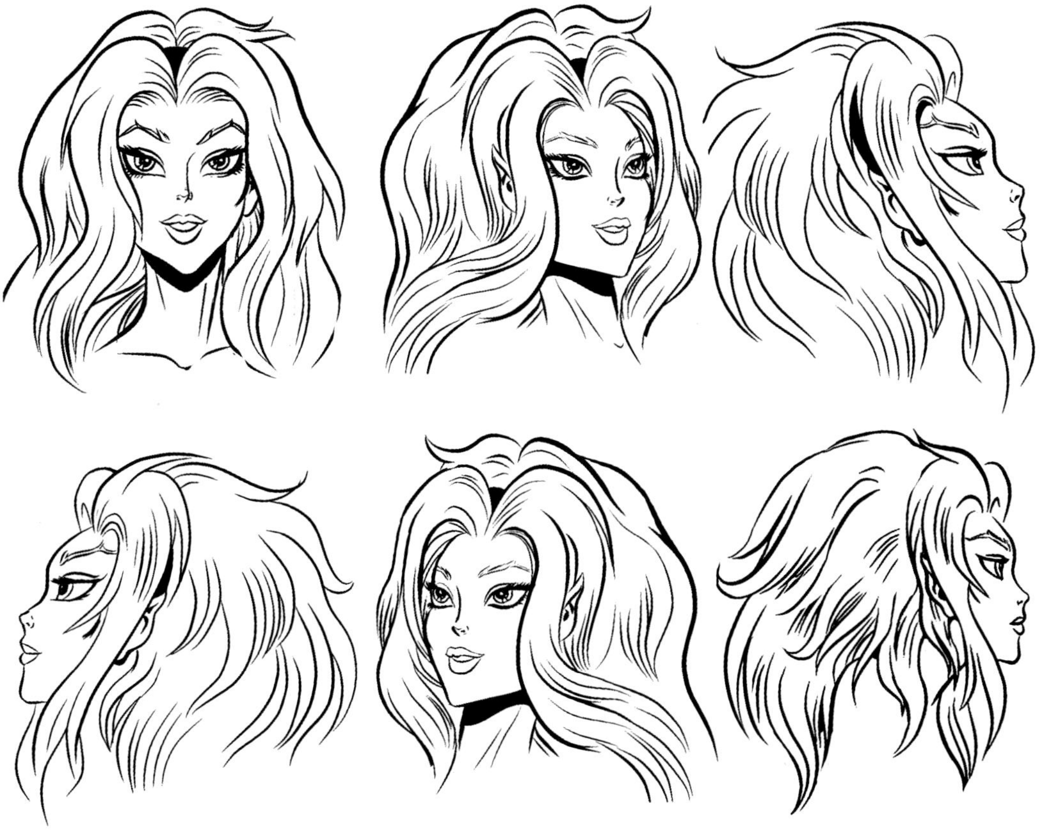

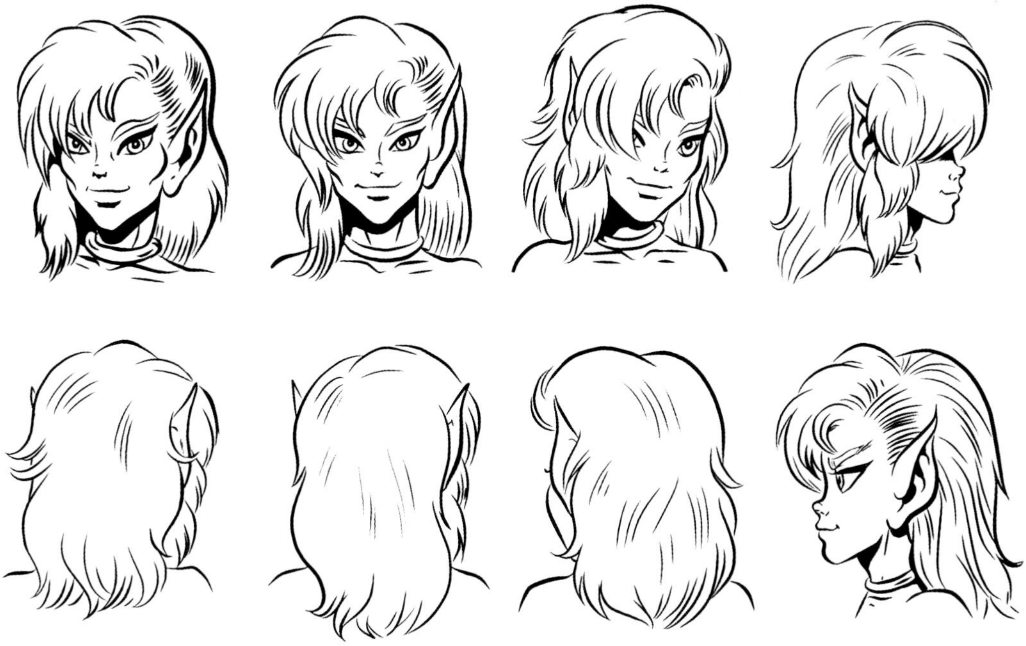

Turnarounds of Jink and Goldruff by Sonny. These are useful in making sure characters look “on model” no matter which angle they’re seen from. There are always subtle differences between someone’s face looking to the right and to the left.

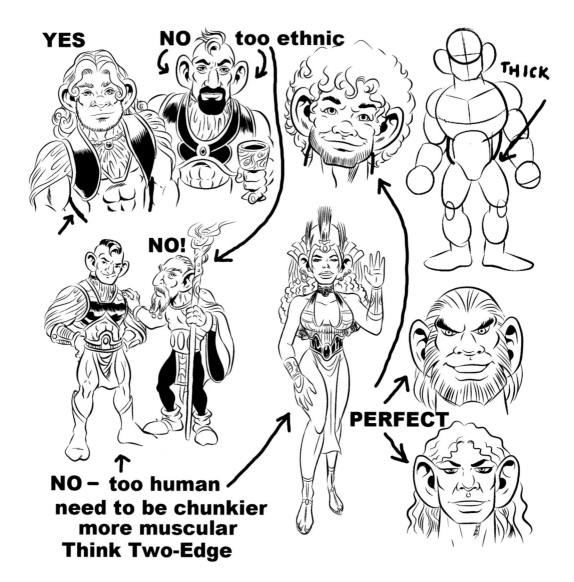

YES

NO too ethnic

THICK

NO!

NO – too human
need to be chunkier
more muscular
Think Two-Edge

PERFECT

Above: This volume ends with the introduction of some hitherto-unknown players, who will have a larger role in the story to come. Based on Wendy's suggestions, Sonny provided a number of design ideas, which Wendy then critiqued and refined.

Opposite: An example of Wendy's pencil layouts. You can see the finished result, with Sonny's finishes and coloring, on page 17.

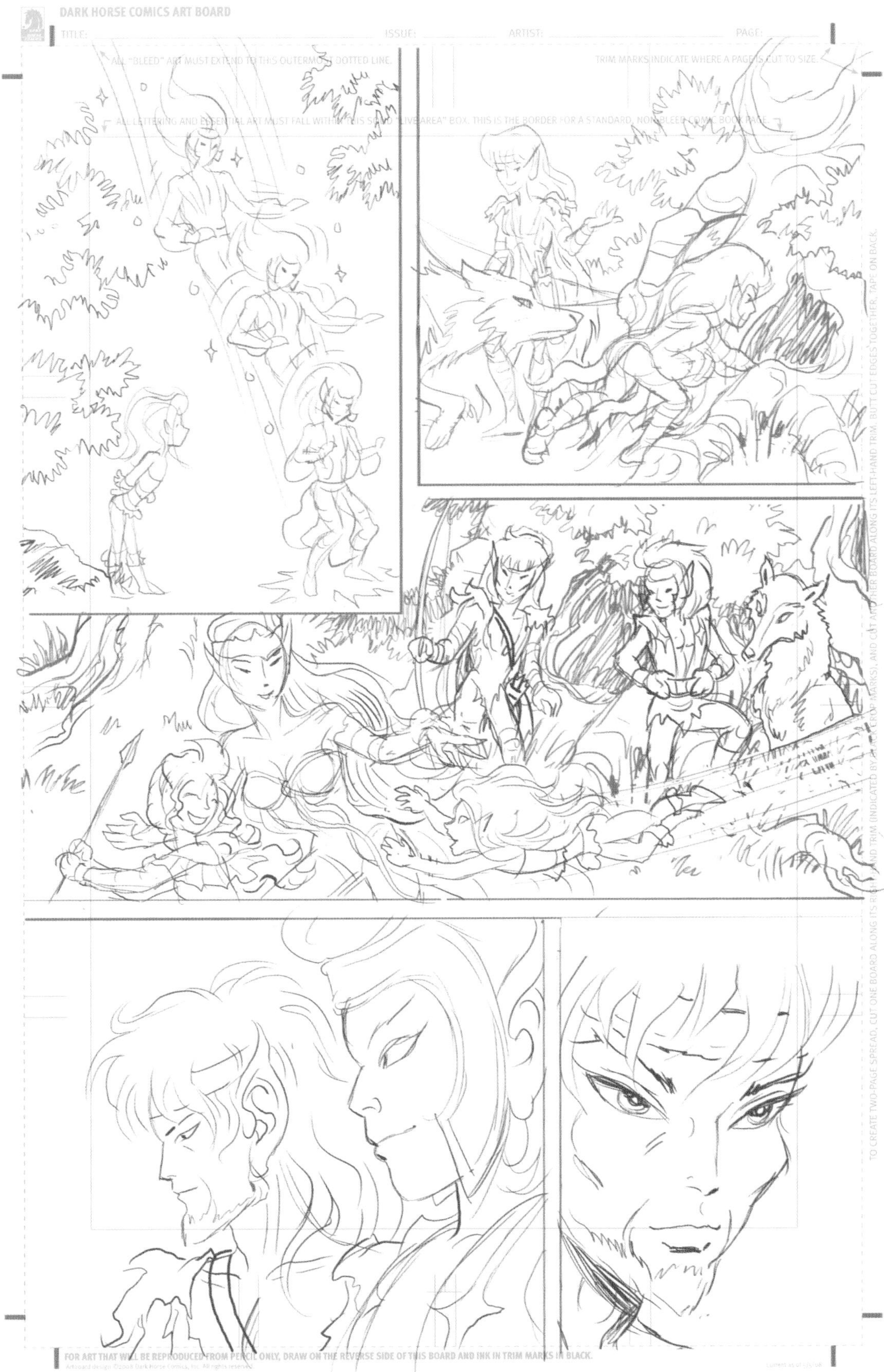
DARK HORSE COMICS ART BOARD
TITLE: ISSUE: ARTIST: PAGE:
ALL "BLEED" ART MUST EXTEND TO THIS OUTERMOST DOTTED LINE.
TRIM MARKS INDICATE WHERE A PAGE IS CUT TO SIZE.
ALL LETTERING AND ESSENTIAL ART MUST FALL WITHIN THIS SOLID "LIVE AREA" BOX. THIS IS THE BORDER FOR A STANDARD, NON-BLEED COMIC BOOK PAGE.
TO CREATE TWO-PAGE SPREAD, CUT ONE BOARD ALONG ITS RIGHT-HAND TRIM (INDICATED BY BLACK CROP MARKS), AND CUT ANOTHER BOARD ALONG ITS LEFT-HAND TRIM, BUT CUT EDGES TOGETHER. TAPE ON BACK.
FOR ART THAT WILL BE REPRODUCED FROM PENCIL ONLY, DRAW ON THE REVERSE SIDE OF THIS BOARD AND INK IN TRIM MARKS IN BLACK.

Above, opposite: For a climactic scene in this volume, the story called for the interior of a weird, semiorganic chamber. On this page is Sonny's rough "intestine-y" suggestion, which Wendy worked into her layout for page 91.

Next spread: Color has always played a major role in setting the mood and tone of *ElfQuest*.

As she prepares the layouts for a given page, Wendy often works with layers in Photoshop. This lets her provide suggestions to Sonny for colors and special effects that he then refines and finishes. Wendy's layouts here are much closer to finished pencils, to ensure that critical facial expressions and body language are just so. These are examples from pages 43 and 57.

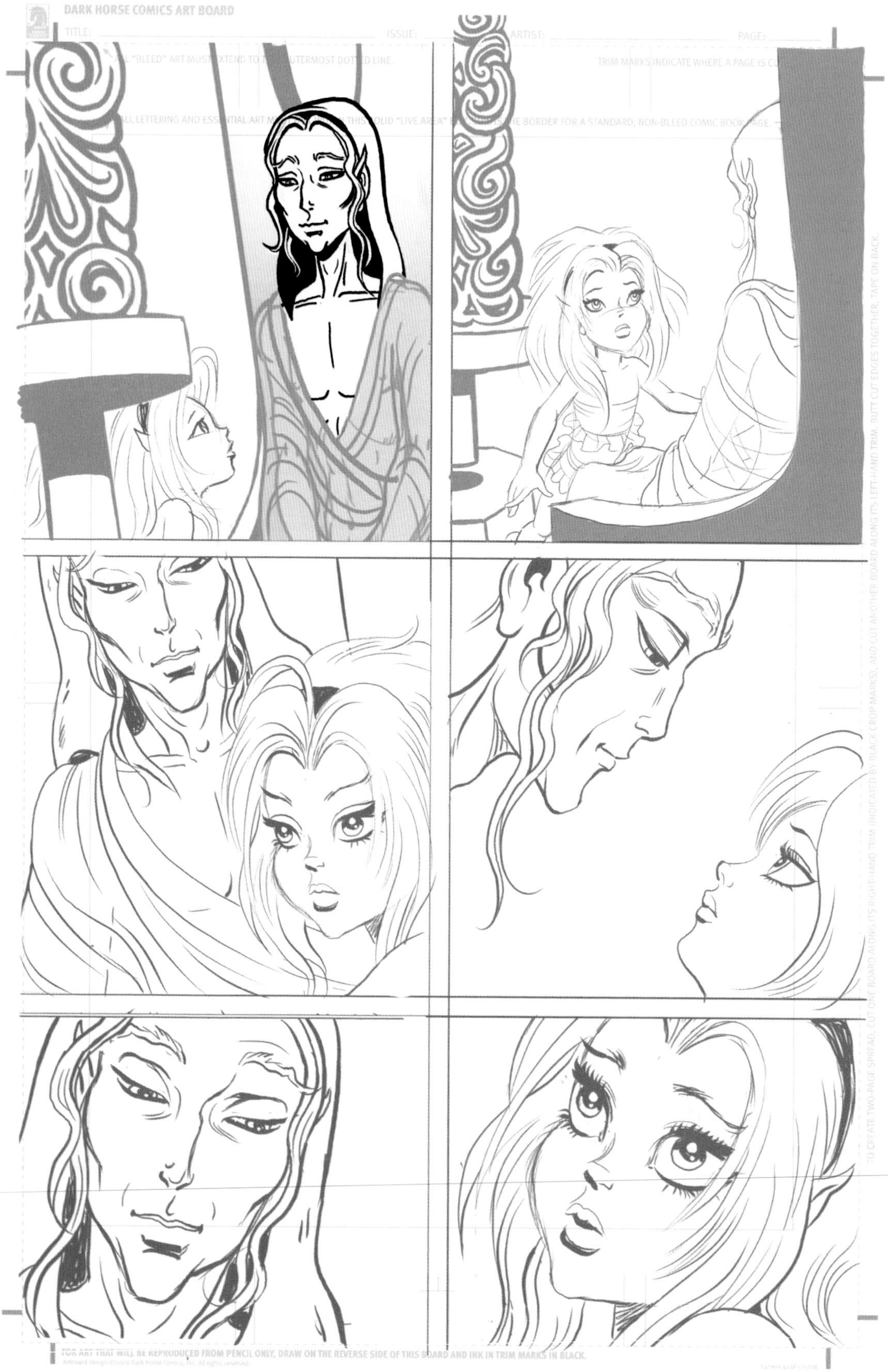
DARK HORSE COMICS ART BOARD
TITLE:
ISSUE:
ARTIST:
PAGE:
FOR ART THAT WILL BE REPRODUCED FROM PENCIL ONLY, DRAW ON THE REVERSE SIDE OF THIS BOARD AND INK IN TRIM MARKS IN BLACK.

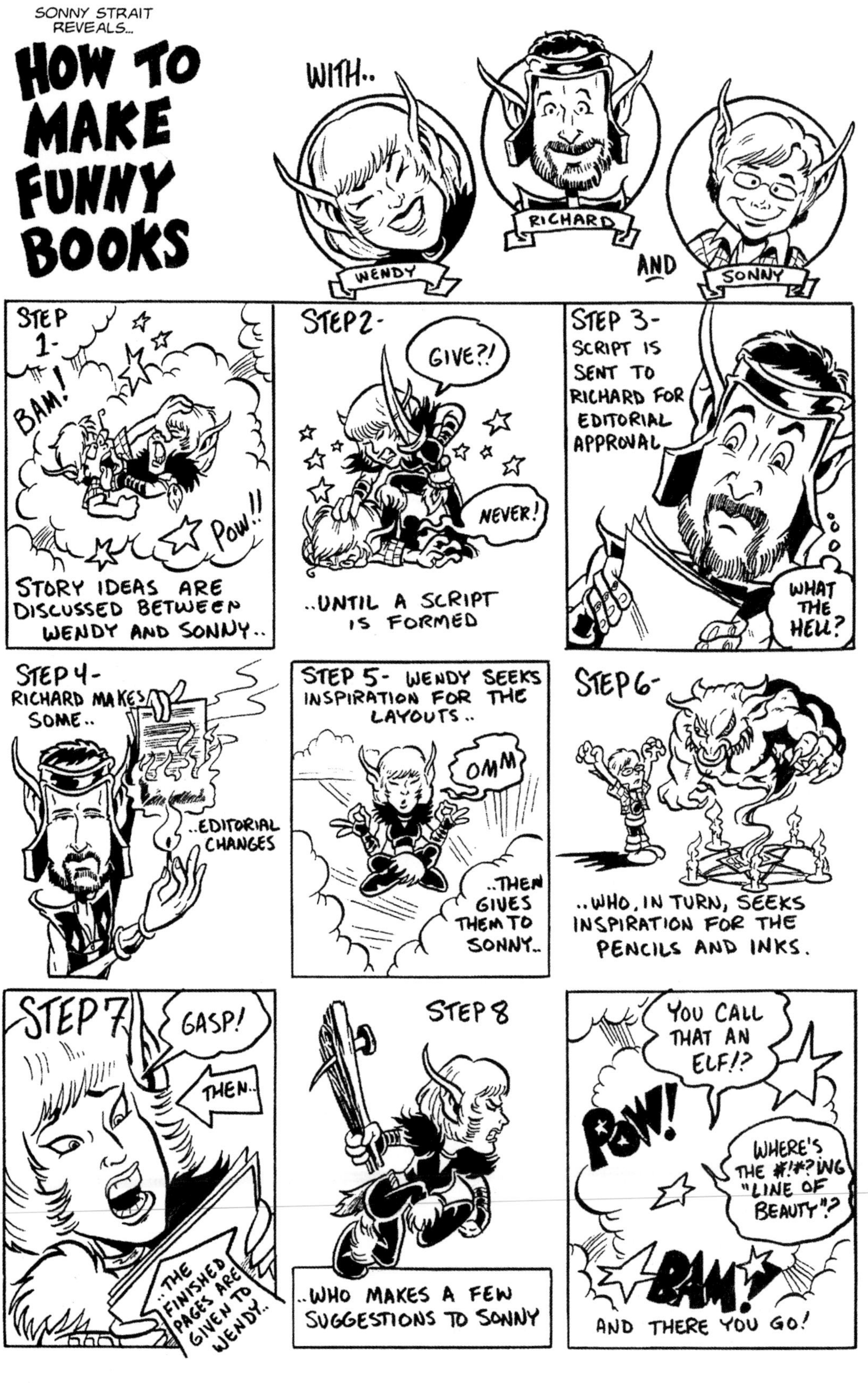
SONNY STRAIT REVEALS...
HOW TO MAKE FUNNY BOOKS
WITH..
WENDY
RICHARD
AND
SONNY
STEP 1-
BAM!
POW!!
STORY IDEAS ARE DISCUSSED BETWEEN WENDY AND SONNY..
STEP 2-
GIVE?!
NEVER!
..UNTIL A SCRIPT IS FORMED
STEP 3- SCRIPT IS SENT TO RICHARD FOR EDITORIAL APPROVAL
WHAT THE HELL?
STEP 4- RICHARD MAKES SOME..
..EDITORIAL CHANGES
STEP 5- WENDY SEEKS INSPIRATION FOR THE LAYOUTS..
OMM
..THEN GIVES THEM TO SONNY..
STEP 6-
..WHO, IN TURN, SEEKS INSPIRATION FOR THE PENCILS AND INKS.
STEP 7
GASP!
THEN..
..THE FINISHED PAGES ARE GIVEN TO WENDY..
STEP 8
..WHO MAKES A FEW SUGGESTIONS TO SONNY
YOU CALL THAT AN ELF!?
POW!
WHERE'S THE #!*?ING "LINE OF BEAUTY"?
BAM!
AND THERE YOU GO!

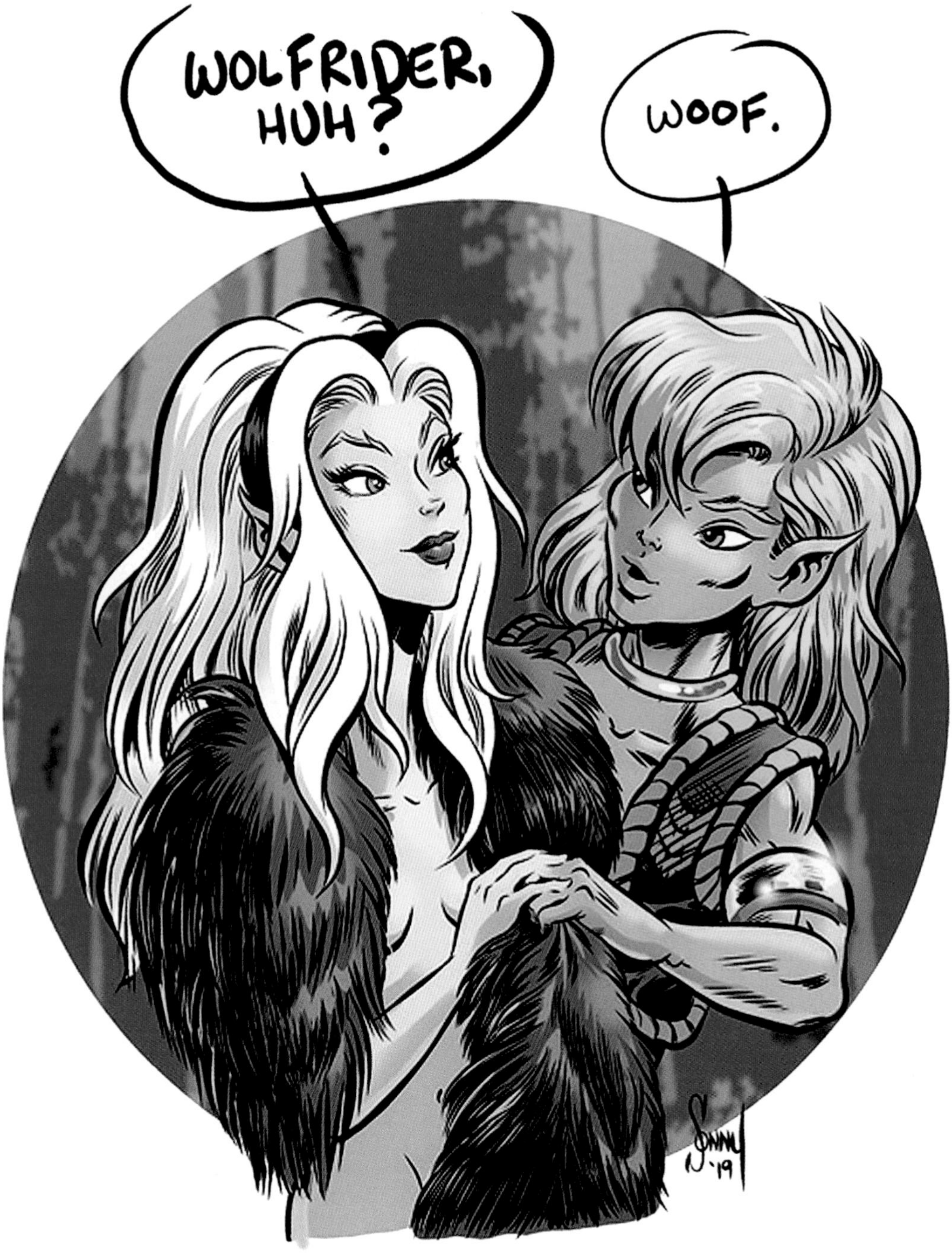
WOLFRIDER, HUH?
WOOF.
SONNY '19

Opposite: Back around 2000, when Sonny began his apprenticeship with Wendy and started working on *ElfQuest*, he drew this tongue-in-cheek "How To" cartoon. But even though it predates *Stargazer's Hunt* by nearly two decades, it turns out the working relationship among Wendy, Richard, and Sonny really hasn't changed much at all!

Above: Jink and Goldruff, in an impish off-camera moment, by Sonny.

ELFQUEST®

DISCOVER THE LEGEND OF *ELFQUEST*! ALLIANCES ARE FORGED, ENEMIES DISCOVERED, AND SAVAGE BATTLES FOUGHT IN THIS EPIC FANTASY ADVENTURE, HANDSOMELY PRESENTED BY DARK HORSE BOOKS!

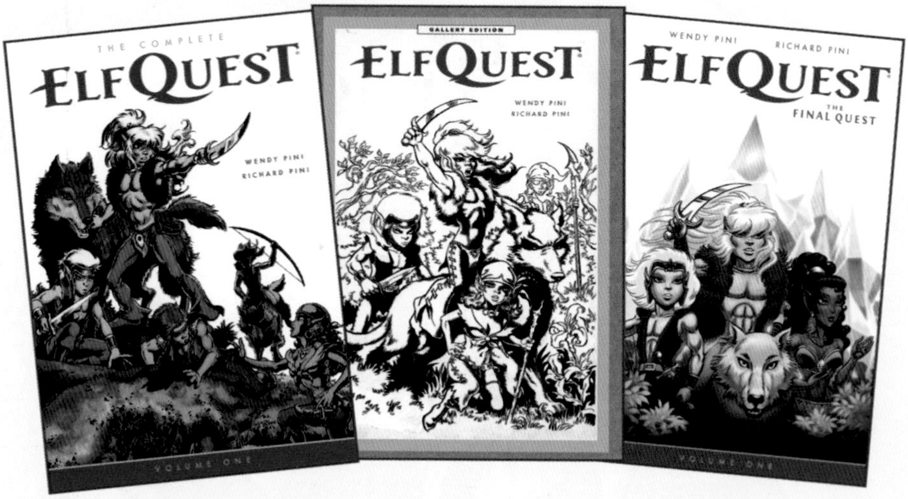
THE COMPLETE
ELFQUEST
WENDY PINI
RICHARD PINI
VOLUME ONE
GALLERY EDITION
ELFQUEST
WENDY PINI
RICHARD PINI
WENDY PINI
RICHARD PINI
ELFQUEST
THE FINAL QUEST
VOLUME ONE

THE COMPLETE ELFQUEST
Volume 1: The Original Quest
978-1-61655-407-1 | $24.99

Volume 2
978-1-61655-408-8 | $24.99

Volume 3
978-1-50670-080-9 | $24.99

Volume 4
978-1-50670-158-5 | $24.99

Volume 5
978-1-50670-606-1 | $24.99

Volume 6
978-1-50670-607-8 | $24.99

Volume 7
978-1-50670-608-5 | $24.99

ELFQUEST: THE ORIGINAL QUEST GALLERY EDITION
978-1-61655-411-8 | $125.00

ELFQUEST: THE FINAL QUEST
Volume 1
978-1-61655-409-5 | $17.99

Volume 2
978-1-61655-410-1 | $17.99

Volume 3
978-1-50670-138-7 | $17.99

Volume 4
978-1-50670-492-0 | $17.99

DARK HORSE BOOKS

AVAILABLE AT YOUR LOCAL COMICS SHOP OR BOOKSTORE
To find a comics shop in your area, visit comicshoplocator.com. For more information or to order direct visit DarkHorse.com